"Did I b

Katie blurted the wo
know if the accusations were true. "Am I the reason you haven't found someone else and married?"

John swore under his breath. "Is that what my mother told you?"

"Yes."

"Don't listen to her." He plastered on a grin. "Do I look like a guy with a broken heart?"

Taking his question seriously, Katie studied him in the dappled green light filtering through the oak tree. She saw shallow creases between his eyebrows and a mouth that used to laugh a lot more than it did now. She saw that something intangible was missing in his eyes. "You look like a man who hasn't found what he's looking for."

Dear Reader,

In *To Be a Family* the hero travels to Bali to claim his six-year-old daughter whose mother has passed away. Why Bali? This beautiful Indonesian island is a popular holiday destination for Australians. It's renowned for its surf beaches, vibrant nightlife and for being relatively inexpensive.

When I first traveled there twenty-five years ago, what I loved was the lush scenery, the intricate paintings and carvings, the colorful local customs and the friendly, gentle people. Oh, and the delicious food! My husband and I hadn't been married long at that time and the trip was almost like a honeymoon.

We returned to Bali last year and stayed in a tiny fishing village just like the one where the hero's daughter lives. The day we arrived we followed a funeral procession similar to the one I've described in the book at a crawl down the winding narrow coastal road.

The village is so small and out of the way there are few tourists and little in the way of amenities. No TV, no internet, no telephone. We spent our days snorkeling on the coral reef right offshore and the evenings relaxing, reading and talking. As I write, we're planning another trip there next month. I can't wait.

I love to hear from readers. Write me at joan@joankilby.com or c/o Harlequin Enterprises Ltd, 225 Duncan Mill Road, Don Mills, Ontario, Canada M3B 3K9. For more info about me and my books visit my website, www.joankilby.com.

Till next time!

Joan Kilby

To Be a Family

JOAN KILBY

Recycling programs for this product may not exist in your area.

ISBN-13: 978-0-373-60732-7

TO BE A FAMILY

This edition published by arrangement with Harlequin Books S.A.

For questions and comments about the quality of this book please contact us at CustomerService@Harlequin.com.

www.Harlequin.com

Printed in U.S.A.

ABOUT THE AUTHOR

When Joan Kilby isn't writing her next Harlequin Superromance title, she loves to travel, often to Asia which is right on Australia's doorstep, so to speak. Now that her three children are grown, she and her husband enjoy the role reversal of taking off and leaving the kids to take care of the house and pets.

Books by Joan Kilby

HARLEQUIN SUPERROMANCE

1212—HOMECOMING WIFE
1224—FAMILY MATTERS
1236—A MOM FOR CHRISTMAS
1324—PARTY OF THREE
1364—BEACH BABY
1437—NANNY MAKES THREE
1466—HOW TO TRAP A PARENT
1681—HER GREAT EXPECTATIONS*
1687—IN HIS GOOD HANDS*
1693—TWO AGAINST THE ODDS*
1772—PROTECTING HER SON

*Summerside Stories

Other titles by this author available in ebook format.

To my wonderful editor, Wanda Ottewell.
You bring out the best in my writing and
inspire me to stretch my wings.
Sometimes you even understand
my characters better than I do!
Thank you so much.

CHAPTER ONE

KATIE GAZED at the children's book section in Summerside Books, pretending she was just browsing, drawing out the anticipation of seeing *Lizzy And Monkey* on the shelf.

She had finished having a coffee and a chat with Josie, the owner of the shop. Now she couldn't wait any longer. The bright red cover was in her peripheral vision. Slowly, slowly, she let her gaze alight. Her breath caught.

Lizzy And Monkey by Katie Henning.

With the cover facing out. *Thanks, Josie.*

She took out her cell phone, glanced around to make sure no one was watching and snapped a photo.

"Katie, hi." John Forster appeared from around the corner of a bookshelf. Six foot four, he had the broad shoulders of a swimmer, the lean build and sun-streaked blond hair of a surfer. With a wink he presented her with his profile, a strong nose and chiseled jaw. "Did you get my good side?"

"Hey, John." She stuffed her phone in her purse.

Of all the people who could have caught her gloating over her book—it had to be her ex-fiancé. If he could still be called that after seven years apart. There must be a statute of limitations on how long someone could be referred to as an ex. Ex-fiancé, ex-lover, ex-friend. Now he was the chief of police in Summerside and her brother Riley's best mate. Someone she didn't avoid exactly, but neither did she spend a moment longer in his company than was necessary for small-town politeness.

His intense blue gaze swept over her from head to toe then returned to linger on her face. "You look great. I like your hair like that. What are you up to?"

Self-consciously she tucked a dark strand of shoulder-length hair behind her ear. He always did this, acted as if he didn't remember they'd broken up. Even though she never gave him the slightest encouragement.

She moved away, pretending to look at other books. "I'm looking for new titles for my classroom."

The long dimples in his cheeks deepened. He pulled *Lizzy And Monkey* off the shelf. "This looks interesting."

She reached out to stop him from handling

her book. Grinning, he backed up, daring her to come after him. She snatched her hand away. "You know about this. How?"

"Riley, who else?" John flipped through the colorful pages. "Congratulations, by the way. I remember you talking about wanting to write, years ago. It's a big achievement."

"Thanks." She made a mental note to kill her brother the next time she saw him. Or at least seriously maim him.

"Why so secretive? You're a published author now. You'll have to get used to publicity. You should have a launch party and sign copies." Somehow he'd edged close enough to nudge her.

His bare arm heated her skin below the cap sleeve of her cherry-red dress. He smelled like bracing ocean winds, sea minerals and memories. Although he didn't surf professionally anymore she knew he still swam in the bay every morning.

Casually she stepped away. His touch didn't affect her one way or another. And they were no longer on flirting terms.

A burst of laughter from a group of teenage girls heading to the in-store café reminded her where she ought be. "I've got to get back to school." She tried to ease past him to get to the central aisle. "Excuse me."

"Katie, wait." He deliberately blocked the narrow space between bookshelves.

"The lunch bell is going to ring soon." Coolly she gazed into his Paul Newman eyes. He didn't bother her. She didn't care. She'd gotten over him long ago. She refused to make herself late because of him. There was nothing he could say that would detain her another second—

"Do you think a six-year-old girl would enjoy your book?"

Except that. Damn it, with a few words she was hooked.

"I wrote it for that age group." Was he teasing her again? On the whole she thought not. The eye glint and the dimples were not in evidence. "Are you asking for one of your nieces?"

"Er…something like that."

It wasn't like John to be evasive. If she wasn't one of his nieces then his current girlfriend must have a daughter. According to her brother, John had broken up with Trudy, his previous squeeze, a few weeks ago. His girlfriends never lasted longer than six months. Whoever she was would be another in a long and endless line of John's women. Katie was inured to that now. She wasn't really interested but writers were curious types.

"New woman in your life, one with a kid?"

Instead of replying he flipped through the

book, turning his attention to the colorful illustrations. "Nice pictures. Riley said you did those, too."

"Is this little girl from around here?" Not in her class, she hoped, her mind skipping ahead to John arriving at school to pick up some other woman's child. Well, it had to happen someday. She was surprised he'd remained single this long. He'd been in a hurry to marry when they'd been going together—maybe he'd finally met another woman who had been able to convince him to drop his role as the town playboy.

"What's the story about?" he asked, still ignoring her questions.

"A little girl and her pet monkey. Sort of *Curious George* meets *Madeleine*."

"I always had a soft spot for monkeys."

She knew that, of course. John was the inspiration for Monkey in the story. Bold, clever, brave. "The monkey and the girl go on adventures together. It's going to be a series." If her latest book proposal was picked up by her publisher. Big if, but she was counting on it.

He closed the book and smiled at her. "Your hair looks really pretty today."

"You said that." She felt nothing, she really didn't.

"Do you have time for a coffee?" he went on. "It's been ages since we've had a chat."

"I can't. I told you. I have to get back to school." She wished he would stop. He never gave up asking her out even though she'd replied with a firm no about a billion times.

"No worries. Another time." He said it as if it mattered not a whit to him, as if all his flirtation was just hot air. It probably was. John didn't seem to know any other way to relate to women.

He held the book out to her, open at the title page. "Will you sign it?"

Katie dug in her purse for a pen. "Who should I make it out to?"

"Tuti. *T-u-t-i.*"

"That's unusual," she said, but didn't make much of it. As a teacher she'd learned not to bat an eye at the odd names parents came up with these days. She propped the book on her knee and wrote:

To Tuti,
I hope you enjoy my book.
Warmest wishes, Katie Henning.

Katie couldn't help smiling as she handed the book back. She'd just signed her very first book. "Do you think the girl you're buying this for will like a story about a monkey?"

He didn't answer for a moment while he read her inscription. Then he looked up at her. His smile had the power to melt hearts. But not hers. "Monkeys are perfect. They live in the jungle near her village."

Katie blinked. "Seriously? She lives near a jungle?"

"Yep." That was it, no elaboration.

Not the offspring of the girlfriend of the moment. Who, then? No, no, no. She was not going to ask about the mysterious Tuti. Writer or not, she didn't care enough about John to be *that* interested.

He tucked the book under his arm and gave her a last lingering look. "I'll see you around."

No, he wouldn't unless it was by accident. Katie made sure she was never at the same social gatherings, despite their mutual friends. The statute of limitations would never be up on his violation after he'd abandoned her when she'd needed him most.

But then curiosity got the better of her after all. As he turned to go, she asked, "Who is Tuti?"

His smile was bland and fixed. But a shadow passed across his eyes. She couldn't read his expression.

"Just a girl I know in Bali," he said.

JOHN TIED A traditional Balinese brown cotton band around his head. He *didn't* know Tuti, his six-year-old daughter. He was about to meet her for the first time at the funeral of her mother, Nena. He was mixed-up and confused, not sure how he was supposed to feel. This meeting was never supposed to happen. What would he say? What should he do? What was going to happen to Tuti now?

Incense wafted over the high stone walls of the family compound. Drumming and chanting floated on the sea breeze. Wearing a borrowed batik sarong beneath his short-sleeved shirt John went through the gates to join the dozens of family and friends behind the funeral tower, a thirty-foot-high golden pagoda-like structure built of wood and bamboo that transported Nena's body.

Women dressed in silk batik sarongs and lace blouses carried offerings of flowers and fruit on their heads. The men wore cotton headdresses and sarongs. The funeral procession slowly wound through the tiny fishing village. There was no crying, no sadness, even though Nena had died prematurely in a motorcycle accident. In Bali, death wasn't a cause for grief but a celebration of a life that had moved to a higher plane.

John recognized Tuti among the throng by the pigtails that stuck out on either side of her head. She also wore traditional clothing and carried her niece, a toddler almost as big as she was. He hadn't had a chance to speak to her yet. He'd arrived late last night and the elaborate funeral preparations, already two days old, consumed everyone's time.

Tuti had no idea who he was. Was there any point in telling her? He'd only come to pay his respects to Nena and to make sure the girl would be cared for.

There'd never been any question that he and Nena might stay together long term. They'd both been clear it was a holiday fling. He'd been on the rebound and Nena, who worked in a souvenir shop in Kuta, a tourist hot spot and part of the surfing scene, wasn't looking for a husband. When she found out she was pregnant, she made her intentions known. She didn't want to live in Australia, nor did she want her child to pine for a father who only visited once a year. It was better to raise the child without John. That had hurt but he'd sent her money regularly and extra whenever she needed it. He would continue to help out Nena's brother and the family.

Being back in Bali, among Nena's people, brought back memories and emotions from that turbulent time. What he'd wanted out of life and what he'd ended up with were, sadly, two different things. He'd wanted a home and family with Katie but instead she'd gotten cancer and broken their engagement. Fleeing to Bali, he'd had a fling with Nena and accidentally fathered her child.

Katie had been near death but she'd survived. Nena, the picture of health, had died at the age of thirty-three. He and Katie lived in the same small town and he saw her frequently, but their relationship was strained. After his affair with Nena, despite telephone and email communication, he'd never seen her again. It was a tribute to the generosity of her family and community that he was now welcomed into her world.

When he'd known Nena seven years ago she'd seemed very Western. Her funeral, and village life on the less-populated side of the island, was revealing a foreign culture with unfamiliar rituals. He didn't know whether nonfamily members were aware he was Tuti's father, but his presence seemed to be accepted.

He joined the procession that wound its way to the cremation grounds next to a temple overlooking the ocean. The coffin was placed in a ten-foot-high wooden bull painted in black and gold standing atop a funeral pyre. The white-robed priest said prayers. There was more chanting, more incense. The dissonant notes of a gamelan orchestra—gongs, bells, xylophones and drums—filled the air.

Someone doused the bull with petrol and set

it alight. Flames shot skyward. Heat pushed the crowd back. Silently, John said a few words of remembrance. He hadn't known Nena long but he'd cared about her. She was gone far too soon.

He glanced around for Tuti. She stood a little apart, on her tiptoes, trying to see through the crowd. Her headdress was askew, her pigtails sagging. Someone must have taken the toddler. In her hands she held an offering of woven palm frond containing boiled rice and marigold petals.

John nudged through the crowd to get to her. He touched her shoulder and mimed picking her up so she could see. She nodded shyly. He hoisted her onto his hip and carried her to the front where he lowered her briefly so she could place her offering by the fire. He didn't know if he was breaking any customs or committing an impropriety but it felt like the right thing to do. Then her small arm circled his shoulders. He blinked and swallowed around a lump in his throat. Tuti was too young to be without her mother.

AFTER THE CEREMONY, the feasting began. John set Tuti on the ground and they made their way to a *bale,* a raised wooden platform where the women were laying out rice, fruits, vegetables and spicy grilled meats on banana leaves.

Wayan, Nena's older brother, was seated cross-legged on the *bale,* his legs tucked beneath his brown-and-purple sarong. At his invitation John kicked off his sandals and climbed up, folding his legs into a cross-legged posture. Tuti brought him a glass of rice liquor.

From previous visits to Bali John knew the Balinese often spent their life savings on cremation ceremonies. He had ready an envelope containing several hundred dollars. This he passed to Wayan. "To help with the funeral."

Wayan nodded his thanks and slipped the envelope into a fold of his sarong. Then he gestured at the array of food. "Please, have something to eat."

John spent the hours until sundown among Nena's family and friends. He spoke with the adults but his gaze frequently drifted to Tuti. Now that the formal ceremony was over she and the other children ran around and played. She was a tomboy, climbing barefoot up a palm tree with her sarong hiked up, revealing pink shorts underneath. He smiled to himself. As a boy he'd spent half his life up in trees. Somehow he'd always imagined his son—when he had one—would be a tree climber. He'd never thought of a daughter that way. Yet here was Tuti, just like him in that respect.

One of Tuti's aunts spoke to her in Balinese

with what sounded like a gentle reprimand. Tuti shook her head and giggled, showing her dimples. The aunt smiled and gestured for her to come down. Tuti just tilted her head and laughed again.

John blinked. Until this moment, he hadn't thought Tuti bore any physical resemblance to him or his family. In appearance she looked much like her mother's side—brown skin, dark hair, almond-shaped eyes. But the way she'd tilted her head just then…she reminded him of his mother.

The realization rocked him. All through Tuti's short life he'd been able to hold himself apart from her. Yes, he'd had the DNA test to prove she was his and he did the right thing with support payments. But he'd done that as though sending money to a sponsor child, as if he had no personal ties to Tuti. Even when he'd first seen her it was easy to feel separate because superficially she looked nothing like him.

Witnessing their connection in the small mannerism was living proof they were connected, that Tuti wasn't just a distant responsibility. She was his daughter. His parents' granddaughter. His brother and sisters' niece. It was a bizarre thing to realize here and now—surrounded by Nena's family—but the foreignness just made the recognition sharper.

Tuti belonged to him. She was part of his family, too. He simply couldn't walk away from that.

"THE CROWD IS BIG," Katie said to Melissa, the woman running the mini writer's festival at the Summerside Library. She peeked through the doorway at rows of chairs filled with children and their parents. "I thought I'd just be speaking to kids."

"You'll be fine." Melissa touched her arm and smiled. "You've got a warm personality. Just be yourself. Let your positivity shine through."

"But what can I talk about that will interest the adults?" Katie leafed through her notes. "I was planning on telling a story about an adventure Lizzy and Monkey had that didn't make it into the book."

"The children will love that. Most authors also talk about how they came to be a writer, what inspires them, their journey to publication, et cetera. The adults will feel they can connect with you as a person."

"At least I won't need notes for that."

Katie followed Melissa into the room and waited to one side of the lectern while the librarian introduced her. A brief round of applause and then a sea of faces—fifty, sixty?—gazed up at her expectantly. She spotted some of her students. Paula Drummond and her son Jamie were also in the audience. Paula, a police detective who would soon be Katie's sister-in-law, winked at her.

"Good morning, everyone." Katie tilted her head, waiting.

Her students in the audience chanted, "Good morning, Miss Henning." A ripple of laughter broke Katie's tension.

"Thanks for coming. Shortly I'll talk about how I came to be a writer but first…" She detached the microphone from the lectern, pinned it to the lapel of her blouse and walked onto the dais. "I want to tell you a story about the time Lizzy and Monkey were walking on the beach and found a pirate's treasure chest…."

For fifteen minutes, the audience listened, rapt. At the end of her story, Katie concluded, "Monkey was sorry to see the pirate ship sail away, but Lizzy was ready to go home for supper. She knew there would be more adventures the next time she and Monkey went for a walk."

Applause greeted the end of her story, allowing Katie time to take a drink of water. She was buzzing on the energy in the room and grinning inside at the response of the children to her storytelling. The reworked version of this particular adventure had gone down well. For her next book she might test the stories on her class, even pass out a simple questionnaire to better refine the story.

"I always wanted to be a writer, from the time I was a little girl," Katie said to begin the second half of her talk. "But I didn't think an author was something that ordinary people like myself became. So because I loved children, I went into teaching." She paced the dais, thinking about her next words. "I would have been happy doing that for the rest of my life. Then when I was twenty-five I was diagnosed with breast cancer. Even though it's so rare at that age, there I was, getting chemo and radiation treatments." She stopped moving and gazed out at the rows of mostly women and children. "It was pretty bad. The doctors, my family, everyone—including me—thought I was going to die."

There was a rustling in the audience, a few low murmurs. She hoped the parents wouldn't think her subject matter was inappropriate for the kids. From her experience children were matter-of-fact about life and death. As long as you were honest and didn't try to sugarcoat the facts, they could handle almost anything.

She glanced out the floor-to-ceiling windows, past the street and the parked cars to a row of gum trees stretching silver limbs into a blue sky. She still recalled how she'd felt after enduring the long months of surgery and debilitating treatments and finding herself still alive.

"Life is a gift." She returned her gaze to her audience, now utterly silent. She smiled, wanting them to see how well and happy she was. "A gift to be treasured more than a pirate's chest of gold and jewels. I didn't die. I got better. The sun seemed to shine more brightly, the colors of the flowers were more vivid. Friends and family were more precious. Even now, years later, every day I wake up is a blessing."

Katie walked back to the lectern and took another sip of water. This was a roundabout way of talking about her writing journey, but she couldn't see how she could take a shortcut and still be authentic. Children and writing demanded honesty.

"From my illness I learned life was too short not to be true to yourself. I loved teaching but I still had a dream of being a writer. How would I feel if I'd been given this second chance at life and at the end of it, I had regrets for what I *hadn't* done?" Her voice vibrated and she held out her hands, inviting a response from the audience. A few heads nodded.

"After I recovered I vowed I'd never again put anything on hold. As soon as I felt well enough, I started to write. Soon I was hooked. Storytelling became my passion. After I went back to teaching, I wrote in my spare time. It was as if all my life I'd been waiting to discover what I really wanted to do—tell my own stories."

A young girl, about seven years old, put up her hand. "Are you Lizzy? Is that what you mean by your own stories?"

"That's a good question. I am like Lizzy in some ways." Katie walked slowly across the dais as she thought out her answer. "When I was younger I had a friend who reminded me of a cheeky, mischievous monkey. He made me challenge myself. To climb trees and cliffs, to swim over my head in the ocean, to be brave enough to take risks."

But when she'd taken a life-and-death risk he didn't approve of—not getting a double mastectomy—well, he couldn't handle that. Which was really unfair considering he regularly risked his life with surf and sharks.

"When this boy and I ventured out together I never knew how the day was going to pan out. As we got older we went rock climbing, paragliding, even bodysurfing at Gunnamatta Beach. It was always something a bit dangerous."

"Weren't you scared?" a boy called out.

"Often I was frightened out of my wits. But I did it, anyway. *Que sera sera.*" She spread her hands wide. "Whatever will be, will be. We can't plan our lives completely. Sometimes we have to trust that things will work out."

Take her writing, for example. She'd thrown herself into it, not worrying whether or not she got published. Lo and behold, after years and a lot of hard work, she'd sold her first book. Before her cancer she'd been a planner and a rule follower. A perfectionist, she liked being in control of her life. It had taken facing her own mortality to know that control wasn't possible all the time. She'd given herself permission to break free, to be more spontaneous. Because you never knew what was coming around the next bend.

"Even with that belief, I don't take chances with my health," she added. "I'm very careful with my diet, only eating organic, whole foods, mostly vegetarian. I see my naturopath regularly and I take special dietary supplements." Some blank faces stared at her. Laughing, she waved a hand. "But you don't want to know all that."

"Do you still have adventures with your Monkey man?" a brunette woman asked, a small smile playing over her lips.

O-kay. That was striking too close to the bone. Some of these people might know that she and John Forster had grown up together and been engaged and put two and two together.

"I have my own adventures nowadays. I've

been in remission for six years but my gratitude for being alive hasn't faded. I regularly take what I call Adventure Days. I get in my car and tootle off down the coast road, heading south on the peninsula. I take my camera and notebook, my hiking shoes and rugged clothing. I'm ready for anything but with no plans whatsoever."

Mostly, though, she found a quiet spot to walk, read and take photos. Maybe write a little. Pretty tame, really. "Any more questions?"

"Where do you get your ideas?"

From memories of her times with John. They'd had so many wonderful experiences together. She didn't know what she would do when they ran out. Her own adventures were all solitary ones.

"Don't tell anyone, but…" She cupped a hand around her mouth and spoke in a stage whisper. "I have an idea tree in my backyard. When I need a new one I go outside and pick it."

An appreciative chuckle ran through the audience. Katie used that to springboard into talking about her writing habits, the way she organized her office, the books she'd loved in childhood. It was a relief to move on to less personal topics.

She worried she may have inadvertently given a wrong impression that she still took part in dangerous activities. Truth was, she hadn't done anything risky in years, not since John. Why was that? Had she gotten scared or just lazy? Or was she simply not the adventurous person she liked to think she was? Maybe she'd only done those things because he'd pushed her and without him she was a wuss.

She didn't like that thought. John didn't rule her life. She'd proved that when she'd had cancer and they'd disagreed on her treatment. She'd stuck to her guns on no mastectomy. He couldn't handle that and had abandoned her. That's when she'd realized she had to rely on herself.

She wanted to be strong. She didn't want to be sedentary and soft. She needed to push herself. And she would. As soon as she thought of something exciting to do.

CHAPTER TWO

A ROOSTER CROWED. John sat up and stretched, his back sore from the thin mat in the unmarried men's quarters of the family compound. He'd booked a hotel room down the road then decided he wanted a closer look at how Tuti was living and make sure she was okay. In the bigger towns Balinese life approximated a Western lifestyle. Here in this remote fishing village time seemed to have stood still for the past fifty years.

Nena's two teenage nephews, with whom he shared the small hut, had already risen and left. Their mats were rolled and stacked against the wall. Just inside the open door was a tray with a teapot and a plate of fresh tropical fruits. He was being treated like an honored guest.

He pulled on shorts and a T-shirt, poured himself a cup of fragrant, fresh ginger tea, and stood in the doorway looking onto the courtyard of the walled compound. Grouped around the outer wall were separate rooms for sleeping, cooking and storage. Judging by the grunts he'd heard from next door, accommodation for pigs, as well.

Ketut, Wayan's wife, was sweeping the ground clean of leaves and bits of palm frond and flowers left over from the funeral offerings. She glanced over and smiled at him but made no move to talk. That suited him just fine. After yesterday's exotic festival of people, color, noise—and yes, too much rice wine—he needed time to himself.

He carried the plate of fruit and his copy of *Lizzy And Monkey* out to the *bale* shaded by a thatched roof in the center of the courtyard. He sat, crossing his legs on the woven mat that covered the raised platform, and reached for a slice of papaya. The compound was peaceful, with a pleasant smell of wood smoke from the cooking fire. A slender young woman in a sarong lit incense sticks on a small shrine in a shady corner. Chickens scratched in the dust at her feet.

Wayan was a fisherman, but from what John could see, the women did most of the work. The men saved their energy for religious rituals and chatting over a glass of rice wine in the evening.

Tuti came through the ornate stone gate that guarded the entrance to the compound. Her hair was again in pigtails and she wore a pink T-shirt and pink shorts. The toddler was once again glued to her hip, which couldn't be good for Tuti's back. But these people were strong, used to doing manual labor from an early age.

She was halfway across the courtyard when she saw him sitting in the *bale*. She paused, uncertain. He motioned to her. Obediently she walked over, adjusting the baby, a little girl with wisps of black hair and a drooly smile.

John held the baby while Tuti climbed onto the *bale*. She took the child back and nestled her between her crossed legs. When he offered her a piece of mango she gave it to the toddler.

"How are you this morning?" he asked.

Tuti smiled shyly, leaving him unsure whether she'd understood him or not.

From his wallet he took out a photo of himself and Nena, a shot of them perched on stools at an outdoor bar on Kuta Beach. He wore a T-shirt and board shorts and had his arm around her. Her black hair was cut short, Western-style, and she wore a yellow dress.

He showed Tuti the photo, watching her face to see if she recognized her mother. And him. She glanced up, her eyes speaking a question.

"Yes, that's your mother—*Meme*." Tuti nodded. He pointed to his photo and then at himself. He started to say, *bapa*—father—then changed it to, *"Nama saya John."* My name is John.

The feeling of connection with her was persisting—growing even—but he hadn't come here intending to claim her. And if he wasn't claiming her there was no point in telling her he was her father. He'd talked to Wayan about this when he'd first arrived and Tuti's uncle had agreed.

It felt surreal even having such talks. He and Wayan had also discussed setting up a bank account for Tuti's support payments so Wayan and Ketut could continue to care for her. Was that enough? It didn't feel like enough. He was Tuti's only living parent. But what was the alternative? Move here and look after Tuti? That wasn't going to happen. Bring her back to Australia to live with him? How could he rip her away from her home and the only family she knew to bring her to a foreign country?

Yet it felt wrong to just go away and leave her behind. Tuti was his family. Family was a big part of who he was. He was close to his parents and his sisters and he loved spending time with his nieces and nephews, teaching them to swim, playing cricket with them on the beach.... They would all adore Tuti.

Tuti stared at the photo of her mother for a long time. Reluctantly she held it out to him. John shook his head and gently pushed it back. "You keep."

She smiled again, her eyes shining. She understood the meaning of his gesture if not the words. John couldn't help but grin back. With her jaunty pigtails and dimpled smile she was cute as a button. He set his teacup on the platform and brought out Katie's book. Tuti edged closer, to peer over his arm. Not wanting to hand it to her while she was holding the sticky baby, he opened to the title page and showed her the inscription Katie had written.

"*Bukuh* for Tuti," he said in pidgin Balinese, pointing to her name. She have him a half smile, half frown, clearly not understanding. Later he would get Wayan or Ketut to explain.

He read the story aloud, letting her look at the illustrations as long as she liked before he turned each page. He wasn't sure how much she understood but she listened attentively and more than once laughed, whether at the story or the pictures, he couldn't tell.

"Do you go to school?" he asked.

Clearly recognizing the word "school," she nodded vigorously, her face lit. In a flurry of movement she handed him the toddler and scrambled off the *bale*. John held the tot in one arm, keeping the book away from her sticky, grasping fingers with the other.

On the ground, Tuti reached for the baby. "Come. School."

John slid off the *bale* and, with the book tucked beneath his arm, he followed Tuti out of the courtyard and down the stone steps to the narrow potholed street.

High on the hillside, set among lush vegetation, a hotel looked out on the ocean. Across the road was an open-air restaurant with just a few rickety tables and a languid ceiling fan stirring the hot air. The village straggled along a mile or so of coastal road, small houses interspersed with homestays for tourists and a few small shops selling dry goods, fresh produce and, outside, liters of gasoline in glass bottles.

Tuti hurried down the road, glancing over her shoulder to make sure John was following. Between buildings, through banana trees and bougainvillea and coconut palms, he glimpsed the curving sweep of a black sand beach. A ragged fleet of outrigger fishing boats with their triangular sails was returning with the morning's catch. At a cleared lot John paused to watch as one boat landed. The fishermen hopped out and, joined by other men waiting on the beach, dragged the wooden hull up the sand.

Tuti tugged on his hand, impatient with his interest in what to her was everyday life. Her destination was nearby, a squat cement building covered in chipped green paint. She walked up to the doorless opening. "School," she said proudly.

John kicked off his flip-flops and ducked his

head to step over the threshold. A table and a chair for the teacher were at the front of the room next to a blackboard on an easel. A woven mat covered the floor, presumably for the children to sit on. An old tin can held stubs of pencils and a plastic basket contained perhaps a dozen dog-eared notebooks. There weren't any desks, or books, or posters depicting the alphabet or the multiplication table, much less anything as expensive as a computer.

He was surprised at how small and ill-equipped the school was. In Bali, elementary school, at least, was compulsory and free. And he'd seen large, modern schools in some of the bigger towns. But Tuti's village was tiny and remote and no doubt couldn't attract the government funding needed for a bigger school.

Tuti bounced on her bare feet, wanting his approval.

John forced a smile. "Good. Very nice. Tuti go to school here?"

She nodded, her grin widening, and held up a finger. "One…year." She sifted through the notebooks and found hers, showing him rows of wobbly Balinese script.

His stomach hollowed. Tuti was so eager to learn, so proud of her tiny school with its acute lack of facilities. How much learning could she do here? Read and write, add and subtract, that seemed to be about it. When he got back to Summerside he would see about sending books, stationery, laptops, whatever he could afford to improve the situation.

Tuti quickly ran out of things to show him. A few minutes later he emerged from the school to see Wayan coming up the path from the beach. He wore a sleeveless T-shirt and shorts wet around the cuffs, and carried a woven fishing basket on his shoulder.

"Morning," John called to Wayan. "Did you have a good catch?"

Tuti, seeing the grown-ups were going to talk, ran back up the road to the compound.

"Yes. Good." Wayan's wide grin showed a gap where a tooth was missing. He lowered the basket and lifted the lid. Half a dozen fish, not much longer than his hand, flopped feebly against a wet palm frond.

John didn't know what to say. If this was a good catch he'd hate to see a bad one. He'd surfed in Bali for years, taking advantage of cheap holidays without giving much thought to the locals who were doing it tough. Nena must have hidden how little money she had, out of pride or embarrassment. It saddened and shamed him that he didn't even know which.

"Tuti showed me where she goes to school," he said, to avoid talking about the fish. "It seems…" he paused, trying to be diplomatic "…small. Is there a larger school in a nearby town, somewhere with more facilities? I'll pay for her fees and transportation. Books, whatever she needs."

Wayan spit in the dust at the side of the road. "Tuti not go to school now. Not important. She stay home and help with the children."

"What?" John was stunned. "But…she has to go to school. To learn to read and write."

"Nena give us money from her job. Now she is gone, Ketut must get a job in the hotel. Tuti look after the baby." Wayan hoisted the basket on his shoulder and trudged off.

John stared after him. And that was that? No discussion? No exploration of Tuti's options? Just shut down her life at the age of six so she could be a babysitter? What would happen to that smart little girl with a thirst to learn, who would never have an opportunity to improve her lot in life? Nena, he knew, would never have allowed that to happen. In their brief, irregular email exchanges over the years she'd been full of hope and plans for Tuti to go to high school, maybe college.

He couldn't let her stay here. But how could he take her away? Wayan and Ketut were good people who would love and care for Tuti as if she was their own. They had little of material value to offer her but they would surround her all day, every day, with loving familiar faces and a home that held a million memories of her mother. Uncle Wayan and Auntie Ketut would be able to tell Tuti stories about her mother as she grew, keeping Nena's memory alive.

What could he give Tuti besides the advantages of an education, good health care and a high standard of living? Okay, that sounded pretty good. But was it enough? He had no wife to soften the edges of his bachelor existence. And there was no one on the horizon. Would material advantages make up for the family life Tuti would have to give up in Bali?

He couldn't imagine not being geographically close to his parents and his sisters. To him, the close-knit family life he'd grown up with was as solid an advantage as school. These days the traditional family with mum, dad and two-point-two kids was more of an ideal than a reality but what was the point of ideals unless you aspired to them? Despite the steady stream of women through his life, he did aspire to the dream of a white picket fence. Whether he would find it in time to benefit Tuti was another matter entirely.

But he had his own family to offer her. He knew they would love her and accept her. She might be sad at leaving Bali in the short term, but now that he knew her future here was so limited he had no choice.

Tuti was coming home with him.

He was acting on instinct, but the immediate relief he felt told him he'd made the right decision.

That evening he spoke to Wayan and Ketut about his plan.

Ketut gazed at the ground unhappily.

Wayan said, "Tuti is all we have left of Nena, my sister."

"I know. I'm sorry. But she's my daughter." He paused and added delicately, "I will continue the support payments in Nena's honor."

Wayan shrugged as if to say that was beside the point. Then he and Ketut talked between themselves in Balinese. They seemed to be disagreeing. John held his breath. Which side would win out?

Finally, Wayan held up a hand. "Tuti go to Australia. Get an education like Nena wanted."

"She will visit us?" Ketut added hopefully.

"Yes, every year," John said, ready to promise anything. He had the right to take her but he wanted their blessing. After further discussion, Wayan and Ketut decided that a cousin from another village would be brought in to help with the baby.

John didn't say anything to Tuti at first, either about being her father or about taking her to Australia. He wanted her to get to know and trust him.

He contacted the Australian Embassy in Jakarta, filled out a bunch of forms and paid extra for expeditious processing of Tuti's immigration documents. Luckily he had holiday time saved, a sympathetic district superintendent and reliable deputies in Riley and Paula.

Over the next three weeks, while he waited for Tuti's visa, he gave her English lessons and taught her how to swim. While her uncle was a fisherman and they lived in a coastal village, Tuti, like most Balinese, was a novice in the water.

The day Tuti learned to float on her back, John decided it was time. When they got back from the beach, he joined Wayan on the shaded *bale* for tea. Tuti started to skip off to the kitchen. John called her back and asked Wayan to explain to her in Balinese that he was her father. Wayan spoke softly at length. When he was finished, Tuti turned to John.

"Bapa?" she repeated, her small forehead wrinkling.

Wayan nodded and said something else in their language.

John smiled encouragingly. It must be hard for Tuti to accept that he, a stranger from a far-off country, was her father. But she took it calmly, almost fatalistically, once she understood. Nena had assured him long ago that she intended to tell her daughter he was a good man. She must have lived up to her promise.

"Ask her if she'd like to come with me and live in Australia," John said to Wayan. "She can go to school and swim in the ocean. She'll have her own room and make new friends."

Wayan conveyed the information. Tuti's face lit at the first few words. She nodded, her eyes shining. "Yes!"

John gave her a hug. He'd had her at the word "school."

KATIE CARRIED a cup of coffee into her home office, the master bedroom of her two-bedroom house. She slept in the second bedroom because the master was bigger and could accommodate both her artwork and her writing.

The easel that she used to create the acrylic paintings that illustrated her books stood in front of the window to take advantage of natural light. Against the far wall a table was littered with palette, brushes and paints. On the other side of the room she'd set up her computer, bookshelves and a whiteboard to scrawl ideas on. People thought that just because there weren't a lot of words in a children's book they mattered less. But the truth was, that made each one matter more.

She slid into her chair and powered up her computer. Lizzy and Monkey were stuck in a swamp where a crocodile was about to eat them. Generally Monkey got the pair into scrapes and Lizzy got them out. This time, however, Lizzy had followed a colorful parrot into the swamp and gotten them lost.

Like all her stories this one had a basis in reality. Years ago she and John had gone out walking after a heavy rain. After hiking through the muddy terrain for a couple of hours, Katie had had enough. Ignoring John's warning against leaving the path, she'd taken what she thought was a shortcut and had gotten lost. Too stubborn to give up, she'd led them deeper and deeper into the bush.

Thinking about John led her to wonder about Tuti. Who was this girl who lived near a jungle? He liked kids. Maybe in lieu of the family they'd planned he'd sponsored a child. Or maybe Tuti was the daughter of friends he'd made in Bali. She knew he went surfing over there every few years. Riley had told her John was in Bali now, on holiday.

It was strange that John had never married. According to Riley, these days he went out with party girls—the antithesis of who she was. Maybe if he settled down and had a family she would find it easier to move on. But the thought of John married to someone else made her chest constrict.

Which was so wrong because she was *over* him. The reason she hadn't gotten serious with anyone else was because she didn't have time for romance with her teaching and her writing.

Speaking of her writing…she needed to buckle down and get some work done. Lizzy was walking in circles while Monkey swung from branch to branch in the trees above her head, saying he told her so. How was she going to get Lizzy out of trouble? On that hike years ago, by sheer luck she'd stumbled on another path that led back to the parking lot. But luck wasn't good enough. Lizzy had to triumph using pluck, resourcefulness and brains.

She wrote in a patch of clear sky so Lizzy could track the movement of the sun and figure out the compass points. That way, knowing the road lay to the west, Lizzy could navigate her way out of the swamp.

The phone rang. "Hello?"

"Hey, Katie," Paula said. "Riley and I are going to try the new French restaurant in the village. Do you want to come?"

"What, now?" She was just getting into the zone.

"It's six-thirty on Friday night. Not a bad time

to get a bite to eat. What do you say? Jamie's at a sleepover birthday party so I'm free, free, free."

"You and Riley should enjoy a night to yourselves. I'd be a third wheel."

"You're never in the way. We want you to come. Please."

Katie glanced at her watch. She would be lucky to make her daily word count and get to the gym before it closed. As well as a healthy diet, she'd adopted regular exercise as part of her rigorous regime aimed at achieving maximum health. "Thanks, but not this time. I have too much to do."

"Has anyone ever told you, you work too much?"

"No," Katie lied. John used to say that to her all the time.

She had to work, to keep writing proposals till another book sold. Her agent had sent out her latest several months ago. Every day she hoped to hear good news when she hurried to check the mailbox as soon as she got home from work. A new contract would add more pressure but without one...well, she wouldn't be a real writer, would she?

She promised to meet Paula and Riley for coffee at the deli on Sunday morning and hung up. Not ten minutes passed before the phone rang again.

Groaning, she reached for the phone. "Hello?"

"Katie, glad I caught you," Adele, her agent in New York, said rapidly. "Have you got a minute?"

Katie hit Save and sat up straight. "Have you heard something about my book proposal?"

"Have I heard something?" Adele brayed out a laugh. "Yes, but first I want to give you some news. Are you sitting down? I want you to be sitting down."

Katie's heart rate kicked up. News that was more important than the publisher's response to her proposal? "I'm sitting. Go on."

"*Lizzy And Monkey* debuted at number forty-three on the *USA TODAY* bestseller list."

"Wow." Katie forgot to breathe. "Just...wow."

"You're on to a winner," Adele chortled.

"Does the publisher know? What did they say about my new idea? Did they like it?"

"Oh, I let them know about the bestseller list, don't you worry. They want to buy your next book—"

"Oh, thank God!" She wasn't going to be a one-hit wonder.

"Plus two more."

"What?"

"They're offering you a three-book contract."

Katie's mouth opened and closed. Lightheaded, she blinked against the spots in front of her eyes. Then she realized she was holding her breath and let it out with a whoosh. "Three-book contract. That's amazing. Are you sure?"

"You'd better believe it. The catch is, they want to release the books bang, bang, bang, to take advantage of your bestseller status and build your name."

"Oh, Adele..." This was a far greater success than she'd ever dreamed of. Well, okay, she'd *dreamed* of hitting the lists but it had been a fantasy. She'd never actually thought it would happen. Now it had. Suddenly a whole new world was opening up to her. She wasn't just a small-town grade-one teacher who dabbled in children's stories. She was a writer.

Adele brought her down from the clouds. "Before you say yes, I want you to be sure this is what you want. I know you're committed to your teaching. We've talked about your career goals and your workload. You only wanted to write one book a year. Are you going to be able to do three books in twelve months?"

"I—" Her chest tightened again. Could she write that quickly? Not just write, but paint the illustrations? Three books. She'd only plotted out one more book. Did she have that many stories in her?

"Do you want some time to think about it?"

She pressed a hand against her stomach and forced herself to breathe out. There was no way she was going to pass up such a golden opportunity.

"No," she said firmly. "I can do it. I *will* do it."

But as she hung up, her bubble of elation burst with a tiny pop. She'd given her word. Now she *had* to do it.

No, she wouldn't give in to anxiety. *Que sera sera.* She, evidently, was meant to be a writer, and a prolific one at that. She laughed aloud, partly with nerves, partly elation. With three new stories to write she would have to have adventures of her own now.

CHAPTER THREE

JOHN BLINKED HIS EYES OPEN. Morning sunlight filtered through the curtains. For a moment he lay spread-eagled across his king-size bed, savoring the sheer comfort of waking up in his own home. A cool, dry breeze drifted in through the open window, bringing with it the scent of pine and eucalyptus and the kookaburra's laughing call.

Their plane had landed at ten last night and it had been after midnight before they'd gotten home. Tuti had fallen asleep in the car. He'd carried her in, still sleeping, in his arms and tucked her into the single bed in the spare room he used as a study.

Now he rose, remembered to put his track pants on, and walked barefoot down the hall to his study. He peeked in the door. The folding cot, crammed between a desk and a filing cabinet, was empty. On the floor, a black pigtail poked out of a bundle of blankets. Her feet were stuck between the legs of his computer chair.

He needed to make some big adjustments

around here for Tuti to feel at home. Starting with getting her a proper bed and dresser and clearing space for her to put her things. Where, in his two-bedroom bachelor apartment he would move his computer and desk, he didn't have a clue. Certainly not in his bedroom. Nothing quelled romance like a workstation next to the bed.

Romance? Huh. With no woman in his life at the moment he didn't need to worry about that. Anyway, with Tuti around, for him to go out at night, come home late, sleep with a woman in his bed… It was simply out of the question. His love life wouldn't come into contact with his daughter's life until and unless he was serious about a woman.

Yep, his romancing days were over for the foreseeable future. Dead in the water at the ripe old age of thirty-five. Overnight he'd gone from being a carefree bachelor to single dad. This was going to be one helluva steep learning curve.

Tuti shifted in her sleep. Carefully, he pushed the chair back and crouched to touch her shoulder. She blinked sleepily. "Hey, Tuti. Why are you on the floor?"

She stared at him.

Because that's where she was used to sleeping, dummy. "Do you want some breakfast?"

Again a blank look. "Are you hungry? Food?" He mimed eating.

She sat up, the blankets falling away, exposing her bare arms in a thin T-shirt. Shivering, she pulled the blanket around herself.

"I'll turn the heat on." The room temperature was comfortable but after living in the tropics she was bound to feel the cold. "May I?" he asked, picking up her faded pink backpack to find her something warmer.

All her clothes were T-shirts and shorts. Her only shoes were a pair of flip-flops. Oh, man.

He showed her where the bathroom was then hunted out an old sweatshirt of his that she could wear like a dress and a pair of thick socks. When she was warm and had a bowl of cereal in front of her he sat down to make a list of all the things she would need.

Clothes. But what kind and how many of each item? What size? He had no idea of how to shop for a child. So he did what any red-blooded male would do. He picked up the phone and called his mother. "Hello, Mum? We're back. Would you like to meet your granddaughter? Frankly, I could use advice."

"Would I?" Alison Forster let out a sound that was half sob, half laughter. "I've been dying for you to get back. In fact, I've been waiting years for this day. It's not the way I imagined it but… I'll be there as soon as I can."

John hung up the phone. His mother had raised three kids and regularly babysat his sisters' children. She would know what to do.

Fifteen minutes later Alison Forster's high heels tapped through the front door in a flurry of feminine excitement. She was all silk blouse, bouffant blond hair, loud voice and a cloud of perfume. In her bejeweled hands she carried bags loaded with dolls, a teddy bear, books and several outfits of warm clothing, including a pair of pink pants and long-sleeved top, socks and two pairs of running shoes.

"I didn't know what size to get but figured I could always bring one pair back. Or take Tuti to the shop with me if neither of these fit. I hope you don't mind me taking it upon myself to buy her some things, but when you rang a couple of weeks ago to say you were bringing her home, well, I just got carried away." Alison glanced around. "Where is she?"

"I don't mind a bit. In fact, I'm grateful." John poked his head into the kitchen. "Tuti, come here, sweetheart. This is your grandmother."

"Hello, darling," his mother cooed and enveloped Tuti in a hug, squeezing her hard. "You can call me Nana. I know we're going to be great friends. We'll make cookies and go shopping and I'll show you where I work—"

John winced as his mother prattled on. She had a huge heart but she could be overwhelming to people who weren't used to her ebullient, extroverted style.

Tuti pulled out of Alison's arms and took a step back. She glanced at John and took another step back.

"It's okay," he assured her. "Don't be shy."

Alison held out a doll and tried to get Tuti to take it. "This is the latest toy, I'm told. All the little girls in Summerside have one. You want to be just like all the other children, don't you?"

Tears started in Tuti's eyes. She bit her lip then, without a word, turned and ran from the room.

"Oh, dear." Alison's manicured fingertips went to her lips. "What's wrong? Doesn't she like dolls?"

"You came on a tad strong." John hadn't realized until now how much his mother must want him to have children. She didn't try this hard with his sisters' kids. He was counting on her to ease him into fathering Tuti, to taking some of the burden of responsibility off him. If Tuti was afraid of her, that wasn't going to work out so well. "It's her first day. Give her time. She'll get used to you."

At least, that's what he hoped. He glanced at the hallway down which Tuti had disappeared. Through work he dealt with juvenile offenders. On the other end of the spectrum were his nieces and nephews—well-adjusted children from loving homes, comfortable if not well-off, who all had two parents.

It brought home to him again how out of his depth he was with Tuti. Not only from another culture, speaking another language, but she'd recently lost her mother. Really, what did he know about raising a kid like Tuti?

"Thanks for the clothes and toys," he said to his mother. "Help yourself to coffee. I'll go talk to Tuti."

He grabbed a teddy bear and some clothes and found her huddled beneath her blankets. Without a word, he handed the stuffed toy to her and waited, using the time to figure out how to explain the strange woman who'd hugged her too hard. He couldn't remember, if he ever knew, the Balinese word for grandmother. After a few minutes Tuti emerged, her cheeks streaked with drying tears. She clutched the teddy bear to her chest and looked at him with huge dark eyes.

"The lady—" John pointed in the direction of the kitchen then at himself. "My *meme*."

Tuti blinked.

"You're *my* child," John tried again. "I'm *her* child."

Tuti looked blank.

He sighed. Should he insist she come out and be polite? He had no idea what child-rearing manuals would say about that. If Tuti were an Australian kid being obstinate, he would probably do just that. But she was far from home, cold, and this was her first day. Instinct told him not to insist on anything. He would make excuses to his mother and ask her to come another day.

"Never mind. Here, let's put something warmer on you." He pulled out the long-sleeved top. "Do you like pink?"

At the sight of the sparkly design on the front of the shirt Tuti got out of the blankets and stood before him, shivering. John helped her dress, wondering what he'd gotten himself into. He'd blundered his way through this time. But if his mother couldn't connect with Tuti what hope did he have?

"GET OUT YOUR notebooks and pencils, boys and girls." Katie pointed to the carefully drawn alphabet on the blackboard. "Copy out the letters in your very best printing."

Heads went down, paper rustled, several tongues were tucked into the corners of mouths as the class of grade-one students got down to work. With a few minutes of quiet Katie sat at her desk and corrected arithmetic assignments.

A knock came at the door. She opened it to John, wearing his police uniform and a grim expression. Her first thought was that something had happened to Riley, and she pressed a hand to her chest to ease a flutter.

He must have seen her anxiety. "There's nothing wrong."

"Thank goodness." Her second fleeting thought, which bothered her in a different way, was how good he looked, his broad shoulders filling out a crisp blue shirt topped by epaulets, and his navy pants with the sharp crease emphasizing the length of his legs.

Then a movement at his side drew her gaze to a little girl clinging to his hand. She was dressed in the school uniform, a blue-and-white gingham dress, one size too big. Her black eyes were huge and terrified. Tear tracks traced her round cheeks. One of the tiny silver circles in her pierced ears was twisted up. And her little pigtails, which stuck straight out from her head, were lopsided and uneven.

Katie's heart melted. Poor sweet thing. Had he found her wandering somewhere in Summerside and brought her to school? Why hadn't he taken her to the office? "Who do we have here?"

"Sorry to interrupt," John said. "This is Tuti. I tried to get here before class began so I could introduce you. But first I had to buy the uniform then I had to get her to wear it. She's not used to hard leather shoes…." He trailed off with a harassed expression. "Tuti, this is Miss Henning. She'll be your new teacher."

Tuti. The girl who lived near a jungle. She looked like she could be Balinese. Had he brought this child to Australia for a visit? Why would he enroll her in school temporarily?

"I don't understand," Katie said. "Who is she?"

John cleared his throat and met her gaze. "Tuti is my daughter."

She stared at him. Surely she hadn't heard correctly. "Your…?"

"Daughter." His hand on Tuti's shoulder tightened protectively. "She'll be six years old next month."

Katie laughed, a slightly hysterical sound. She clapped a hand over her mouth, aware that her reaction was inappropriate. And must appear bizarre to her pupils, not to mention to Tuti.

"I don't understand," she said again. How could he have had a child without her? *Idiot. Of course he could have.* They broke up years ago. He'd left her. Since he'd returned to Summerside he'd never been without a girlfriend for long. He could have fathered a dozen children.

But how was it that she'd known nothing about this Tuti? Who was her mother and why had John brought her here? Did Riley know about her? Questions crowded her mind, confusing her. Emotions she didn't understand made her chest ache. But this wasn't the time or the place to try to make sense of things. The little girl already looked distressed.

Katie collected herself and forced a smile. "I'm pleased to meet you, Tuti. Would you like to join the class?"

The little girl pressed closer to John and turned her face into his waist, her pigtails quivering.

"Does she speak English?" Katie asked.

"A little but she hasn't said a word since she got here three days ago." John's eyes pleaded with Katie. "I'm sure she'll get up to speed quickly but in the meantime she'll need extra help."

"I already have a full class—the administration knows that," Katie said. "She'd be better off with Phoebe Mallon. Phoebe has another English-as-a-second-language student."

"I asked specifically for you. Your assistant principal said it would be okay." When Katie didn't reply to that, he added, "I don't know

Phoebe Mallon. I know you. I know how much you love kids. I want someone who will care about her."

Care about his child with another woman. Really?

Behind her, shifting chairs and whispers told her the pupils had finished their work and were getting restless. Probably curious, too, about the new girl. Dragging this out wouldn't help Tuti. John was right about one thing. Katie loved children and she was a soft touch. She would make room for the girl in her class.

"I'm going to read the class a story, Tuti," Katie said. "Do you like stories?"

Tuti stilled. Then she glanced up at John as if looking for confirmation.

He nodded. "Story…book." He added to Katie, "We've just about worn out the pages on yours." He turned back to Tuti. "Miss Henning is the lady who wrote *Lizzy And Monkey*."

Tuti brightened a little.

John crouched so he was eye level. "I have to go to work, Tuti. I'll come back for you this afternoon." Her bottom lip wobbled. He brushed her cheek with his knuckles. "Chin up," he said, his voice gruff.

Seeing his awkward, tender display of affection, Katie felt a reluctant tug at her heart. Of course she'd always known John would be great with kids. He was a favorite uncle. It made sense he would be a natural as a father.

Tuti looked about to cry. To forestall the waterworks Katie held out her hand to Tuti. "Come with me," she said warmly. "You can sit with Belinda." She gestured to a girl with curly brown hair in the front row. Belinda liked to be teacher's pet but Katie knew she would be kind and helpful. "Belinda, will you come and show Tuti where to sit for story time? Class, this is Tuti. Please welcome her."

The students parroted, obediently if raggedly, "Welcome, Tuti."

Belinda took Tuti's hand, fussy and full of self-importance. "We have to get a chair and go sit in a circle. You can sit beside me." Then she added in a whisper, "Don't cry. It'll be all right."

The children got up and moved to the story circle at the back of the class, the girls talking, the boys pushing. Tuti followed Belinda, holding tightly to the other girl's hand.

John ran a hand through his hair and blew out a heartfelt sigh. "Thanks. I appreciate this."

"I'm doing it for Tuti." Katie fixed him with a stern glance. "We'll need to talk about how best to integrate her into the school community. Please see me this afternoon after class."

John's mouth twitched. "Yes, ma'am."

"This isn't a joking matter." She didn't like

being put on the spot. She didn't like how John had taken advantage of their history. And she didn't like that he'd had a child with another woman so soon after he'd left her. It didn't take a math whiz to calculate that Tuti had been conceived within a few months of his departure. When she was still sick with cancer. He and Tuti's mother must have been making love while she was lying in her hospital bed.

"Yes, I'll do anything for my kids. But get one thing straight. You *don't* know me."

John's lips flattened. "Whatever. As long as we're on the same page with regards to Tuti. I'll see you at three-thirty."

He left and Katie turned back to her class. Belinda was chatting away seemingly oblivious to the fact that Tuti hadn't said a word. Tuti glanced up at Katie, and across the room something tugged at Katie's heart. Oh, no. No, no, no. She wasn't going to fall for John's little girl. She would do her best for Tuti as a teacher but that's where it had to end. For seven years she'd avoided contact with him. The last thing she wanted was a reason to spend time with John Forster.

THE HALLS WERE empty when John returned to Katie's classroom door that afternoon. Was she going to make him write out lines on the blackboard? *I must not bring home foreign children.*

Frankly, he wondered if he'd made a mistake in doing so. It was one thing to feel a familial connection to Tuti and another thing for a bachelor to make a home for a little girl he barely knew and couldn't communicate with.

Last night she'd cried herself to sleep. He'd put it down to tiredness, homesickness and unfamiliar surroundings. He'd tucked her into bed with the doll his mother had brought, but when he'd checked on her in the night, again he'd found her rolled in a blanket on the floor. He'd carried her back to bed. In the morning she'd been back on the floor.

Breakfast this morning was another disaster. He couldn't comb her hair into a proper pigtail to save his soul. He'd run out of cereal and she didn't like toast with Vegemite, or bacon and eggs. In the end he'd found a mango in the back of the fridge.

She had been excited about going to school. Until, that is, she'd seen the huge building and the hordes of children in the playground. He couldn't blame her for being shy—the population of the school was larger than her village—but he didn't know how to deal with it. All his nieces and nephews were outgoing, gregarious kids.

He knocked on Katie's classroom door. She

was a quiet person. She must be able to relate to Tuti.

"Come in." Seated at her desk, Katie was placing big tick marks in a notebook filled with printing practice. "Sit down."

John glanced around for Tuti. She was curled up in a beanbag chair at the back of the room, her nose buried in a picture book. She glanced up, but he motioned for her to stay there while he spoke with her teacher. Gingerly, he lowered himself onto a chair made for a six-year-old, not a grown man, a tall one at that. Feeling ridiculous and at a distinct disadvantage, he waited while Katie finished the notebook she was marking.

She took her time, writing an encouraging note and adding a parrot sticker. Finally she put down her red pencil, closed the notebook and placed it atop the stack on her right. She folded her hands on her desk. "So."

John could still recall his grade-one teacher. Mrs. Renwich had frizzy orange hair, wore glasses on a long chain that sat on her ample bosom and smelled like corned beef. Katie was the complete opposite. Silky dark hair that waved softly around her shoulders, a sweet floral scent, a ready smile and the kindest eyes he'd ever known. Right now she made him more nervous than Mrs. Renwich ever had.

He was still chafing over the way she had said he didn't know her. True, it had been a long time since they'd been together, and she'd undoubtedly changed some. But how was he supposed to know her if she kept refusing to talk to him?

"How did Tuti do today?"

"There are issues. Before we get to those I'm interested in knowing what type of environment she's come from. It will help me deal with her individual needs." Katie lowered her voice. "Have you always known you had a child?"

Since he wanted her help with Tuti, he guessed she had a right to ask. John looked her in the eye. "Yes. I met Nena, that's Tuti's mother, a month into my stay in Bali back in—"

"I know what year you were there."

He cleared his throat. Of course she did. Tuti's birth date was on her enrollment form. Katie would have figured out her conception to the day. "Nena was a lovely person. We had a good time together, while it lasted. The baby wasn't planned, but once Nena found out she was pregnant she wanted the child. What she hadn't wanted was an Australian husband."

He stopped, aware he was giving too much information, justifying himself, explaining more than necessary because of his and Katie's past.

"*Was* a lovely person?" Katie said.

"Nena died in a motorcycle accident. That's why I went to Bali, for her funeral. The women there sometimes ride sidesaddle—in sarongs. Often not wearing a helmet. Half the time hanging on to a kid or a basket of fruit or chickens. It's—" He shook his head. "Never mind. It's the way they do things there. It's just lucky Tuti wasn't with her at the time."

Katie stared at her hands turning the red pen over and over. "You're sure she's yours?"

"Positive." This had to be hard for Katie. They'd talked about having children together many times. Even got around to picking out names. Or he'd tried to. She could never agree with him on when they should start a family. Or even choose a wedding date.

"What made you decide to bring her home with you?"

"I had to." John shifted position on the small chair with a grimace. The edge was digging into his butt. "When I went to Bali I fully intended to pay my respects, make sure she was provided for, and scram."

"But?" Katie's dark eyebrows rose.

"It wasn't that simple. The day after the funeral she showed me where she went to school. It was little more than a shack, with no facilities. I asked her uncle, Wayan, to send her to school in a bigger town and I would pay. He told me she wouldn't be going back to school. She was needed at home to look after her younger cousin."

Katie frowned. "Aren't there laws that say children have to attend school?"

"Yes, but they're not always enforced. School is pretty hit-and-miss for some Balinese. Expats and rich locals attend school regularly. The poor, not so much."

"And is her family poor?"

"They weren't too badly off when Nena was alive and contributing her paycheck. Wayan is a fisherman, but he barely catches enough to feed the family. Nena supported not only herself and Tuti, but helped support Wayan and his family. It's not their fault. The old way of life based on farming and livestock has broken down, fish stocks are depleted and the people are dependent on tourism. But tourism has been down in recent years."

"That's rough." Katie rubbed her thumb over her knuckles. "But do the monetary concerns outweigh the advantages of her living with a family she's grown up with? Surely you could afford to plug the gap that Nena left and let Tuti stay there."

"I'm keeping up payments to the family." John blew out sharply through his nostrils. Katie didn't want to know him, yet she thought she could tell him how to run his life. "I've made my decision. Which, I may add, is *my* decision to make."

Katie tapped her pencil on the desk. "Decisions can be reversed if a mistake has been made."

"I'm not going to chop and change the poor kid. She's staying and that's final." John stopped himself from showing his frustration. Regardless of his feelings, he needed Katie on his side, for Tuti's sake. "I hadn't planned on bringing her back. But when I saw her—" If Katie didn't want to know him anymore he wasn't going to tell how Tuti had reminded him of himself as a child and of his mother. "I couldn't leave her. She might not realize it now or for a few years, but someday she would think back and realize I'd just walked away from her. She would think she didn't matter to me."

Katie went still, her dark eyes simmering. "And now, after seven years, her existence does matter?"

Suddenly the air was charged with the memory of how he'd walked away from *her*. Didn't Katie know that she'd been everything to him? Couldn't she understand that he never would have left if she hadn't pushed him away? They'd gone to the mat over her refusal to get a mastectomy, which he'd been told was the best option to ensure her long-term survival. Instead, she'd tried all sorts of crazy herbal treatments, hours of meditation, eating only raw organic food—he didn't know what all—before finally accepting chemotherapy followed by a lumpectomy and radiation treatment.

Remembering Tuti was in the room, he glanced over his shoulder. She'd left the picture book and was playing with the class guinea pig, poking a sliver of carrot through the bars of the cage. He still didn't know how much she understood and how much of her silence was due to her being overwhelmed by her new life. She seemed oblivious to the conversation.

"Seeing her in person tipped the scales," he went on. "Until a few weeks ago she's been… abstract. Nena had convinced me Tuti was better off if I wasn't in her life at all rather than be a stranger who dropped in every once in a while."

"Personally, I would agree with that."

Katie sat there judging him when she had no idea. No idea. "Maybe it was better, maybe not. But once I'd met her, staying away wasn't better for *me*. She's—" He searched for the words. "She's flesh of my flesh."

Katie made a huffing sound.

His hands fisted on his thighs. "You wouldn't understand, not having a child of your own." Immediately he regretted that low blow.

Her eyes widened. White creases appeared at the sides of her mouth. "Oh, and you've been a parent for all of five minutes."

"Don't take that personally. I didn't understand, either. I still don't, not really." He met Katie's gaze. "All I know is, Tuti and I are connected. I couldn't walk away and leave her."

Katie dropped her gaze to the pencil in her hands. "And does Tuti feel that connection?"

"I don't know. As I said, she doesn't talk."

"Which brings me to the issues I referred to earlier. Today she's spoken not a word, not in English or Balinese. Her mother's death must have traumatized her. Developmentally she's taken a step backward."

John shook his head. "No, I don't think it's that." He explained the Balinese attitude to death. "You should have seen her at the funeral. She wasn't happy but she wasn't overcome with grief either."

"And are you an expert in a child's way of dealing with grief? Her mother's death might not sink in right away. She may need time to process. You should get her counseling."

"How is that going to work if she won't speak English?"

"Psychologists have ways of dealing with children who are pre-language," Katie said.

"Isn't that a specific set of parameters for sexual abuse situations?"

"Maybe that's the side of child counseling you see in police work but there's more to it than that. I'll give you a name of someone." She paused. "You do realize I hope that you can't carry on with your life the way you always have. Kids need a parent to be there for them, especially when they're coping with major life transitions. I recommend you take some leave from work, spend time getting to know Tuti, let her feel safe with you."

"I have work commitments. A major drug investigation is underway—"

"What's more important, police work or Tuti?"

If he said police work, all the arguments he'd just made for bringing Tuti home would be meaningless. But he couldn't afford to take time off right now. Besides, he wasn't going to let Katie dictate how he should handle his own daughter.

"I'll think about it." He rose. "Tuti, time to go home. Come." John knew she understood the word. He tried to make it sound friendly, not an order. She left the guinea pig and started toward her locker at the back of the classroom. "I'll touch base with you tomorrow," he added to Katie.

He and Katie waited in awkward silence while Tuti gathered her lunch box and backpack. All these years he'd wanted an excuse to talk to her. He'd flirted and teased, partly because she wouldn't have a conversation, partly because it was less painful than acknowledging they were finished, that there was nothing left, not even friendship. Now they had a real reason to talk to each other but it was fraught with tension.

No doubt Katie resented the fact that he'd had a child with someone else so soon after they'd broken up. Had she ever stopped to think how she'd made him suffer by making the choices she had? She'd been the one to throw away their future, not him.

"Did she like my book?" Katie asked at length.

"She loves it so much she takes it to bed with her."

Katie's face lit. "I'm glad."

Once upon a time her smile had been like sunshine in his life. Now he looked away.

A small hand crept into his. Tuti gazed up at him, questioning. No matter how she'd struggled against wearing the school uniform, no matter how she'd refused to sleep in a bed, no matter that he had no idea how to deal with a six-year-old girl, not once had she rejected *him*.

From the minute he'd hoisted her onto his shoulders at Nena's funeral she'd trusted him. It was humbling. Yes, he was pretty certain she felt the connection, too.

He cleared his throat. "Tuti, can you say goodbye to Miss Henning? *Selamat tingall.*"

Tuti ducked her head.

"Goodbye for now." Katie leaned down and hugged the girl. Tuti clasped her around the waist. "I'll see you tomorrow."

"We're going to Springvale," John said. "To pick up foods she's familiar with from the Asian market." Seeing Tuti and Katie embracing so affectionately, he added on impulse, "We'll have dinner while we're there. Would you like to come?"

Katie hesitated. For a moment he thought she might say yes. Then she shook her head. "I have work to do."

"Okay, fine." It was a dumb idea, anyway.

"You're going to have to get used to being with her."

"It's not that..." He trailed away. It was, partly. He adored his daughter but he was floundering. Not that he was going to let Katie know that. "Come on, Tuti. Let's go."

Tuti smiled at Katie and gestured to her.

Katie smiled back and waved. "Goodbye."

Tuti shook her head and motioned with her hand to her mouth as if eating.

"She must have understood what I said about dinner," John said.

"And that you invited me. That's good. The more English she understands the easier it'll be when she starts to speak."

Tuti put her hands together in the universal gesture of prayer or pleading. Above her steepled fingertips, her dark eyes danced merrily.

"She knows how to charm," Katie said drily. "Must have got that from you."

"Tuti, Katie is busy. You'll see her tomorrow." He tugged gently on her hand. Her shoulders slumped, but she allowed him to lead her out the door.

"Wait," Katie said.

CHAPTER FOUR

"I'LL COME WITH you after all," Katie said. By his own admission John knew nothing about children, much less little girls. "I'm an expert at buying the healthiest fresh ingredients. When cooking for kids, it's important to have a balanced diet."

John bristled at her comment. "I cook, too. A healthy meal isn't all about googly berries and wheat grass extracts. Tuti won't eat that crap."

"Goji berries." Katie, reaching for her cardigan and purse, stiffened. He had a blind spot when it came to her health choices. "I was only trying to help. By all means, go by yourself."

Tuti's gaze swiveled from Katie to John. Oh, dear. She might not understand every word but she could surely pick up on the tension. John had invited impulsively, and she'd accepted equally impulsively. They'd both made a mistake. But Tuti would be the one to pay.

John noticed Tuti tracking their exchange, too. "No, you're welcome to come along," he said grudgingly. "I'm sure between us we can get what she needs."

Katie hesitated, then nodded. It was too late to back out now. She walked slightly ahead of John down the school corridor. This was her turf. Plus, she needed to maintain some distance. She'd vowed years ago never to go out with him again.

Yet here she was, helping him shop for his daughter. And joining him for dinner. She'd forgotten that part when she'd agreed to help buy groceries.

It was okay. She would handle it—for Tuti's sake. The little girl ran up to her and took her hand. Katie took it with a smile. Her budding affection for Tuti was bittersweet. John hadn't stuck with her to have the family they'd planned. She'd thought he loved her, believed he would be loyal, the way her father had been loyal to her mother when *she'd* had breast cancer. But no, John couldn't handle her illness. He'd gone off and had a kid with someone else.

The fact that Tuti was unplanned didn't make it better. Her mere existence hurt more than Katie could have imagined, almost as if she was being taunted by her own dream. Here she'd beaten cancer, made a great life for herself, written a book even. Yet the husband and children she longed for remained elusive. That husband should have been John. And Tuti should have been their child. But he wasn't, and Tuti wasn't. So much for her dream.

She went in John's car since Springvale was thirty minutes away and it made no sense to go separately. The open area food hall was a maze of fruit and vegetable stalls, seafood, butchers and poultry. Most shoppers were Vietnamese, speaking in their own language. Tuti clung tightly to Katie's hand.

John tried to take her hand, too. She let him but wouldn't relinquish Katie's hand so the three of them wound their way awkwardly through the crowded marketplace. Finally John gave up and let go.

Katie met his gaze. "Don't take it personally. I'm her teacher."

"But I'm her father."

Katie wasn't likely to forget. She could see traces of John in the girl. Not appearance necessarily, but his energy and humor, elements of his personality John seemed to have buried. He'd always been the wild one, an adventurer, blowing where the wind took him, with no clear pathway for the future. After high school he'd drifted in and out of various jobs. Surfing and Katie herself were the only constants in his life.

Then she'd gotten sick and he'd abandoned her to disappear for a yearlong surfing safari.

When he came home he'd gone straight into police academy. Now he lived by rules, enforcing the law, demanding strict discipline of himself and his officers. Only his relationships with women were transient.

Since becoming a cop he'd had to become less spontaneous and more by-the-book. At least she'd gleaned as much from things Riley said. It was too bad. John's zest for life was what had attracted her to him as a young teenager. How many days and nights had she spent mooning over her older brother's hot friend?

She watched him move ahead, his shoulders broad and straight, hips lean and butt tight in navy uniform pants. She stifled a sigh. He was still hot. That hadn't changed.

"This place looks good." John stopped at a fruit stall and picked up a basket. "Just get a variety of produce."

Katie got her own basket and as she put items in, she told Tuti the English name and got her to repeat the word. "You can do this wherever you go," she said to John. "Also, let her watch kids' TV programs like *Sesame Street* where they teach the letters and numbers."

"Maybe I should hire a private tutor." John inspected a papaya, sniffing it for ripeness. "Are you interested?"

"Me?" Katie gave Tuti a plastic bag and

pointed to a display of apples. "Apples. Can you get me six apples?" She held up six fingers. "Six apples."

Tuti carefully placed an apple in her bag without repeating the words. Hopefully she just needed time to adjust and then she would speak.

Katie turned back to John. "I have a job. In fact, I have two jobs, teaching and writing. I've just been offered a new contract for three more books."

John whistled. "Did you accept?"

"Subject to negotiations between my agent and publisher, but yes, I've committed to doing the books. So I won't have a lot of spare time."

"Don't get me wrong, I think it's wonderful that your writing is taking off. But don't you think you're taking on an awful lot considering you're also teaching full-time? You're not going to have much of a life."

What did he know? How dare he make comments on the way she conducted herself. He was no model of appropriate behavior. "I have a good life," she said, glaring at him. "It will only be better now that I have a chance of fulfilling my dream to be a writer."

John faced off with her across the mangoes. "Do you go out? Riley says you don't. When was the last time you had a boyfriend?"

"When was the last time you had a girlfriend

that lasted for more than a month or two?" she shot back. He had no right to be chastising her about her social life. If she went out too little, he went out too much.

"Leave my girlfriends out of this. We're talking about you, not me. Anyway, I'm not with anyone at present."

"I'm sure that won't last—" Katie glanced around, suddenly remembering the reason for this conversation. "Where's Tuti?"

"She's with you. Isn't she?" John swiveled on his heels, looking behind him. "Tuti?"

"You're her father. You're supposed to keep an eye on her." Neither of them were used to watching out for a child. "Tuti! Where are you?"

"She can't have gone far. We only looked away for a few seconds." He pushed through the milling shoppers, moving past the tall fruit bins toward the section of the store that shelved canned goods. "Tuti!"

A flutter of panic ran through her. A few seconds. Was it? Katie hadn't really been paying that close attention. She was used to dealing with children in the controlled environment of a classroom.

She headed in the opposite direction to John, her gaze raking the shop. Small dark-haired children accompanying their parents were plentiful. But no little girl in a blue-and-white gingham dress with pigtails that stuck straight out from the sides of her head. No little girl with a dimpled smile and sparkling eyes.

"Katie!" John waved at her from the fruit and veggie section. "She's here."

Katie hurried to join him. "How did we miss her?"

Tuti was squatting on the floor, her knees up around her pigtails, industriously filling a plastic bag with onions. Beside her were two more bags filled with a mixture of apples, oranges and lemons. Seeing John and Katie standing over her, she smiled proudly and held up her bag to show them.

Katie breathed out, relieved to have found the girl. But her heart sank seeing the bags of mixed fruit and vegetables instead of the six apples she'd asked Tuti for. The girl definitely needed her help.

The question was, at what cost to her, given that she would have less time to spend on her writing? More importantly, how would she cope emotionally with regular contact with John? She couldn't spend an afternoon in his company without getting either annoyed or feeling attracted, despite their many issues. She wasn't sure which emotion bothered her the most.

JOHN CHASED THE last few grains of fried rice around his plate with chopsticks. Katie was gamely making her way through a huge bowl of Vietnamese noodle soup. Tuti had finished her meal and was dangling a toy cat for a baby in a high chair at a neighboring table.

His flare-up with Katie earlier bothered him. For the past half hour they'd been too busy eating to speak. Now that the meal was over the atmosphere had become stifling. But Tuti looked so happy he didn't have the heart to drag her away.

He poured more Chinese green tea into their tiny cups, nodding to Tuti and the baby. "She must miss her niece in Bali. She used to carry that kid around on her hip wherever she went."

Katie took a sip of tea, holding the hot cup by the rim. "Maybe you should go back to Bali and father another child to give her a brother or a sister."

He gave her a hard stare. "That's unworthy of you."

Katie blushed and grimaced. "Sorry. That was uncalled-for. But you have to admit, the timing of Tuti's conception sucks."

"Trust me, I won't be having another kid in a hurry. It's hard enough looking after one kid let alone two."

Katie's eyebrows went up. He clamped his

mouth shut, wishing he hadn't let slip he was having trouble being an instant dad. When Riley had fallen in love with Paula and found a son in Paula's boy, Jamie, he'd been frankly envious of his friend's happiness and new family. Now he wondered how Riley played his role as father to Jamie with such ease. Then again, Jamie was born Australian and Paula was responsible for most of Jamie's care.

"I guess kids cluttering up your bachelor pad will cramp your style with the ladies."

Where did she get this impression he was some kind of lothario? Was it Riley? He was going to have to speak to his mate. "Can you stop with the cracks about my so-called bachelor pad? It's just a modest town house."

"From what I hear it's got a revolving bedroom door. You can't bring a stream of women through with Tuti there."

"I've had *one* girlfriend, Trudy, in the past six months. I'm not with her anymore." Probably a good thing. He had a hard time visualizing the party girl in a maternal light. "I did go out with another woman, Deborah, once or twice but I haven't seen her since I came back from Bali and don't intend to. Although, frankly, it's none of your damn business."

"You asked for my help with Tuti. I'm simply giving you my expert opinion."

"Did I ask for your opinion on my lifestyle? I've already figured out it will have to change." He leaned in to give her a wolfish grin. "Unless your interest in my love life means you're angling to become the next woman in the revolving door."

She rolled her eyes. "While we're having this heart-to-heart, you can stop flirting with me at every opportunity. It makes me uncomfortable."

"Every opportunity? That would be once every three months when I run into you by accident at the pharmacy or something."

"That's four times a year too many." She frowned, tapping her chopsticks on the table. "I can't help Tuti on an ongoing basis if I feel uncomfortable around you."

Did that mean she was considering tutoring his daughter? John smartened up and got serious. "I didn't realize my innocent, lighthearted comments were so offensive."

"They're cheap, throwaway passes. Superficial, the way you are now." A flash of pain crossed her face. "Talk like that diminishes what we used to have." Then she sat back and pushed her empty bowl away. "Not that I care anymore."

Superficial—him? Well, that was news. He had interests, as much as anyone else. Okay, it had been a while since he'd been surfing. He didn't have time what with keeping Summerside safe from criminals and all. If she was talking about the women he went out with, well, they weren't into settling down. That's why he chose them.

"I had no idea I upset you so much," he said stiffly. "I don't know how else to communicate with you. You refuse all overtures. You won't be friends and talk naturally—"

"Friends?" she cut in. "How can we be friends after what you did?"

"After what I did? How about what you did?" He leaned forward. "Or should I say, didn't do?"

"You wanted me to cut off both my breasts," she hissed. "I was right not to, as it turned out."

"That's still a matter of opinion. Yes, you survived and beat the cancer but what evidence do you have that your natural remedies actually worked?"

She spread her arms wide, indicating her fit, healthy body. "The evidence is sitting before you."

She looked good, no question. She always looked good to him, even when she was bloated and her hair had fallen out.

"What if you were to have a recurrence?" She turned her gaze away. He pushed harder. "Would you do anything different?" Still she didn't say anything. "What makes you think you'd be lucky a second time?"

"You don't understand anything." She glanced back, her voice trembling. "If I'd had my breasts removed I wouldn't have been able to nurse our children."

It was on the tip of his tongue to say, they wouldn't even have children if she wasn't alive. He stopped himself. She would never admit she was wrong. If he kept pressing her for an acknowledgment that her choice of treatments hadn't been the safest, or reacted to her accusations about how he'd hurt her, they would keep on fighting.

"Can we please move on?" Katie added.

He was reluctant—they were talking, really talking, for the first time in years. And as far as he knew there was a chance she couldn't even have kids after going through chemo. But he didn't want to fight Katie, he never had. Now more than ever he wanted to be friends. Having Tuti come to live with him and seeing Katie again had stirred his old dreams of a home and family. It was probably wishful thinking but maybe if Katie got to know him again, if they could get past the old stuff, they might have a chance.

The way to her heart was through Tuti. Katie loved kids and she liked to be needed. And

God knows, Tuti needed her. His family, while they were willing to help with Tuti, didn't have Katie's teaching skills. Plus their time was limited. His mother was willing to babysit when she could but she worked, writing a column for the local newspaper. Same went for his sisters, one a lawyer, the other running a café. He could hire a tutor but in spite of Katie's claim that he didn't know her any longer, he did know she had the patience and the resolve and the dedication Tuti needed. Tuti was in a foreign country with foreign customs and limited English. She was overwhelmed and the more familiar faces he could give her, the better it would be. So yes, for all those reasons, Katie *did* top his list of potential tutors.

The family at the next table was getting up to leave, strapping their baby into a stroller. Tuti would be back any second. John wanted a positive connection with Katie so they wouldn't go back to being formal with each other. He took a breath and summoned the kind of courage that didn't get exercised much on the police force.

"It hurts that you don't want to know me." The epithet "superficial" especially had stung. "I'm sorry if I made you uncomfortable. I promise I won't try to flirt with you again. I'm not asking to take up where we left off." *Yet*. "But I would like to be friends."

There, he'd said it. If she turned down his friendship after all that groveling, he would move away from Summerside and never come back. "So…?"

"You're only saying this because you want my help with Tuti."

"I do want your help. I don't deny that. But that's not why I'm flaying myself before you. If you don't have time for her then I'll figure something else out. But just don't…cut me dead when I meet you on the street. Don't leave a party the minute I arrive. Say 'good day' like you mean it. Have a coffee with me now and then." He felt his throat catch and cleared it. "It's not a lot to ask."

"I'm sorry." Her hands clasped tightly around her teacup. "I wasn't aware I was that mean to you."

"Well, you are. People comment."

"I'll try not to do it again." She sucked in a breath, regained her composure. "So, do I have your word—no flirting? No innuendo? No double entendres?"

He grimaced. Had he really been that louche? "None of that. If only you'll give Tuti extra help to bring her up to speed."

Katie tilted her head to one side. The curve of her breasts beneath her draped blouse rose and fell as she thought about it. His mind drifted in an inappropriate direction. Damn it all. He was a man. He couldn't help the way his body reacted. She could ask him to keep his mouth shut but she couldn't control his thoughts.

But he would learn to stay quiet. The comments were more a nervous reaction than anything he really wanted to say to her, anyway. If she actually conversed with him like he was a decent human being then maybe he could respond in kind.

Tuti slid back onto her chair next to Katie and smiled up at her teacher. The little girl couldn't have made a more timely entrance if she'd been scripted. But that just ratcheted up the tension. Katie wouldn't like feeling pressured from two sides.

John sat back and glanced away, as if it wasn't a big deal if she tutored his daughter or not. When, in truth, her continued presence in his life had become of paramount importance to him in a very short space of time.

KATIE WOULD LOVE to help Tuti. But she'd agreed to write three books this year. Plus, she was teaching full-time. And spending time with Tuti would inevitably mean spending time with John. Sure, he'd promised to curb his teasing and flirting but that didn't mean she wanted to be his new best friend. He'd hurt her. Badly.

Tuti's very existence was a constant reminder of the extent of his betrayal.

But Tuti needed her in the here and now, and that was bigger than Katie and John's unhappy past. In only a day Tuti had made her way into Katie's heart with her shy smile and sparkling eyes. Somehow she would find the time to teach, write and tutor Tuti. As for John, she could be friendly without getting involved. "I'll do it."

"Really?" John said, sitting forward. "Thank you."

"But you have to reinforce my teaching," Katie said. "That involves reading to her every night, talking to her as much as possible, explaining things."

"I can do that."

"Even if she doesn't understand every word you say, the meaning will gradually sink in. Children pick up languages easily. Tuti seems very bright."

Tuti's gaze was flicking from Katie to John.

"I'm going to give you extra time after class, just you and me," Katie said, and Tuti beamed up at her. To John, Katie added, "The school will provide a teacher's aide. We should be able to bring her up to speed in a few months."

"I really appreciate this. Let me know what

days and times are good for you and I'll arrange to be home."

"That's not necessary," Katie said quickly. A cozy threesome at John's house felt a little too similar to a family unit for her comfort. With anyone else she wouldn't have even thought that, but with John she didn't want any reminders or allusions to what they might have had.

"I'll take her home with me after school a couple of days a week then drop her off at your place when we're done." Katie reached for her purse among the bags of produce at her feet. "I need to get back. Are you ready to go?"

On the return trip to Summerside Katie pointed out trees, cars and houses to Tuti. The girl listened attentively at first then gradually lost interest to play with her doll.

Katie fell into silent contemplation. Had she really cut John dead at parties? Walked out of the room when he walked in? It wasn't *always* about him, although she would never get used to seeing him with his arm around another woman. She simply wasn't a party person, preferring small groups of close friends. If she was invited to a large gathering, she put in an appearance then often left when the night was still young. She winced to think how others might view her behavior. Riley sometimes gave her a hard time for being standoffish but she put that down to her brother's not-so-secret wish that his best mate and his sister would get back together.

Katie glanced sideways at John, one hand draped over the steering wheel, a slight frown creasing his brow as he gazed at the road ahead. So what if she did snub him? He'd left her to die and gone surfing.

It didn't get much worse than that. And yet…

Seven years on she was still punishing him. She didn't like what that said about her. And it wasn't the way a woman who didn't care behaved.

"It's Tuti's birthday in a couple of weeks," John said. "Would you like to come? My parents are hosting it at their place. They've got the space for all the cousins to run around."

"When is it exactly?" she stalled. Once upon a time she'd felt part of his family, even though the noisy boisterous Forsters were so different from the more reserved Hennings. Acting friendly was one thing but going to a party with him was quite another. Her introverted nature aside, if she went to the party would everyone think she and John were getting back together? That wasn't going to happen. The pressure, the sincere good wishes, might be uncomfortable.

"Not this Saturday but next."

"I'll have to see. I have these insane deadlines now."

"It's going to be Tuti's first time being around the whole family. It would be great if she had a few people there that she knew well."

"Oh, right." Her cheeks burned and she turned away to look out the window. He was asking her for Tuti, not him. Of course. How could she have thought anything else?

"Tuti and my mother haven't hit it off," John went on. "You know how Mum is, so over-the-top. She's trying too hard. Tuti runs and hides every time she comes around."

Katie could relate. She'd been overwhelmed by Alison at first, too, and she'd been a teenager when she'd first met John's mother. Gradually she'd come to appreciate Alison's exuberance, and then to love her as a second mother. "You want me to be an intermediary. Isn't that your job?"

"I've tried. So far it's not working."

"I don't know. The tutoring is within reason. But getting involved in family stuff..." She shook her head.

"Okay. I'm not going to pressure you. Just thought you might like to come for your own sake." He paused. "My sisters ask after you."

Suddenly her chest felt tight. She'd lost a whole family when she and John had split up. His sisters and his mother had rallied around her when she was ill and in the hospital. It wasn't until John had returned to Australia and she refused to make up with him that Alison had turned cool toward her. She understood that Alison would be loyal to John and side with him, but she'd come to rely on Alison's love and support. When she'd withdrawn it, she'd hurt Katie.

She also missed John's sisters, Sonya and Leah. They'd been the older sisters she'd never had. She'd lost touch with them, too. She'd been glad in a way—seeing them had been a painful reminder of John—but it had been another loss. She'd liked his dad, Marty, a fire captain, too. He was easygoing and jovial, a far cry from her bottled-up ex-military father.

Now, through Tuti, John was back in her life and she would have to deal with all those feelings she'd buried for years. In most areas of her life she was confident, happy, cheerful. Yet she'd allowed herself to stay stuck in the role of being the injured party with John. She was weary of it. This behavior made her seem cowardly and, since her recovery, she'd vowed to be bold, adventurous and brave.

She missed being friends with him. Missed their quiet conversations, the laughter, the sense of knowing someone so well they didn't need to speak. For seven years she'd kept John Forster off her radar. Taking on Tuti meant reentering his sphere. It would be uncomfortable at times but she would be lying if she told herself she was doing it only for Tuti's sake. She needed to do this for herself. It was time to learn to see John as just another guy. It was time to move on.

From now on she would go out of her way not to avoid him. It was the only mature way to behave. She would be pleasant and polite. She would have the occasional coffee with him. And she would go to his daughter's birthday party. In return he would simply treat her as a friend. It sounded like a fair deal.

They were approaching the end of the highway and the intersection leading to Frankston. "What day did you say the party is?"

"Saturday, two weeks from now." He shot her a glance. "Two till six."

This was her opportunity to show the Forsters what Katie Henning was made of. So she didn't have a husband or children. That wasn't the be-all and end-all. She'd survived, not just the cancer but the heartbreak, the loss of her second family. She'd gone on to have a great life on her own, a full life, achieving her goals and making a success of herself in not one but two careers.

"I guess I could probably make it."

"Great!" John reached over to squeeze her hand.

Oh, dear. The sudden kick of her heart at his

brief touch wasn't the stuff of friendship. She tugged her hand away and folded it inside her own. No matter what, she was not going to fall for him again.

"HOLD STILL, TUTI." John scraped her slippery hair back with the brush and awkwardly fumbled the elastic around the pigtail. Despite his mother's gifts of sparkly barrettes and pretty hair bands Tuti only wanted her chin-length hair in pigtails. It was damn fiddly and he was sweating beneath his uniform shirt. But so much in Tuti's life had changed, he figured if she wanted to hang on to this one thing, he would give her pigtails if it killed him.

"How's that?" He looked into the bathroom mirror with her, hands resting lightly on her shoulders. The pigtails looked too high on her head, a bit like an alien's antennae. "I'm not much of a hairdresser."

Tuti gazed silently at her reflection, her eyes worried.

"Sorry, sweetheart, they'll have to do." He squeezed her shoulders. "Let's go or you'll be late for school."

He walked Tuti inside to her classroom then drove on to the police station, parking in the back in his reserved spot. Every day he had to face that damn empty lot next door where the station extension should be. Shading his eyes against the sun, he visualized bricks and mortar housing a CSI unit and facilities for half a dozen more uniformed cops. Not going to happen thanks to cuts to the state budget.

He wasn't an empire builder. He just wanted the resources he needed to protect his community. Okay, maybe it was more than that. Lately his job, although rewarding in many ways, had seemed…not enough. The bigger cases kept going to Frankston and growing Summerside station was the only answer he could think of.

Seeing Katie achieve big things with her writing was wonderful but, though he hated to admit it, it had made him more discontent with his own lot. He'd had simple dreams once—to marry Katie, have a bunch of kids and be a professional surfer. His relationship with Katie had gone bust and his surfing dream faded with maturity. He'd turned to law enforcement hoping for a life of action and excitement. But with each rung on the police career he'd had less action and more paperwork. Now he'd risen as far as he could go at Summerside Police Station and he was stagnating, careerwise. He never told anyone that, of course. From the outside his life no doubt appeared perfect—a solid job, nice home, family and friends, great community. To want more would look like he was complaining.

Funny, though, how now that he was ready for change, his life was changing around him. He had custody of Tuti and was reconnecting with Katie. Maybe it was time he did something about his career, as well. He had a family to think about. Okay, she was only one small girl, but being responsible for Tuti made him look at life differently. And if things progressed with Katie—but no, he wasn't going to get ahead of himself. For now he was just glad they were back on friendly terms.

He went inside to collect his mail in the main office. Patty, the young Irish woman in Dispatch, was working the switchboard. "Hey, Patty. Hot day."

"To be sure." Patty adjusted her headset, pushing back red curls damp with perspiration. "The air-conditioning never makes it into this little sweatbox. When are we going to get approval on the extension and upgrade?"

He knew he shouldn't have made his request for funds public, but Patty did double duty as a secretary and had typed the application. Once Patty knew something, the entire station was informed within a day or two. He hated having to explain himself to people. He'd had enough of that following the breakup with Katie and the death of his surfing dream. Nowadays he was more pragmatic, less of a dreamer. Until lately.

Was he crazy, starting to want more professionally just when he was tied down with a child? Except he didn't see it that way. Tuti was a new adventure, a breath of fresh air, reminding him that he'd once wanted more out of life.

"Don't hold your breath." John tugged at his collar. "I think there's a floor fan in the storeroom."

"A floor fan." Patty shook her head dolefully.

John fished his mail out of his pigeonhole and walked down the corridor to his office. Before he got there Paula waylaid him in the bull pen. Behind her, Riley was at a desk, furiously typing into a computer.

"A word, boss?" Paula, tall, athletic and blonde, came forward to meet him. "It's about the Moresco case."

Paula had come to Summerside with a cloud over her head from a past liaison with Nick Moresco, a drug dealer under her investigation who'd fathered her son, Jamie. When crystal methamphetamine appeared on the street in Summerside she'd vowed to put Moresco back behind bars. She and Riley had been working hard on the case, but so far they hadn't managed to gather enough evidence to make an arrest.

"What's the latest?" John said. "Any breakthroughs?"

"Riley and I tailed him to a holiday house

in Rye," Paula said. "We believe he's using the premises to cook crystal meth." She glanced at Riley, checking his progress. "We're applying for a search warrant."

"You going out there today?"

"No, I need to organize the Force Response Unit from Melbourne. That'll take a couple of days."

"What evidence do you have that he's cooking?" John asked. "If you're wrong, you'll send him underground."

"Nick's a city penthouse kind of guy," Paula explained. "This holiday house is tiny and rustic, tucked in the bushes, far from the beach."

"No nosy neighbors to wonder about odd smells," Riley said over the sound of typing. "Nor any great loss if the kitchen explodes and the place burns down."

John envied their excitement at closing in on their lead. Sure he was in charge of the station, but he'd gone into the police force because he was a doer, not a paper pusher. These days his job mostly involved administration and a mountain of paperwork. And keeping a level head. "Sure he wasn't just visiting someone?"

"The property is registered in his grandmother's name. She lives in Palermo, Italy," Paula added pointedly. "We've got him this time, I'm positive."

"Sounds promising. Judge Horton in Frankston is available during office hours to sign your warrant." John clapped Paula on the shoulder and nodded to Riley. "Good work, you two. If you need me to be part of the team..." He tried to keep the wistful note out of his voice.

"Don't worry," Riley said. "We've got it covered."

Of course, they did. But all of a sudden he was desperate to be *doing* something. "Let me know when the raid is going down. I want to be there."

Leaving them staring after him, he carried on to his office. He shut the door with a slam and flung himself in his chair. Files were stacked a foot high on both sides of his desk. Ignoring them, he leafed through the mail. Memos about bushfire safety, notices of upcoming detective courses, the national police newsletter... He flipped through the newsletter to the ads for vacant positions. Not that he was going anywhere. He'd just brought Tuti home to Summerside. She needed to settle in.

He tossed the newsletter aside. Nope, nothing of interest.

CHAPTER FIVE

KATIE IGNORED THE tittering going on in her class to answer the door and let in the sixth-grade girl collecting lunch orders. Normally her students were well behaved, but today the moment her back turned whispers and stifled giggles started. She'd hoped the children would get bored of teasing Tuti, at least until recess when Katie could fix the girl's hair.

Tuti's pigtails did look funny, she had to admit. Done correctly, they adorably jutted out either side of her dimpled smile. She didn't know what John had done today but it wasn't pretty. Not even cute. Tufts of hair erupted from the top of the girl's head at an angle, leaving clumps hanging down that weren't long enough to be held by the elastic. As if that wasn't bad enough, the right pigtail sat an inch forward of the left pigtail. Plus, the left pigtail had a ribbon and the right didn't, adding to the comic effect.

Except that Tuti wasn't laughing. At first she'd smiled in response to the other children's grins and reached out the only way she knew how, by offering them cookies from her lunch, and the use of her precious colored pencils. Gradually she'd realized they were laughing *at* her, not with her. Her sweet smile had faded, replaced by an anxious frown.

Katie glanced over her shoulder. Her heart sank.

Tuti's head was bowed low, her forehead almost touching the top of the table she shared with Belinda. As Katie watched, a tear dropped. Belinda, bless her, rubbed Tuti's shoulder and glared at the class but even she couldn't stop them from teasing. Katie bit her lip. She didn't want to make things worse for Tuti by chastising the class in front of her.

She turned back to the grade-sixer. Miranda was one of the popular girls. Her long shiny blond hair was beautifully but simply styled with a blue hair band that matched her dress.

"Miranda, could you do me a favor?" she said in a low voice. "Leave the order with me for now and take Tuti to the girl's room and fix her hair."

"Yes, Miss." Miranda handed over the plastic container in which she carried the paper bags and money.

Katie called Tuti over and gave her a little hug. "Go with Miranda."

"Come on, Tuti." Miranda smiled and held out her hand. "I'll make you so pretty."

Sniffing, Tuti trustingly placed her hand in Miranda's.

Katie closed the door and turned back to the class. From the shamefaced expressions on most of the children they knew they'd done wrong. Reminding herself that the word *discipline* meant to teach not to punish, she told them a story with a message on treating others as we would like to be treated.

She thought of that lesson and how to approach John about the incident as she drove Tuti home from her English tutoring that afternoon. Naturally she couldn't and wouldn't punish John for making Tuti the laughingstock of the class. But she could teach him how not to.

He opened the door of his town house to her knock, still in his uniform, a beer in his hand. He looked tired, the lines around his eyes more deeply etched than usual. His broad shoulders filled out his blue uniform shirt as nicely as ever but today they didn't seem quite as straight.

"Hey, Tuti," he said. "How did you get braids in your hair?"

Tuti beamed at him then slipped past, kicking off her shoes and tugging at her socks even before she dropped her school bag. She ran down the hall, presumably to her bedroom.

"I got a girl from grade six to help," Katie explained. Miranda had done a fabulous job on Tuti. Two thin braids were caught up in perfect pigtails tied with a rich blue satin that contrasted beautifully with Tuti's glossy black hair. After lunch, several other grade-one girls had returned from the playground with the same hairstyle, although not executed with the same panache.

Katie handed John the reader they'd worked from that he was supposed to go over again with Tuti tonight. "May I come in? There's something important we need to talk about."

John set the reader on the hall table and lined up Tuti's carelessly discarded shoes neatly next to his spit-polished black leather shoes. "I'll just go turn down the stove. Come through to the kitchen."

Katie had never been inside John's town house but she recognized his collection of boomerangs and Aboriginal throwing sticks mounted on one wall of the small foyer. The collection had grown since she'd last seen it in the house he'd shared with Riley in their early twenties. She'd practically lived there herself, coming and going as if it were her second home. She missed those days with a sudden pang—the carefree lifestyle, their still-sunny-looking future, the love and the laughter. Now she was a formal visitor, a service provider, the atmosphere constrained.

Remembering how he liked to keep shoes off in the house, Katie slipped out of her pumps and followed him to the kitchen, where exotic spices wafted from a pot bubbling on the stove. In the doorway she leaned against the jamb and watched him lift the lid and give the contents a stir, a small frown putting creases between his eyes.

"Hard day?"

"The usual." He replaced the lid and turned down the gas burner.

"Tuti had a tough day, too." Katie glanced over her shoulder. The girl wasn't in sight but just in case, she kept her voice low. "The other kids laughed at her, made her cry."

John had been about to take a sip of beer. Instead he set the bottle on the granite counter. "What happened?"

"Her pigtails. I'm sorry but they looked ridiculous. It was really embarrassing for poor Tuti."

"Don't kids have anything better to worry about than another child's hairstyle?"

"Sure they do, like who has the newest video game, or who let out a fart in class. These are kids, John. They can be unbelievably sweet. And they can be unthinkingly cruel."

"But you fixed it, right? Her hair looks fine now."

"Yes, but I can't ask Miranda to do her hair every day."

Wearily he scrubbed a hand across the back of his neck. "What do you suggest?"

"I'm going to teach you to make a proper pigtail and also to braid." She smiled. "Tuti's a trendsetter now. After today, any little girl who doesn't show up to grade one without two tiny braids in her hair is going to suffer."

"You want me to learn to braid hair." He spoke as if she'd asked him to put on a tutu and dance ballet.

"You're a single dad. It's part of what you do. Don't worry, anyone can learn."

Half an hour later, she was beginning to wonder if that was true. Tuti sat on a tall stool in front of the bathroom mirror, eating an ice-cream bar. John, who could splice rope and tie complicated sailor's knots, was all thumbs when it came to braiding Tuti's hair.

"It's so slippery." His blue police shirt was damp beneath his arms and he frowned in concentration, his tongue tucked in a corner of his mouth.

Katie was feeling less than cool herself, crammed into the small bathroom so close to John their elbows bumped. She could feel his body heat and smell the long day in his clothes. If she didn't care about him, why was she so aware of him physically, or notice how he kept glancing at her instead of watching what he was doing?

"You've almost got it. Don't let go of the strands. You're doing well." She had to hand it to him, once he'd accepted that hairdos were an integral part of childrearing he'd stuck to it. "Now, gather the braid and the clump of hair. No, don't just bunch it into the elastic, you have to brush it first so it's smooth."

He fumbled and half the pigtail fell through his fingers. Keeping a tight hold on the rest of the hair, he glanced to her for help. Her arm brushed his and their fingers touched as she gathered up the lock of hair and passed it into his grip.

Golden bristles of his five-o'clock shadow glinted in her peripheral vision. His jaw was set. Katie held her breath. When they'd been together he'd been little more than a gangling youth. Now she was very aware he had a man's strength and air of authority.

Suddenly she saw her avoidance of him over the years in a new light. His smile, his charm, his blue eyes…all were lethally attractive, dangerous given she didn't want to be involved. Now she'd gotten herself into a situation of having to be around him. What kind of an idiot was she? She'd been hurt by him once. Could she trust herself not to fall for him again? She didn't want to take that chance. But what choice did she have? She was committed to helping Tuti.

He pulled the elastic over the pigtail. "Your daddy's doing a good job," Katie said to Tuti in the mirror.

The girl gazed at her quizzically.

"She knows me as *Bapa*." John gingerly let go of the pigtail and stood back. "How's that?"

Bapa. Talk about a cold splash of reality. As adorable as Tuti was, every time she looked at the little girl she was slapped in the face with John's betrayal, with proof that in her hour of need John had abandoned her. She'd thought she knew him but she hadn't really known him at all.

Katie tugged Tuti's pigtail gently to tighten the elastic and tucked a braid into place. "Good effort. Now tie on the ribbons and make a bow." He reached for two ribbons from the collection at random. "No, they have to be the same color."

"Close enough."

"Would you wear socks of two different colors?" Glancing down at his feet, she laughed. "Oh, my God. You are. Can't you tell navy from black?"

"No, I can't." His dimple deepened. "Remember?"

Now that he'd reminded her, she did. Her crack about his socks must have come from her subconscious. The first time they'd spent the night together, at the Forsters' beach cottage, giddy with love, they'd had a silly discussion over his socks. He'd sworn black was blue and vice versa. She never had figured out if he really couldn't tell the difference or if he'd just been teasing her.

"Luckily Tuti's ribbons only give you a choice of blue or white." Even hair accessories had to be in the school colors.

John wound a ribbon onto each pigtail and tied two perfect bows. He met Katie's gaze in the mirror. "Do I get a gold star?"

A corner of her mouth lifted. "You'll pass."

Very casually he added, "Would you like to stay for dinner, as you know, friends do? I'm making Beef Rendang."

Tuti's bright gaze darted between her face and his.

His use of the word "friend" had been a deliberate reminder of her side of the bargain. Katie was tempted, and by more than the rich aroma of ginger, garlic and chili permeating the house. Tuti's origins aside, she *liked* John. Plus, she'd promised not to slight him.

On the other hand, she didn't want to get involved in a relationship again and she got the feeling that's what he was angling after. Yes, she felt an attraction and she enjoyed his company but that didn't make certain issues disappear. Being around him reminded her of the good times, but also of the bad times, the cancer and the treatments. And being rejected not only in her hour of need but also at the moment she had stood up for what she believed in. He hadn't backed her. As much as she might be attracted to him, if being with him meant having to sacrifice a part of herself, well then, she couldn't do it. What if her cancer did recur someday. Would *he* do anything differently? She couldn't risk being hurt again.

Just because they were trying to be friends didn't mean she had to accept every invitation.

"Thanks, but I'm going home to write. My contract arrived today. I really need to get some work done on my book." It wasn't just an excuse. Her deadlines, while exciting, were also scary. She was a tiny bit afraid she'd bitten off more than she could chew.

A refusal was usually his cue to tease her about working too much, and list the menu items in an attempt to lure her to his dining table. Then he would tease and torment until she was struggling between laughing and wanting to slap him.

But all he said was, "Another time, then."

As if it was nothing to him, either way. Just for a second Katie almost felt as if she'd been rejected. But that was stupid. She'd been the one to turn down the offer. She didn't like it when he was too persistent. She'd wanted him to ease up. She couldn't possibly be missing his teasing.

"Off you go, Tuti," John said. "Go change out of your school clothes so you don't get them dirty."

Tuti waggled her head to watch her pigtails bounce, then ran out of the bathroom. A moment later Katie heard the back door slam. Not going to her room to change as she'd been asked. John was straightening up the collection of pink and purple barrettes, scrunchies and hair bands that had bloomed alongside his shaving accessories on the bathroom counter.

Wasn't he going to go after her, make sure she did as she was told? Had he even noticed? Should she say something? Being a teacher, Katie was used to making children behave. She bit her lip to stop from speaking out. It was none of her business if Tuti got her dress dirty and couldn't wear it tomorrow.

She turned to leave. "I can let myself out."

"I'm coming, too. Make sure that rendang isn't sticking to the pot."

She walked ahead of him down the narrow hallway lined with Forster family photographic portraits.

"Which one of our adventures are you going to write about tonight?" John asked.

Katie's step faltered and her cheeks warmed. "I don't know what you mean."

"Come on, Katie. It's obvious I'm Monkey."

He'd guessed. Well, she supposed it wasn't that hard. She'd never expected he would read the book and since no one else knew half the places they went and things they did, she hadn't thought he would find out.

"Well?" John prompted.

She stopped in the narrow hall and faced him. "I probably should have asked you first. Do you mind very much?"

"We had some adventures, didn't we? You really captured the fun we had." In the shadowed hallway he held her gaze, his eyes gleaming.

Memories of sunlit golden days rose up, of them lying together on beaches, in grassy meadows. Her gaze drifted down to his firm lips, curving humorously. Her heart beat faster. She wanted to kiss him. But that was crazy.

She had to glance away. "You didn't answer my question."

"Well, I don't know. You spurned any contact with me yet drew on our shared history for your stories..."

"I'm sorry."

"On the other hand, I'm flattered I played such an important role in your life." His fingertips touched her jaw, turning her face so she had to look at him. "And clearly still do."

"No." She was protesting the intensity of her own feelings as much as his words. She turned and started walking again, urgently needing to be on her way. "Our past is merely grist for the writer's mill."

He followed her. "What will you do when you run out of the past?"

"I'll, why, I'll go on my own adventures." She reached the foyer and breathed a little easier. "I don't need to rely on you now. In fact I'm going on adventures all the time."

"Really? What was the last adventure you went on?" He sounded mildly amused. "I might be interested in trying it myself. And I'll enjoy reading your next book having inside knowledge."

Katie straightened her shoulders. "All right. I haven't done anything nearly as exciting or dangerous as the stuff we used to do together. But I'm going to."

John's smile faded. "You shouldn't be doing

dangerous activities on your own. That's not what I meant. What are you considering?"

Damn. He'd trapped her. She hadn't exactly been planning base jumping expeditions but she couldn't let him think she wasn't capable of acting on her own. "Not life threatening, just challenging."

He crossed his arms. "Like what?"

"Like..." She racked her brains. "Mountain biking. I hear there are some great trails in Red Hill."

"I know those trails. They're pretty gnarly. Have you ever been off road?"

"I ride into the village center to shop or go for a coffee." Her chin lifted. "Sometimes I ride along the chip bark path through the reserve."

He shook his head, chuckling. "In other words, you've still got your training wheels on when it comes to off road."

It was true she'd only ridden her mountain bike on roads and groomed paths. But how dare he call her capacity for derring-do into question? If she wanted to break her neck it was none of his business. "I'll see you next Tuesday. Say goodbye to Tuti for me."

"Don't go off in a huff." John touched her arm.

"I'm not in a huff. I just have to go." She

pulled away, moving toward the front door. "Where are my shoes?"

"Where did you leave them?"

"Right there." Katie pointed to the spot on the marble tile next to Tuti's black Mary Janes.

"Tuti must have taken them. That kid has a mischievous streak." He strode into the lounge room. "She's not here."

Katie went back down the hall and peered around a door into a study where a cot was jammed between a desk and a filing cabinet. "Tuti, where are you? I need my shoes."

No answer.

The screen door slammed. She headed for the back of the town house. The yard was tiny, dominated by a paved patio area and a tall gum tree next to the fence. John stood below the tree, head tilted way back.

Katie hurried to his side and looked up. Way up. Her heart caught in her throat. High among the upper branches flashed a slim brown leg and a swatch of blue-and-white gingham.

"TUTI, COME DOWN." John was trained to stay calm in the face of danger, but his training hadn't prepared him for dealing with his own child in such a situation. He might sound calm—at least he hoped he did—but his heart was racing and only sheer force of will stopped him from bellowing like a frightened bull.

Tuti was about ten feet up the tree. Seeing him, she'd scampered another eight feet higher, her legs and arms stretching impossibly far between smooth-barked limbs. One slip and she would ricochet down like a rag doll.

"Oh, my God. How did she climb so high?" One hand to her throat, Katie shaded her eyes to look up.

"You want a monkey?" he said grimly. "There she is." He cupped his hands around his mouth and called loudly, "Come down right now!" No answer, just a rustle of branches. A twig dropped, bouncing against the trunk to land on the slate pavers. He tried a different tactic. "What have you done with Katie's shoes?"

Katie circled the base of the trunk, scanning the tree. "There they are." She pointed to her black pumps wedged in a fork of two thick lower branches. She turned to John. "I don't care about my shoes. Just get Tuti down."

Did she think he wasn't trying? He couldn't even see the girl. He moved around the tree to get a better view. And almost wished he hadn't. Tuti sat on a narrow limb, her legs swinging, casually holding on to a branch with one hand. With her other hand she mimed eating and pointed to Katie.

John turned to Katie, relief flooding him as a simple solution presented itself. "She wants—"

"I get it." Katie lowered her voice. "But if we give in to blackmail we'll pay long term."

"We?" His attention was momentarily diverted from Tuti. Katie seemed to think she had a vested interest in his daughter. Did that mean she was softening toward him? He didn't think he'd imagined the sexual tension between them in the bathroom, or that moment in the hall.

Confusion stained her cheeks pink. "I mean, you, of course. I'm just her teacher. But I stand to lose authority in the classroom over this." Katie edged away from him and called up into the tree. "Tuti, I can't stay for dinner tonight. Don't worry about my shoes. I'll get them later. Bye."

"What?" John spun around as she started back to the house in her stocking feet. "You want to leave her up in that tree?"

"Please, trust me on this. I know what I'm doing."

"I get what you're saying about blackmail but how can I let her get away with taking your shoes? It's bad behavior." He glanced up to check on the dangling brown legs through the leaves. "This is no time to experiment with child-rearing theory."

"I'm worried about her, too," Katie said. "It's

called reverse psychology. Believe me, I know what I'm doing. I deal with kids all day, every day."

Maybe she had experience on her side, backed up by rational thinking and the wisdom of experts. But he felt the danger to his daughter on a primal level. All his instincts were screaming at him to act. He wanted her down safely and he'd worry about psychology later. Katie couldn't even do a simple thing like agree to stay for dinner. No, she had to turn everything into a matter of principle.

"No," he said firmly. "No way. She's not allowed to risk her silly little neck." *The way Katie had when she'd refused a mastectomy.* She'd defied not just the best medical advice but risked their future together. "Nor is she allowed to try to dictate what goes on around here." Balancing on one foot, he pulled off first one sock, then the other.

Katie stopped walking. "What are you doing?"

"She's not the only one who can climb trees."

"Wait!" She held out a hand. "Stop and think. Jeez, you and she are more alike than you realize—mischievous, impulsive and foolhardy."

"You're comparing me to a six-year-old?" He reached for a lower limb.

Katie put a hand on his arm. "She's a lot smaller than you. She can climb onto smaller branches. If you scare her higher into the tree the danger if she falls is that much greater."

"She won't fall." Katie had a point but Tuti had inherited his agility.

"I'm telling you, this is a mistake," Katie insisted. "You're going about this all wrong."

"She's *my* daughter," he said pointedly. "You might be able to walk away and leave her in a tree based on some theory but I can't."

He'd walked away from Katie when she needed him. He wasn't ever doing anything like that again, not with someone he loved. Holding on to a branch, he planted a bare foot against the smooth gray bark and walked up the trunk until he could throw a leg over a lower branch. He pulled himself up to a standing position, braced between two branches.

"Tuti, come down this minute or you're in big trouble." His voice reverberated through the branches, his fear manifesting as anger. This time he didn't try to sound calm.

"Threatening her won't get you anywhere," Katie called.

"With all respect, butt out. She's my kid."

"You're used to dealing with criminals. And cops who are almost as tough as you are. You don't understand how gruff you sound to a little girl."

"I want to sound gruff." He climbed another

branch, reached for Katie's shoes. "Look out below." He dropped them onto the grass. Then he glanced up through the leaves. He could see Tuti's face and her jaunty pigtails, white ribbons fluttering. Framing her dark head, sickle-shaped gum leaves turned in the breeze and clattered lightly. "Come down. I'm not telling you again."

And wasn't that a pointless empty threat? But he couldn't back down now or Tuti would never respect him. He conceded Katie that much.

Tuti giggled and bounced on her branch. She rocked back, losing her balance. Her eyes widened. John's heart stopped. Just in time she clutched the branch with her other hand and steadied herself. But she'd had a fright. Her dark skin paled and she gripped the branch tightly with both hands.

John focused hard as if he could hold her in place with the force of his gaze. He forgot to be gruff. He forgot everything except the overriding need to make his little girl safe. "Stay where you are. I'm coming to get you."

She nodded, her eyes huge. John scrambled up the tree as if it was a ladder, instinctively knowing where to place his feet and hands, not caring when he grazed his elbow. Moments later he was level with Tuti. The trunk swayed with his weight. Legs braced, he reached out both arms. Tuti released her hold on the tree and dove into his embrace.

John wrapped his arms around her, feeling her small heart beating fast next to his. Then he pulled back and cupped her chin to look into her watery eyes. With a different kind of gruff, he said, "Don't you ever scare me like that again."

Two fat tears rolled down Tuti's cheeks.

John wiped them away with his thumb. "Never mind. You're safe now. Hold on to my neck and we'll go down."

Tuti wrapped her legs around his waist and her arms around his neck. She clung on so hard she almost choked him. Going down was harder than going up. Tuti limited his vision and he only had one hand for the tree because he was gripping her with the other. When he got to the last fork in the trunk he lowered Tuti into Katie's arms then dropped to the ground.

Katie hugged Tuti then handed her back. She said nothing but her eyes accused him of nearly messing up. Yes, Tuti had almost fallen—possibly because he'd scared her—but he'd done what he thought was right. He remembered something his mother had said to him once, "Your father and I raised you the best we knew how." He understood that now. Kids didn't come with a training manual. Katie, for all her experience with her students, couldn't feel what he'd felt.

He kissed Tuti on the forehead and set her on the grass then crouched till his face was level with hers. "You scared me. I was worried you would be hurt. Don't ever do that again."

He didn't expect an answer. Tuti still hadn't spoken since he'd brought her away from Bali, despite several sessions with a child psychologist. But he hoped she would nod to show she understood.

"Okay, Tuti?" he asked, prepared to stay there till she agreed.

"Yes," she whispered. "Me sorry." And then she put her arms around his neck and hugged him tightly.

Something broke free in his heart and he held her closely, struggling not to cry. She'd spoken. Only three words but it was a start. He glanced up to see Katie touch her fingers to her eyes. Part of him wanted to draw her into the hug, to make her part of his little family. But she herself had reminded him she was only Tuti's teacher. Whatever had happened between them earlier it was too soon for an overt display of affection.

Anyway, she'd wanted to walk away. While he didn't agree with giving in to everything children wanted, there was a difference between making a point and not taking a child out of danger. Up until now he'd been relying on Katie to know what to do with Tuti, bowing to her superior experience. This time, she'd been proved wrong.

Her choice of action, as much as Tuti's recklessness, had pushed him to rely on his own instincts. The outcome vindicated his decision. He still respected Katie's knowledge and ability to relate to children but from now on, when it came to his daughter, he would trust the only reliable source for all really important decisions—his gut.

CHAPTER SIX

THE NEXT DAY after work Katie wheeled her mountain bike out of the garage for a test ride before going off road. She'd told John she rode but she couldn't actually remember the last time. The truth hit home in the shape of a flat front tire. Inflating it with a bicycle pump worked—temporarily. Before she was out of the driveway it had deflated again.

She had a repair kit but she'd never used it before. Should she try to patch the tire herself and risk getting out on the trail only for the patch to fall off? Or should she ask for help?

John leaped to mind but she quickly rejected the urge to call him. Just because she was helping him with Tuti and they saw each other regularly now, just because he was handy with tools and would assist her at the drop of a hat, didn't mean she wanted to rely on him in any way.

Especially not after yesterday. He was getting under her skin, just what she'd vowed never to let happen again. The attraction was still there—had never gone away, if she was honest—but that didn't mean she had to act on it. She was happy to help his daughter and to have a casual friendship with John but anything more would be opening a Pandora's box she'd firmly shut seven years ago.

The tree-climbing incident had been an eye-opener to the power struggle she and John were still dealing with. She was positive Tuti would have come down once she knew she wasn't going to get what she wanted. To think that John thought she didn't care about Tuti, or would put her in danger… It stung, professionally *and* personally. It said more about the issues between her and John than it did of who was right and who was wrong in that particular incident. She would never do anything to hurt a child, especially not one she cared about.

And she did care about Tuti despite the history behind her conception. That sweet girl needed her more than her other students. Plus, Katie felt a special connection because they'd both lost their mothers at an early age. But she was also wary of the dangers of letting Tuti get too attached to her—and vice versa—given that there was no future for her and John, not in the way they'd once wanted.

But she didn't have time to think about this now—she had a flat tire to deal with. She could spend hours figuring out how to fix it herself.

Or she could go to Riley, who knew all about bikes, and she could watch and learn.

A quick phone call established that her brother was at home and able to help. Katie wrangled her mountain bike into the back of her car and headed off across town.

Riley was pruning the apple tree out front when she pulled into his long curving driveway a few minutes later. Her father, Barry, his gray hair cut military short, was stacking the fallen branches in a pile to one side. Riley lowered the loppers and climbed down off the stepladder. Barry dusted his hands on his work pants.

"Hey, Dad. Riley." She gave them both a hug then dragged her bike out of her car. "The front tire won't stay inflated."

"This thing is practically an antique." Riley threw up the kickstand and squatted to feel the flabby tire. "No wonder the tires are disintegrating. You've had it since—"

"A long time," her father cut in with a frown at Riley.

"Since I had cancer." Katie gave her dad an affectionate, exasperated glance. "Saying the word won't magically make me sick again. I'm a survivor." Just because her mother died from breast cancer when she was ten and Riley was twelve, her father seemed to regard her as a ticking time bomb, waiting for the disease to strike again. "What do you think? Can it be patched or do I need to buy a new inner tube?"

"Let's have a look. Got a screwdriver?" Riley turned the bike over and stood it on the handlebars and seat.

"Lot of rust on those fenders," Barry said. "Where do you keep your sandpaper, son?"

"In the garage."

Barry took off for the garage. Katie got out the toolbox her dad had given her to keep in her car, gave Riley a screwdriver and hunkered down to watch.

He set about levering the tire off the frame, making sure he didn't puncture the inner tube. "Are you cycling with John?"

"I'm going on my own," Katie said. "Why would you think I'm going with John?"

"He told me you went to Springvale with him and Tuti. And you're tutoring his daughter."

She eyed him through the spokes. "News travels fast in a small town. There's nothing going on between us."

A shock of dark hair fell over his forehead as he worked. "Hey, I didn't say there was."

"So don't make a federal case out of it."

"It was an innocent question." He gave her a wink. "But now I'm wondering."

"Oh, for God's sake." Katie picked up a pebble from the gravel driveway and tossed it back and forth in her hands. “John was against me cycling off road on my own.”

“He’s got a point,” her father said, returning with a sheet of sandpaper. He began scraping the rust off the fenders. “It’s dangerous.”

“I’ll be fine.” Katie frowned. “Why does everyone think I’m so incompetent?”

“Not incompetent. You just have different strengths.” Riley pulled the last bit of tire away from the rim. “John says you two made a pact to be friends.”

Friends. The reality was so much more complicated, as she was finding out. “We’re making a stab at it. For Tuti’s sake.”

“Only Tuti’s sake?” her dad said, rasping away. “Shame. I always liked John. I thought you two were a good couple.”

“I used to think so. But it turned out he wasn’t like you were with Mum—totally devoted, solid and loyal.” Half-jokingly, she added, “You are my model of a perfect husband. I’m still waiting for the guy who can live up to your example.”

Barry stopped his task to frown at her beneath his bushy gray eyebrows. “Hmm.” Then he went on sandpapering.

“Got it.” Riley pulled the inner tube away from the tire. “Let’s take this inside to the sink. I’ll show you how to find a hole in the inner tube by watching for bubbles under water.”

Katie tossed the pebble and stood. “Coming, Dad?”

“Nah, I’ll finish shining up these fenders and give the chain a grease,” Barry said.

“Thanks. You’re the best.” Katie gave him a hug.

Then she followed Riley into the house through to the laundry room. As the sink filled with water her thoughts went back to yesterday and the subtle power struggle between her and John. She’d had no right to discipline Tuti, but she would have thought he would at least respect her experience and knowledge of handling children. And having been drawn into the situation at John’s house she couldn’t ignore it.

“What happens if you have to discipline Jamie for some reason?” she asked Riley. “Does Paula get bent out of shape? Do you agree on an approach?”

Riley turned off the tap and leaned against the counter. “When Paula’s around, I keep my nose out of it. Jamie’s her kid. She’s raised him for six years and knows what she’s doing. I’m just an amateur. Why do you ask?”

“Tuti took my shoes when I was at their house yesterday and climbed a tree with them. John went all Rambo dad on her and scared her farther up. It was dangerous. He wouldn’t even listen to my suggestions. I’ve been dealing with kids in that age group for ten years. By his own admission, he doesn't have a clue."

"He's got a bunch of nieces and nephews."

"It's not the same. I bet he just plays with them. He doesn't have to make them behave."

"True, but..." Riley took the inner tube from Katie and plunged it below the water. "Bottom line, Tuti's his kid. No one wants to hear someone else yelling at their child."

"I didn't yell. It was good cop, bad cop. I was the nice one."

"Did Tuti get down all right?"

"Yes, but she gave John—and me—a scare."

Riley shot her a look. "So what's the big deal? So he didn't listen to you. He still got her down. Getting a little hot under the collar over a simple disagreement, aren't you?"

Okay, so maybe she was making more of this than it warranted. But she was proud of her child-handling skills and John had called them into question. They had a history of clashing on fundamental issues. Yesterday's disagreement didn't feel simple. Had she been trying to push him away because she'd been attracted and that made her uncomfortable? Because she was afraid he was beginning to matter to her?

Katie blew out a sigh. "I was worried about her safety, that's all."

"No, you wanted him to recognize your superior knowledge." Riley cut her a glance. "Admit it, Katie. You like to think you know everything there is to know about children."

"I do know a lot about six-year-olds." She ignored his smirk and pointed to the inner tube. Bubbles streamed upward through three, no four, holes. "That looks bad."

"You'd be better off getting a new inner tube rather than patch this." Riley pulled the plug and let the water drain out of the sink. "What exactly are you trying to prove by going mountain biking by yourself, anyway?"

"I'm just trying to get out and do something fun."

"Liar, liar, pants on—"

"Oh, all right. I just realized that I'm not as adventurous as I used to be."

"When John dragged you along on his crazy exploits, you mean."

"He didn't drag me. I enjoyed them."

"You went kicking and screaming."

"Rappelling and skydiving were scary," she admitted. "But I always ended up having a great time. I want that again."

"He would go with you in a flash if you asked him."

"Why do you push him at me? I don't get that. I'm your sister. He abandoned me when I needed him most."

In fact, she'd been pretty much on her own after John left. Riley had been on duty with the SAS in Afghanistan. Her father, although supportive, couldn't cope with the emotional fallout. Her friends were there for her but that couldn't compensate for the men she loved being absent.

Especially John.

"I don't know why he left you." Riley took his time blotting the wet inner tube on a rag. "I was really pissed at him over that. I wish I could explain, make you feel better *and* exonerate John. But he's never talked about it with me. I only know he loved you and he was in pain, too. In the end I let it go. He's been my best mate since primary school and I've never known him to be anything other than a loyal and caring friend."

Katie didn't want to put Riley on the spot. He was entitled to his friendship with John. But if a woman had hurt *him* badly she didn't think she could have remained friends with that woman. Which might explain why John's mother had withdrawn from her. Except that Katie hadn't hurt John. It had been the other way around. Maybe guys were better able to compartmentalize their feelings. Whatever, she didn't want to fall out with Riley over John. So she said nothing.

"You looked up to him as if he were a god,"

Riley went on. "He's only human. He makes mistakes like the rest of us."

"He never once suggested he thought he made a mistake. In fact, he even went so far as to imply his leaving was *my* fault because I wouldn't agree to invasive treatment."

"He was worried about you. We all were."

"If you're worried, you don't abandon someone."

Riley shrugged uncomfortably. Clearly there was only so far he could defend John. And she knew he felt badly that he hadn't been there for her, either.

He tossed the inner tube in the garbage bin outside the laundry room door. "Go buy a new tube and I'll help you install it. I would go cycling with you, but I'm on standby for a major police op tomorrow."

"It's okay. This is something I need to do on my own." When she and John were together she'd relied on him for all manner of things from organizing their outings to fixing things around the house. It was nice but it meant she'd never really grown up. After John had let her down, she'd recovered on her own, lived ever since on her own. She *was* a survivor. "And next time I'll be able to fix my own tire."

"Katie, you're a one-woman wonder. You

teach, you write, you have a full life. You don't need to prove a single thing to anyone."

"Maybe I have to prove it to myself."

Riley shook his head with a rueful smile. "At least tell us where you're going and when you expect to be back. It's common sense. Don't be some macho mountain bike lady."

Katie snorted at the idea of her being macho anything. But she conceded the point. "All right. I'm going to do one of the easy bike trails in Red Hill. Hardly daredevil stuff."

"If you're not used to riding off road even the basic trails can be tricky. Promise you'll check in when you've finished your ride?"

"I'm not ten years old."

"You'll be in the bush on your own."

"What about this major police op you're doing tomorrow. Does it have to do with a drug raid on Nick Moresco?" She wasn't just stabbing in the dark. The case had occupied the Summerside Police Department for the past six months. "You're not the only one worried about a sibling."

"Not the same thing. I'll be part of a team. Tell you what, I'll check in when I'm done if you check in with me."

"Deal." She could live with that. And he was right to chide her about safety in the bush. Even experienced hikers got lost.

Katie and Riley walked back out through the house. Barry was squirting WD-40 into the bike's gears. "Thanks, Dad," Katie said. "I'll go get a new inner tube and be back shortly."

Riley followed her to her car and leaned down to talk through the window. "I know you were hurt when he left but do you ever think about what *you* did to John? It was a two-way street, Katie. He was gutted when you didn't take all the treatment options you were offered. Forgive and forget."

"Thanks for the advice." She turned the key in the ignition and drove off. She might—*might*—be able to forgive. But forget? Not possible. That would be like forgetting she'd almost died from breast cancer.

But maybe she had been too pushy over John's handling of Tuti in the tree. He had gotten her down safely. And Tuti had certainly learned a lesson. It was clear from the way she held on to John. And she'd spoken her first words since coming to Australia. Maybe he deserved more credit than she was giving him. The least she could do would be to tell him so. That wasn't just an excuse to call him. She was simply being fair-minded.

"*A* IS FOR APPLE." John pointed to the picture in the early-learning book Katie had sent home with Tuti. He held up a shiny red piece of real fruit. "Say it. Apple."

Tuti rested her small hand on his thigh and snuggled closer on the couch. She wore purple leggings and a pink tunic and purple ribbons on her pigtails. "Ap-ple."

Before the tree incident she'd been affectionate but not clingy. Now she was glued to his side. And he was okay with that. She was right where he could keep her safe.

"I like to eat apples." John took a bite and handed the fruit to the girl.

"I…like—"

"To eat…" he prompted.

"—ap-ple." Tuti glanced up, clearly hoping he would be pleased.

He gave her a big smile. "Excellent." His phone rang. "Excuse me, honey." He grabbed his phone off the coffee table. "Hello?"

"Hey, it's Katie."

"Hey." He pressed the phone hard to his ear as if that would bring *her* closer. Despite seeing her several times a week when she dropped off Tuti they didn't call each other up to chat on the phone. "Is everything okay?"

"I wanted to apologize for yesterday." She hesitated. "Sometimes I can be a bit of a know-it-all when it comes to kids. You did a great job getting Tuti out of the tree."

"Thanks." He cleared his throat. "She's right here. Do you want to say hi?"

"I don't want to interrupt anything."

"We're practicing our reading."

"On a Friday night. Good for you, Daddy."

He had to chuckle. Once upon a time he would have been painting the town red. Oddly, he didn't miss the nightlife or the women. Katie was right. His bedroom had been a revolving door. But if these women were so fascinating, why hadn't he settled down with one?

"Did Tuti suffer any ill effects from her fright?" Katie added.

"She's fine." He was the one who'd woken in the wee hours from a nightmare of her falling out of the tree. He'd lain there with his heart pounding, wondering if she wouldn't be better off in Bali. That's when he'd realized how precious she'd become to him. He was pleased she'd started talking. He hoped that meant she was finally settling in.

"Here she is." He passed the phone to Tuti and watched her face light up at the sound of Katie's voice.

He was feeling kind of warm and fuzzy himself. Katie had called him to apologize. And for a little chat. Not to arrange a time for Tuti's lesson or to discuss school. Just to talk. It meant a lot. It meant they were friends. It was a start.

Maybe with time they could be more than friends again. After all, they'd just been pals at the beginning. She'd tagged along when he and Riley had gone exploring. He'd treated Katie as if she was his own kid sister. Then she'd started to grow up, develop into a young woman and he began to see her in a different light. Then one day Riley had a bad cold and it had been just him and Katie hanging out. Without her brother around, John had been bolder. He'd kissed her beneath the big oak tree at his family home. From that day on he'd been smitten.

Tuti said good-night and handed the phone back to him.

"Katie, are you still there?"

"I'm here. I should let you go..."

"How's the book coming along?" he asked, to keep her talking.

"Not too bad. I'm taking a break tomorrow to go mountain bike riding." She hesitated. "Would you like to come with me?"

Damn. If only she'd asked him a week ago. "I can't. I'm taking part in a police operation. You're not still going on your own, are you?"

"Yes." There was a note of defiance in her tone. Then she softened. "But I'm checking in with Riley so don't worry."

"*Bapa* read!" Tuti commanded, finally fed up with waiting.

"Coming, sweetheart." To Katie, he added, "I have to go. You be careful. Don't go off the trail—"

"Good night, John."

The sweet lilt of her voice lingered in his ears as he settled onto the couch and Tuti continued her halted reading. He corrected and encouraged her, stroking her pigtail from elastic to wispy tip.

He hoped Katie would be cautious. He hated that he didn't have any say in her life nowadays. But then, he'd thrown away his chance at that. His life was changing in so many ways—Tuti, another chance with Katie—if he didn't blow it. If she didn't push him away. For the first time in years he had a glimpse of the life he'd always longed for.

THE PAVED PATH ended at a farm gate. Katie straddled her bike, feet planted on the ground and consulted the map. The trail wound over a grassy paddock, along a stream, through the woods, then up a hill to join a second trail that would lead her back to the road. Easy peasy, even for a novice like her.

She got off her bike and walked it through the gate, shutting it securely behind her. At the bottom of the field a herd of black cows grazed peacefully. She adjusted her helmet and scoped out which of the two rutted tracks looked like the smoothest ride down the bumpy slope.

She set off on the left track, jolting along. Yessiree, this was great. Lately her life had become tame. Learning new skills was what kept life interesting.

Red Hill was wetter than Summerside. It had rained here recently—heavily by the looks of the thick mud and long, deep puddles ahead. On either side of the track were broad stretches of waterlogged grass. She hoped she wasn't about to get a "crash" course in mountain biking.

As curious cows chewed cud and watched, Katie approached the first big wet area cautiously. Would her bike bog down, throwing her off? Would her wheels slip out from under her?

Not knowing what would happen was something she hadn't experienced for a long time. It threw her, mentally. She had a split second to decide what to do. Then she realized there was no decision to be made. She couldn't go around, she couldn't go over. She had no choice but to go through.

The bike didn't bog down. The wheels didn't slide out from under her. The cows didn't laugh. Well, they might have smiled a little at her wide goofy grin. This was so great. She'd accomplished something new!

As she progressed along the track, the next

puddle and patch of mud weren't quite so intimidating. Each time she learned a little more about how her bike would respond.

She stopped for a break beside the swift-running stream, swelled by the recent rainfall, and sat on the bank beneath a tree to eat an orange. Just getting out in the fresh air was a good idea. Being by herself didn't bother her. She spent so much time with her students and the other teachers that the silence of the bush, the quiet trickle of the stream and the birdcalls were peaceful.

John would love this.

The thought stopped her. She hadn't come out here to relive their glory days. She'd come to do something on her own. But he'd been on her mind a lot lately. She blushed a little to think she'd called him last night. He'd *sounded* glad to hear from her. She hoped he wouldn't read more into it than she intended. Friends rang each other up. That's all her call was about. And to apologize.

Since John didn't seem to want to leave Summerside any more than she did, chances were good that he would always be in her life one way or another. She'd done a pretty good job of denying that for the past seven years but it was time to get used to the notion. Make peace with his presence in her life. Forgive and forget, as Riley said. Be a bit nicer to John than she had been.

Last night's phone call had been a start. That didn't mean she was going to get involved with him. No sir, she wasn't going to allow herself to fall in love again. But that was no reason to hate him, either. Life was too short, too fragile, to waste on negative emotions. She of all people should know that.

It wasn't surprising she should be attracted to him. He was hot, there was no denying it. And he was a good guy. He didn't have a constant stream of girlfriends because he was a troll and a jerk. As long as she didn't give in to the attraction or let it build they should be able to be friends.

She took a last sip of water, replaced the drink bottle in its holster and set off along the trail. More cows grazed in the sunny patches between the tall trees. The trees gave way to another grassy field. Here was the hill, bigger than it appeared on the map. She came to a halt. No way she could ride up that. It was too steep.

Really? What were all those warrior poses in yoga for if not to develop strong quad muscles? Of course she was going up that hill.

CHAPTER SEVEN

JOHN TAPPED THE steering wheel of his white SUV impatiently, hating that instead of taking an active role in the raid on Nick Moresco's beach house he was stuck watching from the sidelines. The dilapidated weatherboard with the flat roof and peeling paint was almost obscured by a thick stand of ti trees. Somewhere in the bush behind the house, Paula and Riley crouched.

Part of being a good leader meant training his men and women then stepping back and allowing them the freedom and responsibility to do their job. Paula, with Riley as second in command, was in charge. She'd earned it and she was more than capable. But John couldn't help missing the old days when he would have been suited up, ready to storm the house. There wasn't much difference between sitting behind his desk doing paperwork and sitting in a vehicle waiting for others to bring in the bad guys.

He glanced at his watch. Katie was probably on the bike trails right about now. Part of him wished he'd gone with her instead of watching others carry out the op. But he'd committed to being here and he had to follow through.

Over the radio came Paula's terse back-and-forth with the Force Response Unit officers who were decked out in full riot gear with bullet-proof vests, helmets and various weapons, including Tasers and shotguns. In a clearing thirty meters away, the team of four paced outside their black 4WD vehicles, awaiting orders.

Paula and Riley had been after Nick Moresco for five months. There had been many false trails and near misses. Paula was convinced Moresco was manufacturing crystal methamphetamine despite not having found any concrete evidence thus far. If there was no meth kitchen inside the house John would have to consider calling a halt to the investigation. Other issues needed the department's attention.

The radio went quiet. Through the open car window he sniffed the air for the rank odor that came from the chemical reaction. Nothing he could detect but the wind was blowing in the wrong direction. Paula had a lot at stake—months of investigation, regaining her detective status, putting away the criminal who threatened her son…

The radio crackled to life.

John sat up, alert.

"On the count of three," Paula said.

The four black-suited men readied their weapons.

John got out of the car, took a couple of steps, his gaze focused on the Force Response team. Adrenaline poured through his veins, giving him a rush of energy.

"One, two," Paula began. "Three…"

The men charged through the ti trees. A second later came the sound of a door splintering, shouting, glass breaking.

John savagely kicked a stone out of his way. There was no point wishing he could change his decision to move into management. Beat cops didn't make much money. He had Tuti to think of, her education to save for. A bigger house with a backyard would be good, too.

He couldn't even complain to anyone. He felt guilty just bitching to himself. He had a great job. And it wasn't as if he couldn't do the work. He had a knack for leadership and for seeing the big picture when it came to planning and policy.

Over the radio Paula yelled at someone to freeze. He glanced through the trees, itching to follow them into the house. The problem was, he didn't just want to be the ringmaster. He also wanted to be the lion tamer, the trapeze artist and the damn clown all rolled into one.

KATIE TOOK A RUN at the hill. Initial momentum carried her a third of the way. The path petered out. She pushed hard, standing on the pedals, struggling and straining to ride up the lumpy sloping ground. A few meters from the top her bike simply stopped dead. Her feet hit the ground and she leaned on the handlebars, panting.

She hadn't made it to the top. But she'd gone farther than she'd expected.

She got off and pushed the bike the rest of the way to the top. At least once she was over this hard bit the rest of the trail looked easy. Puffing from the exertion, she walked across the top of the hill and looked down the other side, expecting to see a well-worn path that would take her beside the stream back to the road in a big loop.

Oh, hell. The swollen stream flooded the trail for as far as she could see. It looked deep, too deep for her bike. It took her a moment to process the ramifications but finally it sank in. She had no choice but to go…gulp…down the long, steep hill she'd just climbed.

She turned around and walked to study the slope. For a good ten minutes she tried to plot an easy way to ride down. If anything, it looked steeper than when she'd climbed it. And now she knew the long grass hid holes and fallen branches and rocks. She could kill herself going down there.

But what was she going to do, walk down like a wuss? Have John say, I told you so?

He didn't have to know. No one had to know. The cows wouldn't tell.

She would know. And how could she put this in a book if she didn't know how Lizzy felt when she was being brave? Imagination was wonderful, but there were times when it was no match for reality.

She started slowly down the hill, applying both brakes, carefully weaving in and out of obstacles. Twice she stopped and wiped the sweat off her forehead even though it wasn't hot. Each time she had to force herself to get back on the bike.

Halfway down she hit a log hidden in the grass. Instinctively she rose on the pedals, lifted the handlebars and sort of hopped over. Wow. She didn't know she could do that and remain upright.

Then something flipped in her brain. She could do this. She just had to have faith in herself, tap into abilities she didn't know she possessed. Unclenching her white knuckles, she released the brakes and started pedaling. Soon she was flying down the hill, standing on the pedals, bouncing and jolting over the rough ground, scared out of her wits but excited beyond anything.

Whoo-hoo! She felt like a kid again, with a top-of-the-roller-coaster giddiness she hadn't experienced for years, maybe decades. Like a kid, she was living from second to second. The sky seemed a brighter blue. Every blade of grass stood out. The faint scents of wildflowers mingled with cowpats on the breeze blowing through her hair.

She threw back her head and let out an exultant laugh.

Thunk. Her bike hit a rock, stopping dead. Her cry of delight turned to a wail as she flew over the handlebars. The ground rushed up to meet her. Her shoulder hit first, a glancing blow before she came down hard on her foot. Her ankle twisted beneath her. Pain lanced through her leg as she rolled to a halt.

Winded and nauseous, she lay in the grass and mud, her cheek pressed to the sloping earth, struggling to regain her breath. In her peripheral vision she could see the back wheel of her overturned bike spinning uselessly against the blue sky.

She tried to move her leg. Spots danced before her eyes as another jolt of pain sliced through her ankle. Taking a deep breath, she slowly pushed herself to a seated position. Her foot was twisted at a weird angle. With her hands she turned it back to normal. The throbbing began. Gingerly she felt the bones but it was already starting to swell. Whether it was broken or not, clearly she wasn't going to be able to ride out of here.

She felt in her vest pocket for her phone then paused. Lizzy wouldn't call for help. Lizzy would limp along with Monkey making cheeky comments as he swung from branch to branch above her head, alternately teasing and encouraging.

Monkey wasn't here. She was on her own.

The grassy paddock stretched out before her. She wasn't a character in a book. Nor was she stupid. The distance was impossible with her ankle so painful. With a groan for the ribbing she would get from Riley and the scolding from John, she punched in her brother's speed dial number.

PAULA STRODE OUT of the bushes surrounding the house to where John paced beside his vehicle.

"Moresco isn't in there." She was perspiring beneath her heavy gear and breathing hard, her voice tight with frustration. "But I've arrested two male suspects on charges of illegal drug manufacturing."

"Arrested," John repeated. "You mean…"

"They were cooking. The whole house has been turned into a meth kitchen and packaging facility." Now her satisfaction came through. "There are bags of the stuff, stockpiled, ready to be distributed. This is a large scale, sophisticated operation, not backyard hoodlums trying to make a few bucks."

"I'll call the divisional van to take those clowns away," John said, reaching for the radio phone. "And I'll get someone to take a sample into the lab ASAP. We need to match the crystals with the ice sold in Summerside." His role, even in the field, was administrative. "What's happening now?"

"Riley's cordoning off the site to keep out neighborhood busybodies. Then we're going to search the house for something tangible to link Moresco to this."

"The house is in his grandmother's name. You're bound to find other links. Don't worry. We'll put his ass behind bars."

"Damn straight, we will. Boss."

From the pile of jackets in the backseat came the sound of a phone ringing. "Sounds like Riley's ring tone," Paula said. "Do you mind seeing who it is? He's expecting Katie to check in when she finished her bike ride."

John fumbled through jacket pockets until he found the phone. "Hello?"

"John? I called Riley." Katie's voice was tight, laced with pain.

"He's in the middle of something. Are you all right?"

"I took a tumble, twisted my ankle. It's no big deal—"

"Where are you? I'll come and get you."

"Red Hill. The bike trail that runs past Koo Wee Creek."

"I'll be there in twenty minutes. Don't move." He hung up and turned to Paula. "She's hurt her ankle. Tell Riley not to worry. I'll go pick her up."

Before he left, John organized the support crew, calling the lab and the divisional van to take away the prisoners. He pulled in Jackson from off duty to take his place as external coordinator, even though there was little left to do. As soon as Jackson rocked up, John took off for Red Hill, driving like a bat out of hell.

This was his fault. He'd teased her about not having adventures and running out of story ideas. He'd more or less forced her to try to prove something. He should have insisted she wait until he could go with her. If anything happened, if her ankle was worse than she was saying, he would never forgive himself.

This time he would be there for her when she needed him. Whether she liked it or not.

KATIE ENDED THE call. Damn. Why couldn't Riley have answered his phone? Why did John have to be the one to come riding to her rescue? Could her humiliation be more complete? She'd wanted to show him—and herself, of course—she could be strong and adventurous. Instead, she'd made a fool of herself. *I told you so,* he would say. Then he'd quote police statistics about how many idiots broke their necks on mountain bikes every year.

She hobbled to a large rock at the side of the track. Her running shoe was cutting into her swollen left foot. She loosened the laces and winced at the angry purple bruise.

The sun had sunk below the trees and the air was getting chilly. All she wore was a T-shirt beneath a fleece vest. She rubbed the goose bumps on her bare arms. The cows were coming out of the trees and plodding up the hill to their barn. She was sorry to see them leave.

Dusk was rapidly falling. A couple of kangaroos hopped out of the bushes to graze. She checked her watch—nearly half an hour since she'd spoken to John—and strained her eyes to the distant gate. Her ankle throbbed and was hot to the touch. She propped it up on the rock to take the pressure off.

Then she heard a car stop. A door opened and

closed. A flashlight bounced across the field. John called, “Katie!”

She scrabbled to her feet, leaning on her good leg, and waved. “Over here!”

The flashlight beam bobbed across the grass. Below the light strode a pair of long legs.

She’d never been so relieved to see anyone in her life. “Thanks for coming.”

John held the flashlight in his mouth and crouched in front of her to gently probe her ankle. She winced at his touch but his fingers were cool against her hot, swollen skin. “You need to ice that as soon as possible.”

“First I need to get out of here,” Katie said. “How are we going to do this? I was thinking I could sit on the bicycle seat and you could push me—”

“Too slow. Hold this.” He handed her the flashlight. Then he put an arm around her waist, another below her legs, and stood, swinging her off the rock and into his arms.

Startled, she yelped. “Hey, put me down! What about my bike?”

“I’ll send Riley for it later. Shine the light on the path.” He adjusted his grip on her, fingers tight against her thigh. “Put your arm around my neck so you don’t bounce so much. And relax. You’re not going to fall.”

She didn’t want to put her arms around his

neck, or relax into his embrace. It was too tempting. His arms were strong and warm, his chest a solid wall for her weary head. But she could feel his anger even though he wasn't saying anything. Clearly he thought she'd brought this on herself.

And being carried made her feel helpless. She hated feeling unable to control her own destiny. It brought back the days when she was sick from chemotherapy and couldn't do anything for herself.

It brought back the days when John sat beside her hospital bed.

Until the day when he didn't.

A three-quarter moon rose above the trees, shedding silvery light across the path. Up in the barn, cows lowed during milking. John hadn't yet said, *I told you so.* His reticence made her tense. She waited for the scolding she was sure he was just dying to issue. His breath next to her ear, the swish of his boots through the grass, sounded overloud.

"Accidents happen all the time," she said defensively. "I could have tripped over a tree root in the backyard. I could have fallen off my bike riding into the village."

"True. You could have been hit by a bus crossing the street. Or killed by a meteor chunk falling from outer space." John adjusted his grip again. His fingers splayed across her ribs; his other hand held her thigh.

She was being childish about not touching him. Giving up, she reached her arms around his neck. Her fingertips missed his collar and landed on warm, bare skin with the beat of his pulse. She moved her fingers back to the cloth. "Exactly my point."

"No, you've missed the point completely. Those things are out of your control. This wasn't."

"The universe is random."

"You *chose* to go it alone. You didn't need to do that. I should have been with you," he said. "I should have insisted."

Now she understood. He was angry at himself, not her. If anything, that was worse. "You're not responsible for my well-being. It was my choice to make. I'm an independent person."

"When others care about you, when others rely on you to be there, it's not fair to make unilateral decisions."

She was silent, not wanting to go there. He wasn't talking about her ankle. They'd had this conversation before, when she had cancer. There was no resolution to it. Should the situation arise again, she would make the same choices.

Finally they came to the gate. It was only a few more steps to John's vehicle. He deposited her gently on the ground, keeping his arm around her. "Don't put any weight on that foot. Lean on me."

Katie held his arm lightly, but only to keep her balance. She'd learned long ago not to lean on John. She wasn't going to start now.

"HOW ARE YOU doing back there?" John glanced at Katie in the rearview mirror.

Vineyards were silhouetted against the red glow of the setting sun as he drove down the winding road out of Red Hill to the flat coastal plain.

"I'm fine." Katie was slumped in a corner, her injured leg stretched out along the back-seat, a chemical ice pack from his first-aid kit on her ankle.

In the glare of oncoming headlights he glimpsed Katie's face in flashes, her mouth tight, eyes closed. She wasn't fine.

Frustrated by the slow-moving traffic of day-trippers returning to Melbourne, John slapped a flashing blue light on the roof and put his foot on the accelerator. With the siren wailing he bullied his way through traffic. What good was being in charge if you couldn't take care of your friends?

Ten minutes later he pulled into the circular driveway at Emergency. He jogged for a wheelchair parked outside the big sliding doors. When he got back Katie had the car door open. He helped her into the chair and tucked his jacket around her.

"Just drop me off," Katie said. "I could be here for hours and you probably have to get back to Tuti."

"My mother's looking after her. I called and told her not to expect me for a while." John grabbed the handles of the wheelchair and pushed toward the entrance. "I'm not going to leave you alone in the hospital."

"Why not?" she muttered. "You did once before."

His fists tightened on the rubber grips but he pretended not to hear. That was her pain talking. "I know the head nurse in Triage. You'll be given five-star treatment."

"Is she one of your ex-girlfriends?"

"Yeah, that's right. One of my many ex-girlfriends who still adores me and would do anything for me. Even give priority to a brat like you."

In actual fact, the head Triage nurse was a friend of his mother's who'd known him since he was a small boy. He just hoped she was on duty tonight.

In Emergency a young man of about twenty clutched a bloody bandage around his forearm.

Stab wound, most likely. On a gurney next to the wall an inebriated teenage girl waited to have her stomach pumped. John had spent many a Friday and Saturday night here as a beat cop, years ago. He'd seen it all.

But his worst memories involved Katie receiving chemotherapy to shrink the tumor. She must hate this place even worse than he did.

Eileen West was on duty behind the glass cage in Admitting. Her frizzy black hair was threaded with gray but her smile lit when she saw John. "Hey, handsome. Long time, no see." She looked over her half-glasses at Katie. "What have we got here?"

"Suspected broken ankle. Definite pain in the ass."

"Hey!" Katie twisted in the chair to glare up at him.

"How long is the wait?" John asked Eileen. "And can we get a fresh ice pack in the meantime?"

Eileen consulted her book. "Triage will see her in about ten minutes. She should be able to go straight into X-ray. I'll get you an ice pack. Have a seat."

John pushed Katie's wheelchair to the end of a row of chairs and adjusted the leg rest so her foot was elevated. He took a seat next to her.

Across the aisle a mother cradled a feverish toddler in her arms.

"You take me to the nicest places," Katie murmured.

"I know you hate hospitals. Which is why I'm putting up with your bad behavior. Tuti didn't whine this much when she fell and skinned her knee."

Eileen arrived with an ice pack. John took it from her, removed the old one and carefully wrapped the new one over Katie's swollen ankle.

She watched him with a scowl. "Come on, say it. Say, I told you so."

He figured she was angry with herself so she was taking it out on him. She would push and prod until he said it, just so she could be right. Too bad. He felt like being perverse. "I don't need to say it. You're not stupid. You know the score."

"You're thinking it, though, admit it."

With her ice pack securely in place he took the chair opposite. Smiling blandly, he slowly shook his head.

"Now you're teasing me." She stabbed a finger at him. "You promised not to do that."

"You're in a contrary mood," he said mildly. "No matter what I do, I can't win so I'm not even going to try. But now that you mention it—"

"I knew it." Triumph flashed across her face. "Knew you couldn't resist."

"Next time you do something risky, take a friend along."

"I was fine on my own. I just need to get better at mountain biking."

"I would have come with you if you'd waited a day. Why are you so determined not to need anyone?"

"I've learned through experience to rely on myself."

His smile faded. Even though they'd become friends again she still didn't trust him. That hurt. "You know I care about you. Even when you piss me off."

"If you cared so much—" She glanced away.

He wouldn't have left her when she was critically ill.

Nope, he wasn't going to go there. Not now. Not when she was tired, injured and in pain. That was no basis for a rational discussion. They'd never seen eye to eye on the issue of her health. And right now, she just wanted a reason to be mad at him. She wanted to push him away. Well, it was working.

"I'm going to get a coffee. Do you want one?"

"No, thank you."

John went over to the vending machines and pushed coins into the slot for a hot drink he didn't want. Yes, he'd left her behind. But not because he didn't care, or because he was a coward, as she seemed to think. He wished they'd had it out back then even if it meant saying things they regretted. Better than regretting words left unsaid.

He'd never told her, or anyone, his reason for leaving. In hindsight it seemed dumb, even egotistical. He'd thought if he took himself out of the equation, if she wasn't trying to keep herself whole for him, then she would have the mastectomy. He'd loved her so much he was willing to risk their relationship to save her life. He'd gambled and lost.

He hadn't even told Riley his rationale, because Riley couldn't have kept it a secret from his sister. And he definitely couldn't have told Katie. His ill-fated scheme wouldn't have had a chance of working if she'd known why he was leaving. But she hadn't reacted the way he'd hoped. Even after he'd left she'd stubbornly refused to have the operation. Later, when he'd come home, she'd banished him from her life. He'd tried to explain then but she refused to even talk to him, much less listen.

He sipped his coffee by the machine, keeping his eye on her. Seated in the wheelchair with her leg up, fighting fatigue and pain, she looked vulnerable but defiant. He'd always admired her spirit. She saw herself as a scaredy-cat but she was stronger than she knew. She'd proved that by staring cancer down without flinching. That was the annoying and endearing thing about her—she did the wrong thing for the right reasons. Or was it the right thing for the wrong reasons? Whatever. Deep inside she was at odds with herself. But she couldn't see it.

A nurse with a clipboard appeared at Katie's side. "Katie Henning? I'm here to take you to Radiology."

John walked back.

"Thanks," Katie said to him. "You can go. I'm sure you want to get Tuti and go home."

"No, I'll stay."

"Please don't. I'll phone my father to come pick me up after I've had the X-ray."

"Ready?" The nurse spun the chair toward a broad corridor and a pair of swing double doors.

No doubt Katie expected him to leave. She didn't believe she could count on him for anything. Which only went to show how little *she* knew *him*. He settled in a chair and sipped his coffee. When it came to Katie he'd had a lot of practice waiting.

TWO HOURS LATER Katie returned through the double doors to the waiting room, an orderly pushing her wheelchair. Her foot was encased in a boot cast. The crutches she'd rented from the hospital rested across her legs.

She was about to ask the orderly to take her outside so she could phone her father. And then she saw John. He was slumped in the hard plastic chair, eyes closed, hands clasped across his chest. His blond hair was rumpled and his jaw bristled with golden stubble. He appeared to be dozing.

She'd been so sure he would leave after the bitchy way she'd treated him. But he hadn't. Her throat tightened. For a moment she thought she would cry. She knew she was just emotional because she was tired and aching and cranky. But deep inside something in her let go, as if a band around her chest had eased slightly. He hadn't deserved the way she'd treated him earlier.

It hit her then. Deep down she'd been hoping he would prove he cared by waiting for her. Prove what he hadn't proved seven years ago.

She blinked, trying to push away her emotion.

Was she an idiot to still hope that he loved her with the unconditional love she longed for, the kind her parents had had? Him staying for a couple of hours in Emergency didn't prove anything. It was too damn little, too damn late.

"Over there, please," she told the orderly, directing him toward John. He parked her at the end of the row and left.

In sleep, John's closed eyelids looked vulnerable, his firm mouth younger and softer, almost as if they'd gone back in time.... She couldn't resist lightly stroking his forearm, warm skin covered in blond hair. "Hey," she said softly, then removed her hand before he woke up.

John's eyes blinked open, startlingly blue, instantly alert. He glanced down at her foot. "Not broken then?"

"Just a bad sprain." She grimaced. "I tore a ligament."

"Come on. I'll take you home." He started to get up.

She touched his arm again and this time she left her hand there. "Thanks for waiting. And for everything."

He covered her hand with his own. "It's no big deal."

"Still. I appreciate it." Her hand felt warm and secure sandwiched between his arm and his palm. She didn't even care that she might be sending the wrong message. "I'm sorry I was so awful."

"I'm used to it."

Through the tossed-off humor Katie heard the grain of truth. "Seriously, I really appreciate you coming. I hope I didn't interrupt anything important."

"Nothing much." His thumb stroked her wrist, the rough pad grazing her pulse.

A tingle traveled up her arm and spread in a warm glow. The pain relievers must be kicking in, making her giddy. "Tuti must be wondering where you are."

"I checked in with my mother. Tuti's fine." But he got the hint. He stood and pushed her wheelchair toward the exit. "Still think your bike ride was worth it?"

The rush of bouncing down the hill came back to her, overcoming her fatigue. "I haven't experienced anything so exciting since we rappelled down that rock face in the Blue Mountains. It was wonderful. I felt like a kid again."

"Really?" There was amusement, and a slightly wistful note, in his voice, as if he was too world-weary to know what excitement was anymore. But he wished he did.

"Absolutely. I would do it again in a heartbeat. In fact, I will do it again. As soon as my ankle heals."

"Next time, I'm sure you'll be more careful."

"Where's the fun in that? Danger is much more thrilling."

He chuckled. "That's my girl."

For a moment she wished that were true, that she was his again, that they would plot their next adventure together, not as a way to keep her safe but just because that's what they did.

Then they were outside and the cool evening air hit her face, bringing clarity. Not going to happen. She didn't even want it to happen. Why indulge in futile fantasies?

John's SUV was waiting in the pickup zone. "If I know you, you'll somehow make this into Monkey's fault."

"I've been working on that already. Monkey taunted Lizzy about being a wuss until she had to prove she could have adventures without him."

"But she learned her lesson this time, didn't she?"

"She proved she has the guts to go after what she wants. To venture out completely on her own."

"That was never in doubt." John set the chair brake and opened the passenger door.

She *could* survive on her own, could even have adventures. But it would be a lot nicer having them with someone. With John's help she climbed into the passenger seat. He squeezed her knee, setting butterflies loose in her stomach. Suddenly she missed what they used to have with a fierceness that took her breath away.

CHAPTER EIGHT

JOHN PULLED UP in front of Katie's house. It had been a long day and he was tired and still had to pick up Tuti. But he couldn't leave until he was sure Katie was okay.

"Don't move until I come around to help you," he said. "I don't want to have to take you back to the hospital because you've fallen and broken your other leg."

Being Katie, she had the door open and her crutches poised to hit the ground by the time he got to the passenger side. He took the crutches from her and put an arm around her waist. Her scent, ripe with dirt and sweat, was earthy and warm.

"I'm going to have to learn to do this by myself," she grumbled as he swung her down from the vehicle.

"You don't have to learn tonight when you're tired and sore. Walking on crutches is harder than it looks."

"I guess you would know." Standing on her good foot, she placed a hand on his shoulder for balance while she positioned a crutch beneath her arm.

She was referring to the time when he was fifteen and she thirteen and he'd fallen out of her parents' apple tree and broken his leg. It had been embarrassing for a guy who prided himself on his athleticism and, in particular, his tree-climbing ability. "Did that make it into one of your stories?"

"Not yet." She let go of him and set off up the path to her front door, one awkward step at a time. "I couldn't figure out a good reason for a monkey to fall out of a tree. I mean, really. You of all people."

"Maybe Monkey was distracted because he saw something luscious but out of reach."

"What do you mean?"

"Maybe he saw Lizzy sunbathing in a bikini."

"Huh?" She jerked, lost her balance and started to topple.

John caught her, his arms closing around her. She went very still. "A purple bikini with white polka dots," he said, his mouth next to her ear. "It's etched in my memory. That was the first time I saw you as a girl and not as Riley's pesky kid sister. It was the beginning of my love affair with your breasts," he added huskily. "They were barely buds but oh so sweet and firm and high."

"Stop." Her voice was breathy and her legs wobbled, but she still had enough strength in her arms to push him away. She took a breath and tackled the steps, planting her crutches and dragging herself up behind. "I was going to offer you coffee but I've changed my mind. You're a pervert."

He grinned as he climbed the stairs after her. Getting a rise out of Katie never failed to amuse him. "Not a pervert, just a red-blooded teenage boy. What were you doing strutting about in a bikini where you could be sure I would see you?"

The pink in her cheeks deepened. "I was not strutting. I was—oh, you're doing it again. Good *night*." She fumbled with her key in the lock.

He took the key out of her hand. "I'm coming in with you." He opened the door. "While you shower I'll make you something to eat. Soon as you're settled, I'll leave. Promise."

"But—"

"No arguments. Or I'll come in there and scrub your back."

She threw him an exasperated look and hobbled down the hall, no doubt too tired to fight him over it. Was he a hopeless case or what? Still mooning over Katie Henning like a schoolboy when she'd made it more than clear she wasn't interested.

He went into the kitchen and flicked on the light. A cream-and-gray cat leaped off a chair and arched its back, green eyes wary.

"What's your name?" He bent to scratch behind its ears and the creature purred. "I'll bet you're hungry, too."

He searched the laundry room and found a bag of premium dry cat food. After taking care of the cat, he checked the fridge for human food. Organic vegetables and fruit, a big jar of fish oil, free-range eggs, biodynamic organic yogurt… When had she turned into a health nut?

Oh. Duh. Well, good to see she was taking care of herself. But the bottle of micronutrients and extracts of obscure algae made him uneasy. He hoped she wasn't still putting her faith in quack medicines and dodgy pseudoscience to keep healthy. He hoped she was doing regular breast exams and whatever else her doctor recommended as routine screening. He started to put the bottle back and his hand stopped in midair.

He didn't trust her to take care of herself.

Sobered by the realization, he took ingredients out of the fridge. He peeled and chopped and whisked and sautéed. She needed someone to look after her. Was anyone making sure she did the right things? He would ask Riley. Or maybe Paula would have a better idea. The two women were close.

Fifteen minutes later he flipped out an omelet containing enough vegetables to choke a rabbit. He added a garnish of strawberries and blueberries for extra goodness.

"Smells good." She stood in the doorway, resting on her crutches, wearing pajamas printed with cats. Her wavy hair hung dark and wet around her shoulders.

"Yeah." Only he was referring to the fresh scent of her shampoo.

Her cat rubbed up against the boot on her leg. "Hey, Lulu," she crooned as the feline sniffed the casing. "It's all right. I'm going to be all right."

"Madame." John set a plate of food before her, nodded at her thanks, then brought over two mugs of herbal tea.

"I thought you were going home as soon as you fed me."

"Soon." He sat opposite and sipped the tea. But first he was going to tell her the truth about why he left, even if it made her hate him worse than ever.

KATIE FORKED UP a bite of tender omelet. Part of her wanted him to leave so he wouldn't stir up muddled feelings. Part of her enjoyed his company. And that was dangerous. "This is delicious. But you've made a man-size meal. Want some?"

"Maybe just a bite." He opened his mouth expectantly.

She didn't know whether to laugh or be annoyed at his cheek. Well, she did owe him. Cutting off a hunk, she held it out. He leaned over. As his mouth closed around the bite of food his gaze met hers.

Would those blue eyes never lose the power to dazzle?

She dropped her gaze. "How's Tuti?" she asked, because it was safer than asking why he was still there.

"She's such a little monkey—and I don't just mean climbing trees. She's full of mischief."

Katie smiled. "Wonder where she got that from?"

Frowning, he wrapped his hands around his mug. "But she worries me, too. I heard her crying the other night, after I'd put her to bed."

Katie put down her fork, her appetite diminished by the thought of little Tuti in pain. "What's wrong? Do you know?"

He shook his head and shrugged.

"She's probably sad about her mother's death." Katie knew how that felt. She'd been ten when her mother died and the bottom had been ripped out of her world. With her father devastated and Riley pretending he didn't care, she was left to struggle with her grief on her own. Her father had poured all his devotion into her mother. And that was right and as it should be.

"Could it be you've glossed over the grieving process because of what you know about Balinese traditions? Maybe you thought she would recover more quickly?" John stiffened, no doubt taking her comment as criticism. It was true, she didn't think he'd taken Tuti's loss seriously enough although she knew it wasn't out of any lack of caring. "Her mischievousness might be her acting out because she doesn't know how to deal with her feelings."

"I told you, they view death differently in Bali."

"Maybe so," Katie said. "But she's still a small girl who's lost her mother and no doubt misses her terribly. She might understand the religious and cultural meaning of death. But the reality is that her mother isn't there to give her a cuddle when she falls down, to kiss her good-night."

"I'm there. I comfort her when she hurts herself."

"That's good. I can tell Tuti adores you. But it's not the same as knowing your mother will never hold you again." Even now the thought brought pain. She missed her mother every day of her life. Her heart ached for poor little Tuti.

John stared at the table. When he glanced up, his eyes were clouded. "I'm doing my best. I can't do anything more. Nena's gone. Nothing can change that fact."

Katie's heart reached out to him. He was trying so hard, probably wondering why he still couldn't get it right. But was that even possible when it came to raising kids? With the best intentions in the world parents still made mistakes.

"Do you talk to her about her mother—Nena?" Speaking the woman's name aloud, her voice sounded odd to her own ears. She'd thought she didn't feel any jealousy. Now she was aware of a dull ache behind her breastbone when she thought of John making love to another woman barely a month after he'd left Katie's sickbed.

A healthy woman. A woman who had given him a child.

It was a long time ago. Get over it.

But it was hard to get over something she hadn't had time to process. She'd tried to set aside the hurt for the girl's sake but it was only buried, not banished.

"I probably don't talk to her about Nena

enough," he admitted. "There's not a lot of time by the end of the day what with school and work, getting dinner, doing her reading, getting ready for bed… I had no idea how much time it takes just doing the basics of looking after a small child." He paused. "Katie, there's something about those days that I want to tell you—"

"First, what was Nena like?" She didn't really want to hear, but if she cared about Tuti she needed to be able to talk about the girl's mother without hostility. During her illness, she'd learned that when the pain was intense, she had to lean into it. Only by pushing through could she get to the other side, to a place of calm.

John shook his head. "You don't want to know."

Meaning, he didn't want to tell her. Was that guilt talking? Their feelings didn't matter, not compared to Tuti. "Yes, I do. The more people Tuti can talk to about her mother, the better."

"Well…" He scratched his head. "She was a lot like you."

"Like me?" Katie went still. "How do you mean?"

"Self-contained. Not reserved exactly but she was self-sufficient. She enjoyed my company but made it clear she didn't need me. Not in the long term."

And that's what *she* was like? No way. She'd adored John, wanted to be with him every moment of the day. "*I* needed you."

"You did and you didn't. I know you loved me but there was a small part of you deep inside that you held back. That you kept...separate. It's okay. I accepted it. I don't think you meant to hurt me. It's just the way you are."

Withholding. He'd thought she'd been withholding. Katie made herself take another bite of the cooling omelet because she didn't know what to say to John's accusation. Withholding. That's not how she saw herself at all. She gave every scrap of love and warmth she had to her pupils, to her family, and she'd given it to John when they'd been going out.

"I didn't know that when we were together," he added. "I only realized it much later, after I was away from you and had a chance to reflect."

"I had no idea." Nor did she understand or even believe it. How could something that big, that fundamental, be true and she not know it about herself?

"Now, about what I wanted to tell you—"

"Hang on. I'm struggling with what you just said. Can you give me an example of me holding back?"

"I don't mean you were passive-aggressive or anything. You were always warm and loving. But if we disagreed you didn't want to talk about it. Instead, you tried to smooth it over and sweep things under the carpet."

"I don't believe it's necessary or good to dwell on problems," she said uncomfortably. "People disagree, sure, but that doesn't mean they have to argue and get angry."

"Our final argument was about life-and-death. Of course I was angry when you refused to discuss your treatment or change your mind."

"Let's not go there." A topic that divisive wasn't open for discussion, not when their relationship was so fraught with emotional minefields. "You still haven't given me an example of me being too self-sufficient."

"Okay, whenever I tried to pin you down for a wedding date, you would discuss the pros and cons of different seasons but never come to a conclusion about the best time. So we never set a date. When I talked about having kids someday you raved about how much you loved children but never said when we would start a family."

"We were in our early twenties, in no hurry," she protested. "We had our future ahead of us."

"What does it hurt to talk about it, to plan, to dream?"

"I had dreams." Marrying John and having a family, being a writer, teaching and working with children. She'd worked hard to fulfill those dreams. Could she help it if the first one took two people to make it come true? When one of those people left how could it happen?

Unless John had left because he didn't feel she was fully committed. But that was crazy. She'd wanted to marry him since she was sixteen years old. That hadn't wavered until the decision was taken out of her hands by his abrupt departure. Then it had been as though someone had died and she'd gone through all the stages of grief. By the time he'd returned she'd detached from their love and arrived at acceptance. She was cured of cancer—and of her love for him. But before that she'd been as committed as he was.

Now he was saying she hadn't been, or that he hadn't felt it. If true, this negated her image of herself as someone who lived life to the fullest, loving and laughing with abandon. The bigger question was, was she still withholding a part of herself? How could she tell? Currently there was no man in her life. Maybe that in itself said something about her.

But she wasn't finished asking about Nena. Hopefully, like lancing a boil, it would be painful but the wound would heal cleanly. She had to brace herself to ask the next question. "Did you love her?"

"I knew her for three months. I don't fall in

love that quickly. When I do, I stay in love for a long time."

Did he mean he was still in love with her? Something flared inside that for once she couldn't—or didn't want to—squash. A glimmer of hope that what they had wasn't dead after all, that with a little fanning of the flames they could resurrect the spark.

But could they, really? Did she want to go there? She was healed. Why pick at the scab, reopen the wound? Suddenly she felt very tired. Her foot ached and she wanted to go to bed.

John seemed to sense her change of mood. "I should go."

"You were going to tell me something."

"It's late. Another time."

Katie grabbed the crutches and hobbled after him out the front door onto the veranda. She stood beneath the porch light, questions still buzzing in her brain. "When you found out about Tuti did you consider going back to Nena, trying to make it work?"

John sighed. "I did. But Nena was smarter than I was. She knew we liked each other but without love that wasn't enough, not with all the cultural differences we would have had to overcome. She didn't believe I would stick around. She didn't want Tuti being devastated when I left, as she was sure I would inevitably do."

"But if she'd said yes, *would* you have stuck it out?" For some stupid reason she hoped he would have tried at least. Better he'd left her when she was sick because his love wasn't strong enough than that he was a person who couldn't be counted on.

"I've asked myself that over the years. But until I'm actually put in that position, I can't say. Who can say staying with Nena would have been the right thing to do? Marriage is difficult and messy at times. It takes solid love and commitment to see it through, even in the best of circumstances."

Katie propped herself against the rail and set her crutches aside. In bad circumstances even greater love and strength were needed. Her father had been a rock for her mother, never wavering all through her long illness, remission, then recurrence and final stages when the breast cancer traveled to her ovaries, then to her spine and then everywhere.

"My parents had a perfect marriage. There was no messiness. My dad gave my mother unconditional love and support, even when she refused a third round of chemotherapy. That was her choice and he respected it." She'd hoped for that kind of unconditional love from John but he hadn't measured up.

"Are you so sure about that?" John looked

skeptical. "No one really knows what goes on behind the scenes in a marriage."

"*I* know." She didn't like him doubting her parents' love. Without that ideal to strive for, her whole grievance against John would come tumbling down and the past seven years they'd spent apart would have been a huge mistake. But he *was* wrong. He didn't know her mother and father the way she did. "One thing I never understood. Why, if you loved me as much as I thought you did, did you leave me? You've never wanted to talk about it. I can only assume you felt so guilty—"

"Guilty? No, I was angry you wouldn't do everything possible to get well. It's like you were giving up on yourself, on us and our future." He gripped her shoulders. Beneath the porch light shadows darkened his eyes. "I did try to talk to you about it when I came back to Summerside seven years ago. It's what I've been trying to tell you all night."

"How dare you be angry because I didn't want to chop off both my breasts?" She pulled away from him and got onto her crutches. "How do you think it feels to be a woman and lose one of the most important elements of femininity? You just admitted you were in love with my breasts from an early age. How long could I have held you with no breasts? And if I lost you, what other man would want me? Angry? *I* had a right to be angry. Not you."

"That's from your perspective. If you'd died, what difference would it make if you kept your breasts? I watched your mother die. I saw what that did to you and Riley. To your father. I didn't want to watch *you* die."

She drew herself up as tall as she could on her sore ankle. "I'm very much alive, in case you hadn't noticed."

"Oh, I've noticed." All at once the atmosphere changed, became charged. He moved closer. Before she knew what was happening his warm, firm lips pressed against hers. Her mouth opened and his tongue slipped inside. Blood surged in her veins. She felt fully alive, just as she had rushing down the hill on her mountain bike. Then just as she was about to push him away, his lips softened and lingered.

Katie felt like crying and didn't know why.

"I was angry," he said, easing away. "But there was more to it than that. I left so you wouldn't keep your breasts for my sake, so you would get the mastectomy and live. I'm so grateful you survived." The back of his knuckles brushed lightly down her breast, grazing her nipple. "I'm glad your breasts did, too, despite the fact I still think you were wrong." He sucked in a breath. "There, I've finally told you. Before you ream me out for being an idiot, I'll go and you can rest."

Before she could react he'd backed away, stepped off the porch and was striding to his vehicle. The motor started.

She watched his taillights move off down the street. Her lips still tingled with the imprint of his mouth.

He'd left to try to save her? That was crazy. But she believed he meant it. It was just the noble nutty kind of thing he would do.

She'd been so sure she was over him. And she had been.

And yet…with one kiss he'd set her alight.

But she was confused. What had the kiss meant to him? He went out with a lot of women. Kissing her might have been simply the way he closed an evening. Or a way of closing out the past. It didn't necessarily mean he was attracted to her.

He'd said he was angry. Did that mean he hadn't forgiven her for not taking him back seven years ago? Had he confessed just to get this off his chest? He hadn't stuck around to find out what she thought about it all.

The truth was, she didn't know what she thought.

She went inside and closed the door. The evening had raised more questions than it had answered. Slowly she made her way down the hall. Baby steps. Wait and see. Don't rush into anything. *Que sera sera.*

WHY HAD HE gone and kissed her?

John thumped the steering wheel as he drove away from Katie's house. He'd taken her by surprise. She hadn't been ready. The circumstances were all wrong given the nature of their conversation. But he hadn't been able to help himself. They'd been talking, openly and honestly for the first time in years. And standing on the porch in the dark, feeling her so close, the years had fallen away. He'd kissed her without thinking.

He slowed to make the turn onto his parents' street to pick up Tuti. And reminiscing about perving at her in a bikini? He winced. Not cool. Not a mature relationship based on more than sexual attraction. Which was what he wanted to have with her.

At first he'd simply wanted her to be civil to him. Then he was content for them to be friends. Now, now he wanted much more. He wanted Katie back in his life permanently. He was falling in love with her again, or, more accurately, doubting that he had ever fallen out of love. And he wanted her to love him.

Brief as the kiss was, it reminded him of everything they'd once had. And all that he'd lost.

One little kiss with Katie was worth more than all his sexual adventures in the intervening years combined.

The anger between them still festered away below the surface. He thought he'd forgotten, gotten over the past. But ever since Tuti's arrival memories and emotions had been surfacing.

Like his lack of security in their relationship. It had been only annoying when she wouldn't commit to a wedding date. Terrifying and out of control when she was sick with cancer and possibly dying. All he'd ever wanted was for them to be together and raise a family. He'd thought he had her…and then she'd slipped away from him.

He felt a glimmer of hope that he and Katie could forge a new relationship, one based on the present and not the past. They'd both moved on with their lives, accomplished important things on their own. Now they needed to approach the future from a different perspective, without always harking back to the past. He needed to not second-guess her, always expecting she would balk at the last hurdle. It would be hard to do but Katie would be worth the effort.

He pulled into his parents' driveway and hurried up the path. He knocked once and let himself in. Every light in the house was ablaze. A Disney movie was playing on the TV in the lounge room. The radio was on in the kitchen, barely audible over the sound of his mother and father squabbling good-naturedly, as was their habit. Also in the conversation was another voice he couldn't place. No sign of Tuti.

He walked through the house, glancing into rooms. And stopped in the doorway of the kitchen. His mother was seated at the table, addressing brightly colored invitations. His dad was on Skype talking to someone while his mother kept interrupting with her two cents. Tuti was lying on the tiled floor, sleepily stroking the cat.

"Mum, Dad. Sorry I'm so late." He bent to touch Tuti on the shoulder. She glanced up and smiled. "Hey, sweetheart."

"Get a second estimate on that transmission," Marty Forster was saying to his laptop computer.

John glanced at the screen and recognized his dad's sister, Gena, in Brisbane. He waved hello. "Hey, Aunt Gena. Dad's right. Get another estimate."

"Mechanics see a single woman walk in the garage and rub their hands in glee," Marty went on. "Crooks, the lot of them."

"They're not all crooks," Alison objected, licking an envelope. "Gena can handle herself. She's not stupid."

"Did I say she was stupid?" Marty huffed. "I said mechanics are crooks."

"They're not *all* crooks—" Alison began again.

"I've got to go," John said. "Tuti needs to get to bed."

"Of course she does." Alison reached around to hug Tuti, but the girl sidestepped into the safety of John's arms. Pressing her lips together, Alison turned back to the invitations. "I'm almost finished," she said brightly. "Tuti, you're going to have the best birthday party ever."

John noted the thick stack of invitations. His mother turned every social occasion into a major event. Tuti wasn't prepared for this. "How many people are you inviting? I thought it would be just close family."

"Plus a few friends. You having a daughter is a big deal."

"Have you got an invitation there for Katie? I can give it to her myself."

Alison frowned. "Do you really want her there? She's—"

"She's giving Tuti extra help with her English skills," he said, cutting his mother off before she could say anything mean about Katie in front of Tuti. "Tuti is crazy about her."

"What about you?" His mother's blue eyes

searched his. "Don't go getting your heart broken again."

"No fear of that," he said lightly. Even though he could still taste Katie's lips and feel the soft skin of her cheek beneath his fingers. "We're friends, that's all."

His mother had been almost as gutted as he when Katie hadn't taken him back. She was prejudiced against her. No way was he confiding in her about his hopes for a new beginning with Katie.

Alison sniffed. "She's got you running after her again, rescuing her, waiting around the hospital till all hours. Was anything wrong with her ankle in the end?"

"A bad sprain. She's on crutches." John gently pushed his daughter in the direction of the hall. "Go get your backpack and put your shoes on. Then wait for me at the front door. I'll be right there."

When she'd left the room John pulled out a chair next to his mother. "You used to be fond of Katie. Said she was like a daughter to you."

"That was before." Alison grudgingly handed him an invitation. "I suppose she can come if you and Tuti want her."

"We do." His mother was only being loyal out of love for him, but her antagonism added another layer to his conflicted emotions. It made him realize that while part of him wanted to explore a fresh relationship with Katie, to see where it took them, part of him agreed he would do well to keep his distance.

Their breakup seven years ago had been the first time he'd faced the loss of something really important to him. Katie, despite saying she loved him and wanted to marry him, had disregarded his feelings and dismissed his fears about her long-term health. If she'd truly loved him she would have found a way to compromise.

And what about her comment tonight about her father's perfect love for her mother? She'd said as much years ago when they were teenagers, but he'd put that down to the romantic idealism of a young girl. Clearly she still thought that way. But how much would Katie know about what went on between her parents? She'd only been ten years old when her mother died at a relatively young age. Barry Henning's love for his wife had been enshrined in Katie's eyes as perfect and unsullied. How could he compete with that?

"Bapa!" Tuti called from the front door. "Tie shoes."

"She hasn't learned that yet?" Alison shook her head.

"She's only had laced shoes for a few weeks.

Give her a break." He shifted impatiently. "I should go help her."

"Let her try a little longer," Alison said. "I want to hear about you and Katie. Are you dating?"

"Don't make a big deal," his father said. "If John says they're just friends, that's what he means."

"It's not that simple, though, is it?" his mother said. "You're fooling yourself if you think you're over her."

"It is complicated," John admitted. "We have a history. But neither of us is interested in getting back together." Truth was, he didn't know how to read Katie's response to his kiss. She'd seemed confused by it and by his parting words. Well, she'd confused him plenty in the old days. He took the envelope and rose. "Can you do something for me?"

"Anything, you know that, darling," his mother said before licking an envelope.

"Be nice to Katie at the party." Before she could protest he held up a hand. "I've seen how you snub her." Since Katie had done it to him, he knew how painful that was. Despite everything, he would spare her that if he could.

His mother sighed and set another completed invitation on the stack. "I'll try."

He changed the subject. “How was Tuti tonight?”

“She’s very standoffish. Such a quiet little thing.”

“You’re too loud around her,” Marty interrupted his Skype conversation to remonstrate. “You scare the poor kid.”

“*I* scare her? Who put on *Bambi* for her to watch?”

“How was I to know Bambi’s mother got shot by a hunter? I don’t watch kid’s movies.”

Alison rolled her eyes. “When Bambi’s mother died, Tuti ran out of the room. It took me half an hour to find her. She was outside, hiding in your old tree fort.”

“Katie thinks she’s grieving for her mother.”

“Of course she’s grieving.” Alison tutted. “Poor thing.”

“And that she misses her Bali family.”

“She’s got us. We all adore her. I really want this party to be special. I’ve hired a bouncing castle and a clown—”

John groaned and dragged a hand over his face. “That’s very generous of you. But I told you not to go overboard. She’s not used to a big fuss being made of her.”

While Tuti could be outgoing around people she knew well, she was shy in large groups. His mother knew that. But he also understood where his mum was coming from and tried to be forgiving. When he and his sisters were growing up his mother had worked full-time as a journalist. She'd put in a lot of extra hours just to be on the same playing field as her male colleagues. Consequently she seemed to feel as though she'd missed out on her children's youth and was determined to make up for it with her grandchildren.

"She'll have a terrific time," Alison said firmly.

Tuti ran back into the room, her pack on her back. Grinning, she pointed to her running shoes. The laces were knotted in a tangled bow. Not perfect but she wouldn't trip.

"Good effort." John seized the opportunity to get away.

On the way home in the car he asked Tuti, "Are you looking forward to your birthday party?"

"Grandma hurt my ears."

"Grandma means well. She wants to make you happy."

Tuti shrugged and turned to look out the window at the dark streets. Her reflection in the glass showed a downturned mouth, sad eyes. He thought about how quiet the Balinese were, never raising their voices even when angry. His family was good-natured but loud, and his parents, though they loved each other deeply, squabbled constantly. It was hard to listen to sometimes but it didn't mean much. Storms blew in and blew out.

But Tuti wouldn't understand all the nuances. It was going to take time for her to get used to his family. Katie was right, she undoubtedly grieved for her mother. Seeing his father on Skype had given him the idea to put her in contact with Wayan and Ketut.

His mind circled back to Katie. Kissing wasn't any part of the pact they'd made for their current relationship. Technically speaking, he hadn't broken his promise—that only covered sexual innuendo and teasing. But he couldn't afford to put her off. He needed to be in her good graces for Tuti's sake.

But just for a moment she had kissed him back. He would hang on to that. In the meantime he would try to take things slowly. Maybe he needed to cool it for a while. Katie wasn't like the other woman he'd gone out with. She was a long-term proposition.

CHAPTER NINE

KATIE MADE IT through the school week somehow but by Friday afternoon she was relieved to come home and prop her sore ankle on a footstool. She booted up her laptop to do a search on Balinese spiritual beliefs. The Balinese were Hindus and believed in reincarnation she found out. Tuti would derive some comfort from believing her mother's soul had been reborn into another life. But the girl must still be sad. She knew from her own experience a person couldn't leapfrog over grief.

Oh, here was something. Apparently inside the family compound was a spirit house or *sanggah taksu,* believed to house the spirits of the family's ancestors. When a member of the family died, the priest conducted a ritual and family members made offerings to invite the part of the deceased spirit that stayed on earth to enter the shrine.

Katie looked at the photos of tall narrow terra-cotta shrines with thick thatched roofs. Where was she going to find one of those? She tapped in a new search. A dozen links popped up. Wow. You could get anything on eBay.

A closer look revealed that the shrine was actually a garden lantern in the shape of a Balinese spirit house. But if she took out the light and made a few other modifications, it would be close enough. She tapped in her payment details then paused before she hit the buy button.

How was John going to feel when she showed up at his house with a shrine for Tuti's dead mother? Would he accept her help or would it look like interference? She was only the girl's teacher, after all.

But if she was going to be friends with John then she wanted a deeper relationship with Tuti, too. Plus she felt an affinity to the motherless child and couldn't bear to think of her being unhappy. With her background she was in a good position to help John help his daughter to heal.

Over the past week she'd only seen John when he came to pick up Tuti. Was it her imagination or was he keeping those moments as brief as possible? Did he regret kissing her? Or was he feeling uncomfortable about something he or she had said? They'd covered so much ground the night of her bicycle accident that it could be either. His comment about her being unable to commit had floored her. She hadn't even realized she'd refused to set a date for their wedding.

All she'd ever wanted was a love as deep and true as her parents had. They'd never fought, never raised their voices in angry dispute. If they didn't agree on a point they discussed it calmly and rationally. And then her father, a military man who'd commanded a platoon, found ways to give her mother what she wanted without losing face. Because he loved her that much. And understandably so—Mary Henning had been a goddess. Beautiful, serene, wise, talented. She somehow found time to be a professional cookbook author as well as a loving wife and mother.

Katie had thought she'd found that perfect love with John. He was smart, handsome, brave, and had more integrity than anyone she'd known barring her brother and father. But as her illness progressed it had become clear he hadn't really loved her, not as much as she'd needed him to. That's what it boiled down to. She hadn't been "enough" for him. Not pretty enough, not worthy enough. Not adventurous enough. Whatever he'd been looking for, she hadn't been it.

So why had he kissed her? What did he want from her now?

And what was up with his "noble gesture" of walking away so she would rethink her stance on the mastectomy? It was easy to be noble from a distance. Especially now that she was okay. She wriggled her sprained ankle and made a face at the lancing pain. Then she rolled her shoulders and felt the tension from hours at the keyboard every night after dinner.

So what if she hadn't been ready to commit? Who said there was a timeline? It was a good thing she hadn't married him if that's the way he acted when she got sick. And he actually thought just by leaving he could change her mind about her treatment? No, it was good they hadn't married. Divorce would have been a lot more drawn out and painful than him simply walking away.

She'd done the hard work: recovering, getting healthy, surviving. Not for John—he'd left, but for her own sake. And she *was* successful. She was alive, goddamn it, when all the doctors—and John—thought she wouldn't make it.

She was still trying, trying so hard to be all she could be, to be indestructible. And he had the audacity to complain that she wouldn't set a date for their wedding. If she hadn't been enough for John as she was then, she didn't know what more she could be now.

"IT'S A SPIRIT HOUSE, a *sanggah taksu.*" Perched on a chair in the foyer, Katie launched into an explanation of what she'd read on the internet.

John circled the thatched roof shrine sitting in his foyer. He had a rough idea of what a spirit house was and while this wasn't authentic it was close enough. And it was very nice that Katie had made an effort considering she was still limping around on crutches.

"I went to Springvale and bought some offerings." Katie opened her tote bag and removed sticks of incense, a banana leaf, a container of cooked rice and a marigold.

"You've gone to a lot of trouble. Thank you." Mentally he kicked himself. Why hadn't he thought of this? He was more familiar with Balinese traditions than Katie. Why hadn't he been a better parent?

"Where is she?" Katie asked. "Can I show it to her?"

"She's on Skype with her aunt and uncle in Bali." It had taken a week and several phone calls but he'd arranged for them to go to the internet café in the next village at a prearranged time. "You should show her while her aunt and uncle are online. They'll be able to tell her more about the rituals."

He picked up the spirit house and carried it into his bedroom, close to the desk opposite his bed. His home office had ended up in his room, after all. "Tuti, look what Katie brought you, a *sanggah taksu* for your mother's spirit."

Tuti turned away from the computer screen. Her eyes widened. Then she began chattering volubly in Balinese, gesturing to her aunt and uncle to look at the spirit house. John didn't think he'd ever seen her this animated.

He and Katie stood just out of the camera's range. He put his arm around her shoulders and nuzzled her neck. She smelled delicious, like a field of flowers. "Have you been avoiding me?"

She turned her head and her big dark eyes were looking into his. "I thought you were avoiding me."

"Well, maybe I was giving you space." He searched her face. "Are we good?"

She laughed nervously. "Now there's a loaded question."

Before he could pursue that Tuti hopped off the chair and went into a flurry of activity. Wayan and Ketut appeared to be instructing her. Tuti laid a small ball of rice on the banana leaf and decorated it with marigold petals. She took a stick of incense out of the package and looked to John. "Fire, *Bapa*. Please."

While he dug in the desk drawer for a book of matches Tuti ran out of the room. She came back with the photo he'd given her of her mother. She propped it against the back of the shrine behind the rice and marigold petals.

John lit the joss stick and the delicate scent of sandalwood filled the room. Wayan and Ketut began to chant, soft and low, the fluid words weaving a spell. Tuti put her hands together and bowed her head. Silent tears rolled down her cheeks. John felt a lump form in his throat. This was the same little girl who hadn't cried at her mother's funeral. Appearances could be deceiving.

Katie pressed a tissue to her nose. "Excuse me." She hurriedly left the room.

John followed her, shutting the door behind him to give Tuti privacy. Katie was dabbing her eyes. "Are you crying or do you have a cold?"

"There were some tears. Poor little Tuti. But I also have a cold."

"You look tired." Now he noticed that her eyes were bloodshot and fine lines of strain radiated from the corners of her eyes. "If you're sick you should be at home, resting."

"Don't worry, I won't get too close to Tuti. I wouldn't want her to catch a cold and be ill for her birthday party."

"I was more concerned about you."

"I'm fine." She pulled a plastic pill bottle from her purse and shook a handful of tablets of various shapes and colors into her palm. Carefully she sorted them, separating out three, all different. "I'll get a glass of water."

John followed her into the kitchen. He handed her a clean glass from the cupboard. "What are those pills you're taking?"

Katie ran water from the tap. "My naturopath recommended them to boost my immune system."

His hands curled into impotent fists. Her reliance on alternative medicines was a hot button for him. It didn't matter that he had no right anymore to have a say in her health care; nor had she given him any reason to be invested. But he couldn't help his reaction. He believed in traditional medicine not this mumbo jumbo. "You believe in what those witch doctors say?"

"Witch doctors? Come on, John, that's harsh. This is the twenty-first century." She popped the first pill.

"I've read reports that natural remedies can act against legitimate medications with bad effects. At best they're ineffective, at worst they could hurt you. I hope you also see a real doctor."

She gave him an odd look. "I have a cold, not a terminal illness." She tossed another tablet into her mouth, took a drink and swallowed. "These have vitamin C in them plus a whole pile of other good things." She started reading the packaging. "Spirulina, echinacea..."

All items which at most had only anecdotal evidence for their effectiveness. Next she'd be telling him she could meditate her way out of a head cold. The faith she placed in her natural remedies, the way she bandied about the phrase "terminal illness" so glibly, was worrying. She'd been clear for six years, but she still had a higher-than-average risk of cancer recurring and would for the rest of her life. If that happened would she handle it any differently than last time?

"Why does it bother you so much what medications I take?" she demanded.

"You have to ask? I almost lost you once because of your...your crazy notions."

"You lost me because you walked away."

"I told you why I walked."

"It seems to me that was all about *your* crazy notion."

"Given another chance I might not take the same tactic but I would just as adamantly lobby for the most conservative treatment."

"I've been taking care of myself for quite a few years. I'm doing a pretty good job, too." She jabbed him in the chest. "You've been pestering me to be friends or something for years. In all that time have you ever asked yourself whether you're prepared to accept me as I am?"

He stared at her.

She rattled the pill bottle. "This is who I am. Herbal medicines and organic food. Naturopaths and homeopaths. Anyone and anything that I believe can keep me well. Maybe that's your problem. Maybe you still see me as someone who's sick."

He blinked. Could she be right?

The sound of Tuti crying in the other room tracked across his radar. "Something's wrong."

The Skype screen had frozen in the middle of the ritual for Nena. Tuti's aunt and uncle's images were a pixilated blur, their mouths open and unmoving. Tuti clicked the mouse over and over, not knowing how to get them back. She spoke in her own language, distraught far beyond what was reasonable.

"Tuti, sweetheart, it's okay. We've lost the connection, that's all." He put an arm around her while he repaired the connection. He got Wayan and Ketut back on Skype and helped Tuti dry her tears. Then he went looking for Katie.

He found a note on the hall table atop a book. "I also brought this over for Tuti. Read this to her. I'll see you both at her party."

The book was for children who'd lost a loved one, to help them deal with their grief. John shook his head. Once again Katie had beat him to the punch on something beneficial for Tuti. He could only be thankful she was in his life and that she cared about his daughter. He thought he knew something about coming face-to-face with the fear of losing a loved one. But she'd lost her mother. He knew nothing compared to her.

And yet, after her mother died, her fear had been realized and was over. Presumably she'd found some closure. For him the fear was ongoing. Because of Katie's family history she would always be at greater risk of cancer. Her attitudes hadn't changed as she'd grown older; they'd become more entrenched. If she got sick again their whole conversation would pick up where they'd left off.

Didn't she see? Just because she'd survived once didn't mean she was indestructible.

KATIE PAINTED THE wrapping paper for Tuti's birthday gift herself. Cheeky brown monkeys swung from palm trees next to a sandy beach lapped by blue waves. She had fun shopping for Tuti and was tempted to shower her with gifts. But she'd reined herself in knowing John wouldn't appreciate his daughter being spoiled. In an import shop she'd found an adorable family of brightly painted wooden cats from Bali sitting up like people on a couch.

Anticipating seeing Tuti's face light up kept her humming all morning. Her ankle was improving although it ached after standing on it all week. Her cold was better, too, no doubt thanks to her special supplements. Take that, John Forster! But with her first deadline looming, the party would seriously cut into her plan to write all weekend.

And yes, face it, she was nervous about seeing John again after running out without saying goodbye the day of the Skype session. But he had a nerve calling her naturopath and homeopath witch doctors. Especially considering she'd been in remission and perfectly healthy for over six years.

She carefully placed the cat family in the center of the paper and began to fold and tape.

How dare he try to control her health choices when the last time he tried had proved disastrous for their relationship? How much nicer if he'd simply given her a hug and said he hoped she felt better soon? Given her some credit for being able to take care of herself.

As much as she was looking forward to seeing Tuti, she rather dreaded the coming encounter with John's mother. The last time she'd run into Alison in the grocery store the woman had looked right through her as if she wasn't there. The experience had shaken her. She was used to everyone liking her.

She considered just dropping off the present and going straight home. Her sprained ankle would be a good enough excuse. But she wanted to go for Tuti's sake. From things John let slip Katie knew the party was going to be bigger than *Ben Hur*. Tuti was easily overwhelmed by people and excitement.

The party was to begin at two that afternoon. At a carefully calculated 2:15 p.m. Katie arrived at Alison and Marty's beautiful two-story home in an exclusive neighborhood. She figured by this time Alison would be fully occupied with her other guests and she could slip in unnoticed.

Her red dress wasn't conducive to blending in with the furniture, but pride dictated that she make herself as attractive as possible to compensate and distract from the crutches and the ugly bandage around her sprained ankle.

She pressed the doorbell. Please let John answer. Or one of his sisters, or his father, anyone but—the door opened—Alison.

Perfect. Katie forced a smile. "Hello."

"There you are, Katie! We thought you weren't coming." Alison's smile was effusive, her manner warmly welcoming as Katie entered the foyer. "It's been so long since we've seen you. Come in, come in."

What was going on? Was she drunk? Katie leaned in cautiously as the other woman gave her a peck on the cheek. A cloud of perfume enveloped her but there was no alcohol on Alison's breath. Warily, Katie hugged her back, conscious of a pang for the years when they'd had almost a mother-daughter relationship.

"How have you been?" Katie stopped short of saying *I missed you.* Was Alison sincerely trying to mend their relationship or was her friendliness just for show on Tuti's birthday? She really hoped it was genuine.

"Oh, you know me. I'm always fine." Alison led the way into the crowded lounge room. Adults filled all available seating while children ran in and out. "Put your present on the table and come and sit down. John told us all about your poor ankle. There's tea or coffee or soft drinks. Marty's got a bar going in the kitchen if you'd like something stronger."

"No alcohol, thanks, but I wouldn't mind a cold drink." Katie waved to a mother of one of the children in her class. "Where's Tuti? I'd like to say happy birthday to her."

"She's out back on the trampoline. That was our gift to her. We figured if we're going to be babysitting regularly she would need something fun to do while she was here." Alison removed a bag from a chair and pulled it out for Katie. "Sit down, you poor thing."

"Thank you." Katie lowered herself and propped her crutches on the wall next to her. Through the kitchen doorway she spotted John's sisters putting food onto platters. "Sonya, Leah, it's so good to see you both."

A flurry of exclamations and hugs ensued. Katie chatted with them while they worked and got fully caught up on their kids, jobs and husbands. Katie in turn told the story of her sprained ankle.

Alison poured her a tall glass of iced lemonade from a frosty jug. "There you go."

"Thanks," Katie said warmly. "That's so kind of you. I'll rest a bit then go see Tuti."

"She'll be thrilled you came." Alison plucked an olive off one of the platters. "She talks about you all the time. Katie this, Katie that. She thinks you're wonderful."

What was wonderful was hearing Alison, who'd once been so important to her and then so cold, pass on this information. Katie smiled up at her. "The feeling's mutual. I adore Tuti."

A warm hand cupped her shoulder. "Glad you could make it." John's short blond hair was shiny, his jaw freshly shaven, his eyes very blue.

"Thanks for inviting me." Katie sipped her lemonade.

John pulled out a chair and sat next to her. At a glance from him, his sisters and mother picked up the platters and moved into the backyard. "What happened the other day? You ran off."

"I had to go. You were busy with Tuti…."

"I appreciate the trouble you went to over the shrine. It meant a lot to Tuti. And the book on grief." He took a breath. "Maybe I wasn't dealing with things the way I should."

"You're doing a good job. It's not easy to think of everything."

"Well, you were right. Can we leave it at that?"

"Well…" She leveled him a direct look. "No apology for giving me a hard time about my choice in medicine?"

"I won't apologize for having your best interests at heart." He held up a finger as she opened her mouth to protest. "Don't spoil the party by arguing."

"In that case, I'll go outside and say happy birthday to Tuti."

"Uh-uh-uh. You promised not to run away when I came into a room." He dropped his hand to her strapped ankle. "How's the foot?"

"It doesn't throb anymore. I can stand on it without crutches for short periods."

"And your cold? Can I get you anything—a

box of tissues, freshen your drink? I'll be your personal butler. Anything you want, just ask." John got up and dragged over another chair, covered it with a cushion off the breakfast nook and lifted her bandaged ankle onto the cushion. "Is that better?"

"It's great. Thanks."

He was purposely being charming. And it was working. She couldn't bring herself to remind him he'd promised not to flirt. In the old days he used to overwhelm her with pampering. She'd end up laughing and exasperated, batting him away. But she'd loved the attention. And now? She still enjoyed him. But she was wary of getting used to the royal treatment again. Who knew when he might suddenly withdraw it. And himself.

He grabbed himself a cold beer from a bucket of ice, nodding at the shrieks of children's laughter coming from outside. "It's a zoo. I don't know where my mother found all those kids."

"She's gone to a huge effort for Tuti."

John twisted off the beer cap. "It's too much. Tuti's not used to the attention or all the presents. I don't want her upset. Or spoiled."

"It will take more than a few presents to spoil Tuti. Don't be mad at your mother for indulging her. It's a grandmother's right."

"Speaking of my mother, I hope she's behaving?"

Suddenly she knew what had happened. He'd told his mother to be nice to her. It was thoughtful of him—but wrong. Alison would only be more resentful of Katie if she had to pretend to like her. Suddenly she felt tired and sad and disappointed. She'd thought all her old wounds had healed. She'd thought she no longer cared whether Alison liked her or not. But then Alison had hugged her and she'd almost cried because it had felt like she was coming home. To know that Alison was only pretending was awful.

"You don't need to protect me from her," Katie said quietly. "We'll work things out if we're able to. If not, her being nice because you asked her to won't help."

"In other words, she's gone over the top, as usual."

"I'll survive."

"Of course you will, because that's what you do." He gave her a smile, as if trying to make up again.

Here was the opening—if she decided to take it—to tell him why she'd made the decision not to have a mastectomy. After him telling her why he left she thought he deserved an explanation in turn. She didn't want him to think she was a crackpot. But who wanted to talk about breast cancer at a child's birthday party? It wasn't a sexy topic. And she'd noticed several attractive women here today. She already had a bum ankle. She hated that in his mind she would always be the sick girl.

"Come along, everyone," Alison said, poking her head into the room. "Tuti's opening her presents."

Katie and John followed the rest of the guests out back. Tuti sat atop a picnic table surrounded by gifts, her eyes wide, her round cheeks flushed. She was overexcited, a little frightened by all the attention and confused as to what she should be doing. Katie felt for her and wished she could help. But this was Alison's show and she didn't want to risk her wrath by interfering. She cringed as Tuti edged away when John's mother sat next to her to hand her presents. Despite everything, she couldn't help but feel sorry for Alison.

"Excuse me, Katie, I'd better get in there," John muttered, and pushed through the crowd to join Tuti. "May I help?" he asked his mother. Without waiting for an answer he sat between Tuti and Alison and became the go-between.

There were so many presents and half of them seemed to come from John's mother. Tuti was starting to lose it. She ripped off the paper, barely looking at each gift before thrusting it aside and demanding another. John whispered in her ear. She merely shrugged. Katie winced. What should have been a simple celebration with close family had turned into a circus.

Tuti was handed Katie's present. The hand-painted wrapping was torn off and flung on the ground. Katie braced herself for Tuti to toss the gift aside just as she'd done the plastic dolls and jewelry-making kits. But when Tuti saw the cats she went still. She tugged on her father's arm to show him. John had picked up the wrapping paper and was examining it. He looked at the cats then pointed Katie out to Tuti. Across the other children's heads, Tuti beamed at Katie.

Katie's heart filled. Misty-eyed, she smiled back. No matter what happened between her and John, she would never be *just* Tuti's teacher.

When all the presents had been opened, it was time for barbecued lamb and salads. The music was turned up and the adults spilled into the backyard, sipping wine and beer. The children piled into the bouncing castle or jumped on the trampoline.

Katie didn't feel like drinking and she'd had enough socializing for the moment. She went in search of Tuti, knowing she would be someplace quiet. It took an introvert to recognize another one, something that Alison didn't get. She found the girl in Marty's den, sitting up at her grandfather's desk playing with the Balinese cat family.

"Hey, Tuti," Katie said softly from the doorway. "Do you like your present?"

"I like very big." Tuti arranged the cats in a circle.

"You like it very much. What do you say when someone gives you something?"

Tuti beamed at Katie. "Thank you."

"You're welcome." Katie took a seat in an easy chair next to the fireplace and watched Tuti play for a few minutes. "There are a lot of people here today."

Tuti flashed her an anxious glance, as if worried Katie might send her back out. "Many peoples."

"Your grandmother loves you very much." She never thought she'd be pleading Alison's case, but Tuti needed her grandmother even if she didn't know it.

Tuti shrugged and continued to play.

"You know, if you don't run away from her all the time, she might give you some space."

Tuti glanced up, puzzled. Hmm, how to explain "space"? "She might not sit so close or try to hug you all the time. She might not talk to you so much and expect you to talk. People don't understand that you need to be alone sometimes."

"I didn't realize I was so annoying."

Katie twisted in her chair.

Alison stood in the doorway. Her blue eyes, so like John's, shimmered, not with tears but with resentment.

"Oh, dear. I'm sorry. I didn't mean—"

"Yes, you did," she said curtly. "We're ready to sing happy birthday to Tuti. Tuti, would you like to come and blow out the candles on your cake?" Alison glanced at Katie with an unfathomable look before turning back to Tuti. "Or would you like to play by yourself a little longer?"

Tuti looked like she didn't know what she wanted.

"Why don't you come in for a moment," Katie suggested to Alison. "Tuti, can you show your grandmother your cat family?"

Tuti nodded.

Alison started to go to her side, hesitated then sat across the desk from her. "Do they have names?"

"*Bapa*, *meme*, Wayan, Made, Nyoman, Ketut," Tuti recited mother, father, followed by the Balinese names commonly given to the first, second, third and fourth children in a family.

"Those are lovely." Alison watched Tuti line the cats up on the couch in order of size. When Tuti put them in the wrong order she opened her mouth to correct her. Then she caught Katie's eye and pressed her lips together.

After a bit of rearranging Tuti got the order right all by herself. Satisfied, she looked at her grandmother. "Cake?"

"Cake." Alison rose and held out her hand.

Tuti slid off her grandfather's big leather chair. She ran past Alison's outstretched hand and threw her arms around Katie's neck. "I love you." Then she ran out of the room.

Alison froze, her face flushing brick-red. Her fingers curled in on her palm.

"She's only a little girl," Katie defended. "She doesn't mean to hurt you. She'll come around."

"Save your advice for someone who wants it." Alison gave a haughty sniff. "Everyone thinks you're so wonderful. But it's your fault John won't stick with any woman for long. What he went through with you scarred him."

Katie stared. Where was this coming from? Had John talked to his mother about their relationship? She agreed John had changed. But life-and-death situations often had that effect. How did Alison think *she'd* felt?

"I am not responsible for his playboy lifestyle!"

"You broke his heart when you wouldn't reconcile. Now you've wormed your way into his life through Tuti. If you hurt him again—"

"He left me when I needed him most. *He* broke *my* heart."

No question about it now, Alison's earlier display of affection had been completely phony. It hurt all the more because the affection between them used to be genuine. Oh, why hadn't she stayed home and worked on her book? If she'd done that she wouldn't be having this conversation.

"Really? Then why hasn't he ever married and had a proper family?"

"I don't know." She shook her head, hurt and bewildered. "You're being unfair."

Alison walked out, clearly not prepared to listen to any more. Katie sat very still, her hands clenched in her lap. How could Alison have said those things? They were untrue—they had to be, calculated to hurt her. She hadn't damaged John. It was unthinkable.

"Katie, there you are!" Sonya appeared in the open door. "Come on. We're singing happy birthday." She hustled Katie back to the backyard. A plate with cake and a glass of champagne were pressed into her hands.

Smiling faces were all around but she was close to tears. Could Alison be right? Had she ruined John's life? In focusing on getting and staying well had she been that self-absorbed that she hadn't noticed he was hurting?

She slipped away from the group to a quiet corner of the yard separated by a hedge and sat on the wide swing made for two beneath a big old oak tree. She and John used to sit here on moonlit nights….

As if she'd conjured him, he came around the hedge.

CHAPTER TEN

"AHA, I FIGURED YOU would have gone into hiding by now. Tuti really likes those cats. Are they from Bali?"

"What? Oh, yes, they are." She kept her face averted. Her emotions were close to the surface.

He walked around the swing and bent to narrow his gaze at her. "What's wrong? Did my mother say something to upset you?"

Katie knew better than to criticize his mother. He could complain about her all he liked but he wouldn't appreciate her doing it. "It's no big deal."

John sat next to her on the swing. "Tell me."

Fearing she might cry for all she'd had, and lost, not just John and his family, but the core of who she thought she was, she took a deep shaky breath. Still she couldn't speak.

John took her hand. His grip was warm and comforting, his thigh and shoulder pressed against hers. "What did Mother do?"

"Did I break your heart?" she blurted. "Am

I the reason you haven't found someone else and married?"

He swore under his breath. "Is that what she told you?"

"Basically."

"Don't listen to her." He pasted on a jaunty grin. "Do I look like a guy with a broken heart?"

Taking his question seriously, Katie studied him in the dappled green light filtering through the oak tree. She saw shallow creases between his eyebrows and a mouth that used to laugh a lot more than it did now. She saw that something intangible was missing in his eyes. "You look like a man who hasn't found what he's looking for."

His smile faded. "Maybe I haven't. But look, stuff happens." He glanced down at her hand, still nestled in his. In a low voice he asked, "Did I break your heart?"

Her voice was even quieter. "You know you did."

"Maybe we weren't ready, have you ever thought of that? You were only a couple of years out of university, in your first teaching job. As for me, surfing wasn't panning out and I had no idea what else I wanted to do with my life. Then when you got sick, I was scared. Scared of having to watch you die. The way we all watched your mother die."

"I—"

"But you know what I think? I think your cancer was just a smoke screen, a scapegoat for our breakup—although you made some dumb decisions about your health. Still are, in my opinion." He held up a hand. "I know. I have no right to tell you how to live your life."

Not if they weren't together. Because being committed meant compromise. She'd compromised by going with chemo and radiation therapy when she'd really wanted to pursue unproved, alternative therapies. What concessions had he made? "How could my cancer be a scapegoat? You just said that's why you left. You couldn't deal with my illness."

"Even before you got sick you couldn't commit to marrying me. Then when you were sick, you wouldn't do everything possible to get well for us. At least that's how it appeared to me." He gazed down at their linked hands. "Sounds selfish to me now. Selfish people aren't ready to get married."

"If we truly loved each other what does timing matter?" she said. "If you truly loved me you would have stuck around no matter what."

"I did love you. I just don't think you loved me enough to do everything in your power to stay alive."

How long would he have loved her if she

didn't have any breasts? A virile twenty-seven-year-old surfer surrounded by buxom blondes in bikinis? Even after all these years she feared the answer so much she couldn't ask the question. There was no point in asking. How could a person reply to that truthfully?

"People grow and change," he maintained. "What works at one stage of life doesn't necessarily hold true for always."

"So me getting sick saved us from the heartbreak of marrying too young and regretting it later. Is that what you're saying?"

His gaze was steady. "Maybe."

She felt sick to her stomach. He'd just confirmed everything she'd always suspected. He hadn't believed in their love the way she had. He *hadn't* loved her enough. Maybe that's *why* she hadn't been able to commit.

And yet, she had to acknowledge that she must not have believed in his love if she'd thought he would leave her for a hot surfer chick if she was disfigured.

"Why did you kiss me the other day? Are you playing with me? The way you've been playing with women for the past seven years? I'm not like those women."

"I know that. You kissed me back, don't forget."

"Reflexive action."

"Oh, yeah? How long do you want to keep me dangling on this hook, Katie? Because I'm over it."

"Dangling? I've been clear all along I didn't want a relationship."

"Yet you haven't found anyone else, either. As long as you are available..." He shook his head. "I don't know what I'm saying. You're right. You were clear. We're over."

Exactly what she'd been saying for seven years. So why did it hurt coming from him? *Had* she kept him dangling, secretly liking that he flirted with her, as if, should she change her mind, she could have him whenever she wanted? Her own motives were as confusing to her as his.

"Why did you kiss me if you didn't want to deepen our relationship?" She needed to hear him say she meant something to him. Because, like it or not, she was getting in deeper. And she wanted him to go there with her.

"Because you looked beautiful in the porch light. Because your mouth trembled just..." He touched the corner of her lips. "There. Because you were in pain but pretending not to be. You were sweet and strong and vulnerable." His eyes bored into hers. "I want to kiss you again right now."

He slid his arm behind her and grabbed the

rope on her other side. Then leaned in and pressed his lips against hers. Her lips parted and she tasted champagne on his tongue. The sun burned through the leaves onto her forehead, shoulder and thigh. As the seconds passed all sensation faded but the movement of their mouths together, the slow dance of their tongues, his hand molding her breast…

She didn't hold back but opened herself to his kiss, moving her hands up his shoulders to loop around his neck. She leaned in, showing him there was still a spark. More than a spark. Desire flared, hot and sweet.

He drew back, his eyes hot and serious. "Oh, Katie."

Her heart was pounding. It felt as if they were on the cusp of something important. If only they had the courage to make the leap from dancing around feelings to declaring them.

From the leafy branches of the tree came a giggle.

"What was that?" Katie asked, craning her neck.

"Tuti," John said, sliding off the swing. "Is that you?"

Tuti poked her head out of the leaves and giggled again.

"Come down from there." John dragged a hand down his face. "Jeez. That kid."

There was a rustling and a second later Tuti swung down from a lower branch and dropped to the ground. A leaf was stuck in her hair and her pink party dress was dusted with bits of bark.

"You little monkey." Laughing, John tried to grab her.

She scampered away, giggling, and disappeared around the hedge.

John let her go. "At least she came down this time when I asked her to." He returned to the swing again and pushed off, setting them in motion.

Katie clutched the rope to keep her balance, leaning back to look up at the layers of green. Like the leaves on the tree a million questions surrounded their relationship. But they all boiled down to the one thing. Did she want to take a chance on falling in love with him again? Oh, who was she kidding? She was already falling in love with him. The real question was, should she say something?

"Stop, I'm getting dizzy."

"Pansy ass." But he stopped pumping. Gradually the swing slowed.

There was no easy answer. The intense moment following the kiss had passed without clarifying matters. In the aftermath she was only more confused about her feelings. And his. He'd more or less confirmed that he hadn't found what he was looking for. But why, when he seemed to have it all, at least on the career front?

"I never congratulated you on making senior sergeant and becoming the big cheese around the Summerside Police Department."

If he was surprised at the change of subject he didn't let on. Maybe he was relieved. "That happened over a year ago."

"We haven't talked much."

He threw her a glance as if to say, *Whose fault is that?*

"So, do you like the position?" she persisted.

His gaze turned wary. "What made you bring that up? Has Riley said something?"

"No." Why was he so cagey? Had she touched on a nerve? "It's just not the sort of job I ever envisaged you doing."

He started the swing going again, gently. "I like being a cop. I probably wouldn't mind being a detective. But just between you and me, paperwork sucks big-time."

"Tell me about it. I love teaching but administration tasks eat up more and more of classroom time. But you're running your own show. Can't you delegate or something?"

"To who? To get back on active duty I'd need to move to an even smaller station in the outback where I could be chief cook and bottle-washer." His head lifted, as if he was actually considering it and could smell the freedom of it.

Katie felt oddly panicky at the thought of John not living in Summerside. He'd always been here. He was a fixture. Who would keep the town safe if he wasn't in charge? "Would you do that? Leave Summerside and your family and friends?"

"I don't know." He started swinging again. "There's Tuti to think of now. And also—" He stopped to look at her, searching her face.

"Also…?" Was he going to say something about them? Did she want him to? Yes, her heart cried. No, her mind responded. He'd basically said it himself—they'd grown up and moved on. It was too late for them. Wasn't it?

While she waited, breath held, he glanced away and the moment passed.

When he spoke again, his voice was neutral and even. "What about you? Are you going to continue teaching now that you've got a big book contract?"

"It's too soon to quit my day job. I have no idea if I'll make enough money to support myself. In some ways I'd love to write full-time. But I'm afraid I'd miss teaching."

"You work too hard."

"Yes, and I should be getting back to it." She glanced at her watch. "Weekends are the only time I can put in long periods of uninterrupted writing."

"Don't go yet." He touched her arm. "We're going to play cricket with the kids."

She laughed. "I can hardly run around on the grass."

"You could keep score." Lightly, he stroked her cheek. "Stay. Please? Tuti would like it. I would like it."

While she dithered, lost in his eyes, a woman came around the hedge. Tall and willowy, with flowing blond hair, she glanced at Katie briefly then her gaze rested on John. "Are you John? Paula sent me to find you. Your mother wants to get the cricket game going and for you to organize the kids."

"Sure," John said easily, turning on the dimples. "This is Katie. You must be one of Paula's Carlton friends."

"That's right. I'm Candice," the woman said, flicking her hair back. "How did you guess?"

"I'm a cop. Must be my training."

Katie stared at him. *Oh, please.* Anyone John didn't know was unlikely to be local. Anyone who was a friend of Paula's most likely came from Carlton, where she'd lived before Summerside. This wasn't detective work; this was… flirting.

"Let me guess…." John looked Candice up

and down, tapping a finger to his chin. "Senior Constable?"

Katie almost snorted in disgust. Since Paula was a cop, her friends were most likely cops. Too easy.

"Wrong." The blonde threw her head back and laughed. "I'm a massage therapist. Paula and I went through an intensive course together."

"Interesting," John murmured. "Do you play cricket?"

"I love cricket," Candice said.

This had gone on long enough. Katie rose suddenly. The swing tipped. John slid off the wooden board. "Oh, look at the time. I've got to go."

"Katie?" John scrambled to find his feet.

"You go ahead and play cricket. I need to work, anyway." Katie limped over to her crutches propped against the tree. She couldn't compete with a blonde, beautiful, cricket-playing massage therapist. Nor did she want to try. John was only hanging out with her to kill time or because he felt guilty about his mother's rudeness or because he wanted to keep in her good books for Tuti's sake....

"Katie, come back," John called. "You can watch."

"No, that's all right." He meant watch the

cricket but what she'd really be watching if she stuck around was John flirting with Candice. She shouldn't mind—he was a free agent and she was used to him carrying on.

But she did mind. The green-eyed monster had taken her over. Had she really thought he might want to renew their relationship? Ridiculous. He'd as much as said he'd only kissed her on impulse. He'd simply had another impulse today. She wasn't his type, never had been, even though she'd tried to keep up. He was a people person. She needed alone time. He was a natural athlete. She struggled with most athletics.

As she moved away, she glanced over her shoulder. He was standing by the swing, looking torn. If he had any feeling for her at all, even friendship enough not to want to see her humiliated, he would come after her.

"Your girlfriend is leaving. Aren't you going after her?" Candice's amused voice carried across the lawn.

"She's not actually—" He groaned. "Katie, wait up."

KATIE FLUNG THE crutches forward, felt them bite into the soft ground and swung forward a giant step. No, she wasn't his girlfriend. That's the way she wanted it. But hearing it come out of his mouth, to an attractive woman he'd just been flirting with, was infuriating.

She could travel surprisingly fast on the crutches. But not fast enough to outrun John.

"Katie, stop!" John stepped between her and the gate, lifting her hand away from the bolt she was trying to wriggle loose. "Why are you running away?"

"I'm not running. I'm leaving because I'm tired and I want to go home. Is that reason enough?"

"What was going on back there? You weren't jealous of me talking to Candice, were you?" He dared to sound amused.

"No," she said automatically, because she would never admit it. "I need to work. Excuse me."

He didn't budge. "You were fine until I was called away from you. As soon as you weren't the focus of my attention you wanted to leave."

"Oh, come on. I'm not that immature."

"I don't know that it's immature, just… What the hell, it *is* immature."

Didn't he know it was embarrassing for a woman when a guy she's with flirts with another woman? But that presumed they were a couple. And they weren't.

But she wanted them to be.

"If you want me to stay, then sit with me.

Let someone else organize the cricket." *Don't flirt with any girl who walks by.* "Do you really want to play?"

"Well..." Again, he looked torn. And annoyed. "Why do I have to choose? It's like you're testing me. And I'm pretty sure I'm going to fail. If I haven't already."

"Testing you? Don't be ridiculous." Of course she wasn't testing him. But if he couldn't even give her his undivided attention for a couple of hours then he must not like her very much. She'd kissed him back, leaving no doubt how much she wanted him. She'd made herself vulnerable and then he'd...left. Not physically but he might as well have, the way he'd zoomed his attention in on Candice.

"This is my parents' house," John argued. "Tuti is my daughter and I'm a co-host. If there's a cricket game I should be playing. It's only polite."

"You're right. I'm probably just tired. You do what you need to do." She tried to sound as if she didn't care, as if she wasn't testing him, and that the outcome didn't matter to her one way or the other. When in reality, it mattered too much. "I need to work anyway."

"You need to take it easy. To relax for a change. If you don't want to watch cricket, at least go home and rest."

"Sure, I'll do that."

"Will you, or are you just saying that?"

"I said I would." But of course she wouldn't. She had deadlines. But she hated confrontation. She wasn't used to fighting. In her family if people disagreed they quickly dropped the discussion. John seemed to *want* to argue. How did anyone live like that? "Thanks for the party. Say goodbye to Tuti for me."

He slid the bolt back and held the gate open for her. Katie moved down the path along the side of the house and around to the front. She was confused and upset and not entirely sure why. It wasn't really about Candice. She knew John was unlikely to start anything with her when he was so focused on Tuti. Katie hadn't exactly pried but she had her sources and the word was, John hadn't gone out with anyone since he'd brought his daughter home from Bali.

John was following her. "I didn't pass, did I? Back then when you had cancer. I failed spectacularly."

"Yes, you did," she said through gritted teeth as she negotiated a couple of steps down to the driveway. "Any man who really loved a woman would have stuck by her. You said you wanted to marry me. What are the wedding vows again? In sickness and in health?"

"It seemed to me you were choosing sickness."

"What nonsense." There was no way they would resolve this because they both thought they were right…even though she was and he wasn't. "Never mind. That was all a long time ago."

"Yes, it was." He was waiting for her at the bottom of the steps, blocking the way to her car. "But unless we talk about it we won't come to an agreement."

"You're arguing, not talking. You seem to thrive on it."

He gave a short laugh. "Okay, we'll do it your way. We'll change the subject. Are you going to make your deadline?"

"I'll make up for lost time on the school term break."

"Tuti and I are going to my family's beach cottage on Phillip Island over the break. I'm going to teach her to surf."

She shook her head at his abrupt change of subject. "Surf—are you kidding? She's only six."

"I was four when I first got on a boogie board. Of course I'll keep her close to shore. Come with us."

"I beg your pardon?" Surely she hadn't heard that last bit correctly.

"Spend the holiday with us. You can do nothing but write. I'll make all the meals. If you have time in the evening you can spend it with Tuti and me. Or just Tuti if you're still mad at me."

She stared. "Why?"

"Because Tuti would like it if you came. And because after all you've done for us I'd like to give something back. Consider it a writing retreat. You don't even have to talk if you don't want to."

"I…I…"

"You see? You can't think of a single reason why you can't go."

She had plenty of emotional reasons but voicing them would be admitting she had feelings for him. She searched for a logical reason she couldn't go. Damned if she could think of one. "Didn't you just take three weeks of holiday? How can you go away again so soon?"

"I have months of vacation time banked up. The district commissioner is badgering me to use it." John opened her car door. "So I'll take your answer as a yes."

She was tempted. The beach cottage held so many good memories. It was where she and Riley had shared happy holidays with the Forster family when they were younger. Later, she and John first made love in the little bedroom at the back to the sound of the waves pounding on the shore.

But going away with him and Tuti would open the door for her and John to take their relationship to another stage. She wasn't sure she was ready.

"I'll think about it," she promised as she started the engine. "And let you know."

JOHN ENTERED THE police station through reception the following Tuesday morning just after seven o'clock. Paula had called him at home at six-thirty with the news that she'd arrested Nick Moresco and was bringing him in.

Patty, her headset askew in her mass of red curls, was fielding calls as fast as her fingers could push the buttons.

"What's up?" John feigned ignorance, knowing Patty loved to be the source of information.

"They got Moresco." Her blue eyes lit up as bright as the switchboard. "Summerside Police Department. How can I help you?" She redirected the call and returned to John. "He's right here in the station. A ruddy drug lord. But he's no 'lord' now. He's looking mighty defeated." With a satisfied grin, she fielded more calls.

Smiling, John punched his security code into the door and entered the inner offices. Uniformed night-duty officers milled around the bull pen with the day shift, reluctant to go home and miss the most excitement Summerside P.D. had seen in years.

Paula stood over her prisoner, a man in his early fifties with thinning dark hair going silver at the temples. His olive skin was pale and there was a cut on his right cheek. Handcuffs held his fine-boned wrists together. Paula kept one hand on the butt of her Smith & Wesson.

"Good work, Detective Henning," John said to Paula. He glanced at Nick Moresco. "You'll be transferred to Frankston P.D. as soon as the paperwork is complete. Their holding cells are just that little bit less comfortable."

"Your officers have made a mistake," Moresco said disdainfully. "I'll sue for false arrest."

Paula shook her head. "No mistake."

"Manufacturing illegal substances, namely methamphetamine, dealing said substances, including to minors..." John ticked off the offenses. "This will be your second conviction. You won't see the outside of prison for a good ten years or more."

Moresco jerked at his handcuffs and muttered under his breath. John ignored him to speak to Riley. "I'd like to see you in my office."

He headed down the corridor, feeling oddly flat. Which was wrong. His officers had captured a significant criminal, earning them and the station recognition. More importantly, the streets of his beloved village, and the wider community, were safer. And yet…

He gazed out the window of his office onto the main street, his thoughts going back to that part of his conversation with Katie about his job. She was right. He hadn't found what he was looking for. Her insight surprised him. They hadn't been friends for years, yet she somehow knew he felt unfulfilled.

Patty had left his mail on his desk. He leafed through the latest police newsletter. Flipping to the vacant positions, an ad caught his eye. What at first looked like a travel poster—white sand, turquoise water, palm trees—turned out to be an ad for a command posting in Tinman Island off the tropical north coast of Queensland. Tinman was a resort island on the Great Barrier Reef renowned for native wildlife, outdoor sports and surfing. There would be administrative duties but the successful applicant would also be on the ground, doing active police work. Just the sort of dream job he'd described to Katie.

Was this fate? From Tinman Island it was a short flight to Bali. He could make a fresh start, get out of his rut. And if Katie would come with him—

Katie hadn't even accepted his invitation to the cottage. She would never leave her family, her teaching, the town she'd grown up in to move clear across the country. She tried to be adventurous but she wasn't, not really. She was brave when she needed to be, but her idea of a good time was curling up with a book. That was okay with him. He liked that she was a homebody. Wherever she was felt like home. He would find it hard to leave Summerside because of her, even if they were never more than friends.

Except that he wanted more than friendship. He wanted her to be his wife and the mother of his children. She was quite simply, the love of his life. He could no longer kid himself. Without her he was rudderless and adrift.

Riley knocked on his open door. "Boss?"

John dragged his gaze away from the newsletter. "I'm taking off for a week to Phillip Island with Tuti."

"Nice." Riley sat and leaned forward, hands on his knees. "Good thing we got Moresco before you left."

"Yes, it's one less thing to worry about. I've already gone over a few things with Paula." He shuffled papers, found the file folder he'd set aside and passed it to Riley. "This is a list of active cases and the officers assigned to them. You'll be acting station chief while I'm gone."

Riley's eyebrows shot up. "Not Paula?"

"She's got enough on her plate liaising with

the task force on the Moresco case. Making the arrest is only the beginning."

"Well, then, the other guys." Riley ran a hand over his short dark hair. "Jackson, Crucek, Delinsky—even Stan Grant has more seniority than I do."

"They're not former Special Forces. You bring skills to policing they'll never have." John leaned back. "Have you thought about applying for detective?"

That brought a gleam to Riley's dark eyes. "I have. Paula and I talked about it. But what about the budget cutbacks?"

"We've got a state election in two weeks with a good chance there'll be a change of government. Who knows? We might even get the go-ahead to expand the station. So, are you up for the challenge?"

Riley grinned. "Hell, yeah."

"You've earned it." John leaned back, the official portion of their conversation over. "Guess it'll be a relief around your house now that Moresco's under lock and key."

"Paula and I will be able to get on with our lives. Set a date for the wedding, make a decision on where to live. To me it's a no-brainer—my house now that I'm finished renovating it. But women these days don't give up their independence easily."

"Tell me about it." John blew a gusty sigh. "I guess we shouldn't complain since that's part of what we like about them."

Riley cocked his head. "Are you referring to anyone in particular?"

John hesitated. "I invited Katie to come to the beach house with Tuti and me."

Riley's eyebrows rose. "Did she say yes?"

"Not exactly. But she didn't say no, either. She's your sister. What do you suppose that means?"

Riley laughed. "You're asking me? I guess I'd say she's open to being convinced. Are you asking her so she can continue tutoring your daughter?"

"I just think she's got a lot going on with the deadlines and her ankle slowing her down. I figured that I could take care of the day-to-day stuff for a couple of weeks and she could write and relax and spend time with Tuti. Maybe even have a little fun. I'm not going to push the schoolwork while we're on holiday, though. Tuti's only six. She needs a break."

"So it's nothing to do with you and Katie starting up again?"

John hesitated. This was a touchy subject with Riley. "Would that be a bad thing, in your view?"

Riley studied him gravely. "You know you're my best mate."

John nodded warily, sensing there was more coming.

"And if I had anything to say about it, you'd have been my brother-in-law years ago." Riley looked down at his hands. "My mother died after refusing a third round of chemo."

"I know. I'm sorry," John murmured. "Her death was a hard one."

No one understood just how hard it had been for John though, not even Riley and Katie. He'd been the unofficial third child of the Henning household, spending more time at their house than at his own. Mary Henning was more nurturing than his own mother, and she'd taken him under her wing like another of her own chicks. She'd fed him after school, helped with his homework, driven him and Riley to soccer practice when his mother was at work.

Watching the warm, vibrant woman waste away during her long battle with cancer had been almost as agonizing as if she were his own mother. But she wasn't. With the focus of sympathy on the Henning kids no one had thought to help him through the grieving process.

"If I hadn't been shipped off to Afghanistan when Katie got sick I'd have helped you try to talk sense into her about her treatment," Riley went on.

"She's so stubborn. I'm not sure she would have listened to you, either."

"I forgave you the first time you left my sister in the lurch," Riley continued as if he hadn't spoken. "But if you were to hurt her a second time— Let's just say, in the SAS they taught us to kill a man with our bare hands." Riley met his gaze. He looked every inch the battle-hardened soldier who could, and would, take him apart if justified.

John accepted the threat as his due. He didn't blame Riley but he'd never wanted to hurt Katie. "If I were lucky enough to have a second chance, I wouldn't leave her again."

"I tend to believe you. But how do you know?"

He would die himself before he walked away from Katie again. But he took Riley's point. *He* knew. But actions, not words, convinced men like him and Riley and, more importantly, Katie. Not that he wanted to test his conviction by Katie getting sick.

Maybe asking her to go away with him was a mistake. Alone together in the evenings after Tuti had gone to bed there would only be one thing on his mind. If she wanted the same thing, if they made love—his body tightened at the thought—and then their relationship fell apart for *any* reason, she could still get hurt. Hell, he could get hurt, too, but that he could handle.

What he couldn't handle was being responsible for Katie's pain. Not again.

"I just know."

"All I'm saying, mate, is be careful with my sister."

"You can count on me."

John sat staring at the wall for a long time after Riley left. What if taking care of Katie meant leaving her alone? What if he couldn't make her happy?

No, he could. Deep down, he believed they were meant to be together. This was his chance to step up. He would win her, no matter what it took. He wanted to be able to offer her something bigger than a week at the beach, although that would be a start. He wanted to give her a whole new life. Not because her life at present wasn't good. But for the two of them to be together, maybe Summerside wasn't the best place to live. Bad memories might be holding them back. With a fresh start things could be different.

He fished out the newsletter and went over the requirements again for the post on Tinman Island. Then he booted up his computer and began to update his résumé.

CHAPTER ELEVEN

HER BRAIN WAS paralyzed. It had simply stopped functioning. Katie stared at the blank computer screen and tried not to panic. But she was stuck, blocked by a knotty problem in the story. Her fountain of creativity had dried up like a billabong in a ten-year drought.

On the desktop calendar her deadline was highlighted in screaming yellow. That usually got the juices flowing. Not today. Not yesterday, either. Or the day before. Had she burned out as a writer? Wasn't it too soon for that? She'd only written one book. Why on earth had she agreed to a three-book contract, to be delivered in one year?

It didn't help that she was having trouble sleeping. The past few nights, ever since Tuti's birthday party, she'd tossed and turned, alternately reliving John's kiss and going over in agonizing detail every word of his flirty exchange with Candice. Her imagination might be on the blink but her memory was working way too well. What if she hadn't been at the party?

Would he have been even friendlier to Candice? Paula said he wasn't dating but maybe he'd simply been too busy with Tuti. The two kisses he'd shared with her wouldn't mean much to a man who dispensed them all over town.

Katie couldn't think about the party without remembering those awful, hateful words Alison had spewed at her. She understood the dynamic of a mother's defense of her offspring. She'd seen plenty of that with the parents of her students. But she'd almost become a member of Alison's family. She hated that there were bad feelings between them. Tuti could have been the link that drew them together, except that Alison was jealous of her relationship with her granddaughter. Surely that would change if Alison learned not to crowd Tuti.

Katie indulged in a little fantasy of joining John and Tuti and John's parents at the beach cottage. She would be an intermediary between Alison and Tuti, bringing grandmother and granddaughter closer, and as a result, bring herself back in Alison's good graces.

The fantasy became problematic when she mulled over the sleeping arrangements. She could easily see herself and John sharing a bedroom but not with Alison and Marty across the hall—

She shook her head back to reality. Alison and Marty weren't going.

Should she go? She wasn't usually this indecisive, but this simple getaway would throw her and John into intimate surroundings. Was that what she wanted? Were they ready?

Katie rose from her computer and walked over to the window. Old Mr. Neilson across the street was painting the trim on his redbrick house a bright peach. The man must be color-blind.

Hmm, could she use that in her story somehow? What if Monkey was color-blind? Except that she'd started thinking of Tuti as Monkey and from her drawings at school she knew Tuti loved color.

Tuti would be at the beach cottage. After she went to bed it would be just her and John… No TV. No internet. What would they do with their time? Perhaps a romantic glass of wine on the porch watching the sun sink into the ocean. Followed by cuddling on the couch in front of the wood-burning stove. And after that…

Oh, *now* she had ideas. *Now* her imagination was working.

The doorbell rang.

Paula stood on her porch holding a pizza box in one hand and a bottle of red wine in the other. As if on cue, Katie's stomach rumbled.

"Did I dream you?" Katie stepped back to let her in.

"I know you only eat certified organic but we'll sprinkle the pizza with chia seeds and call it health food." Paula bustled straight through to the kitchen and set the food on the table. She gave Katie a critical once-over. "You've lost weight. So don't tell me you don't have time to eat or I'll have to tie you down and force-feed you."

"I'll eat. And I'm not fussy tonight. I'm ready to gnaw my own arm off." Katie got wine-glasses down from the cupboard and opened the bottle while Paula got out plates. The smell of the pizza, Paula's friendly banter…it was such a welcome relief from her lonely desperation that all at once she choked up, overwhelmed by a lack of sleep, anxiety and emotional overload. "Thank you for coming. I've been s-so—"

"Hey, hey, hey." Paula drew her into a hug, stroking her back. "It's going to be okay."

Katie gulped and knuckled her wet eyes. "I know. Sorry—"

"Don't apologize." Paula pushed her into a chair and handed her a glass of wine. "You've been working too hard. And spending too much time by yourself. You lose perspective. I remember what that was like."

Paula didn't intend to be smug but her tone held an unconscious complacency as she recalled her singleton days. Katie didn't resent her happiness—after all, she'd gained a friend who was like a sister to her. And she was happy that her brother had found someone so perfect for him.

But she did envy Paula—the love she shared with Riley, the companionship, the home life, the family. Katie shook her head. *Quit feeling sorry for yourself.* She had a job she loved—two jobs she loved. Family, friends… She didn't understand where her discontent was coming from. For years she'd been fine on her own—until John had reentered her life, bringing Tuti with him.

"Not alone. I spend all day with twenty six-year-olds." She caught Paula's eye and grinned sheepishly.

"Case close." Paula handed her a plate loaded with two big slices of pepperoni pizza.

"Ah, my favorite guilty pleasure." Katie took a bite and ate hungrily, surprised at how quickly she downed the first slice. "Congrats on arresting Nick Moresco, by the way." She added cautiously, "How is Jamie taking the news that his father is going to jail?"

Paula took a big sip of wine. "Riley and I took him to counseling. He's surprisingly calm and accepting. When Moresco snatched Jamie from his grandmother's birthday party, he lost some of his appeal," Paula said wryly. "Plus having

Riley adopt Jamie helps a lot. As far as Jamie and I are concerned, Riley's his father now."

"That's great. You're so lucky to have found each other."

"What about you and John? I hope asking doesn't bother you."

"No, I don't mind." Katie told her about John's invitation to the beach cottage. "I just wish I could decide whether to go or not."

"Give me the pros and cons." Paula grabbed a pad of paper Katie had been making notes for her story on. She flipped to a clean page and looked up expectantly. "Pro."

"I need to meet my deadline and John promised to let me do nothing but write with a bit of time for Tuti."

"Good one. Con?"

"Being around John and Tuti would make me want to play, not write."

"Hmm, in my opinion that would be a pro." Paula frowned at the paper. "Next?"

"A change of scenery could free up my writer's block."

"Excellent. Con?"

"The beach cottage is where John and I first made love."

"Again, that sounds like a good thing."

"Except there's so much unresolved between

us. Bad memories might get stirred up as well as good memories."

"We'll call it a con for the sake of argument. Pro?"

"I need to relax. I'll have a better chance of doing that with John taking care of the mundane stuff like cooking." Before Paula could say anything, she added, "But that's also a con. Relaxing means I'll let my guard down. Anything might happen, if you know what I mean."

Paula grinned. "Girl, all you've proved is that you don't understand the concept of con. What's the bottom line here? What's your gut feeling?"

Katie shut her eyes and looked inward. What she saw she wanted so badly it scared her. She and John and Tuti having a beach holiday, just like a real family. With a week in a secluded setting, they might be able to figure out whether they had something real and lasting.

"Katie?"

She opened her eyes. "I want to go."

"That's good."

"Not necessarily. I want it too much."

"Are you falling in love with him?"

Katie hesitated. She'd barely admitted it to herself. Saying it aloud to Paula would mean her feelings were real. Worse, she might have to do something about them. "I think so."

"You think, or you know?" Paula pressed.

"You are such a cop." Katie laughed and pushed a hand through her bedraggled ponytail.

Paula reached across the table and squeezed her hand. "Don't be afraid. Being in love is the best feeling."

Katie smiled. *Oh, yeah.* Despite the fact that John didn't live up to her standards of love, she couldn't help the stomach flutter when he looked at her, the quickening of her pulse at his touch. The hope that somehow he would overcome her doubts and fears and prove himself worthy. The desire that she would be "enough" for him, that he would want her and her alone. If all that was love, then yes, she'd taken that leap.

But. There was always a "but."

"I'm not sure I want to love him. As I said, John and I have issues we can't seem to overcome."

"Riley told me John regrets leaving you and that he thinks John still loves you."

"Really? John said he loves me?" Ridiculous, the way that made her heart pound.

"Not exactly. Riley *thinks* he does. John hasn't come out and declared his feelings in so many words. Guys don't, though, do they?"

"I'm not sure I want him to be in love with me." Her voice dropped to a whisper. "Not if I can't trust him to be there for me."

Paula met her gaze soberly. "John is the only

guy on the Summerside police force besides Riley that I would trust with my life."

"That's in relation to your job." Katie toyed with her second slice of pizza. "What if I got cancer again? He thought he was doing the right thing when he left but I honestly don't know which was worse, the illness or being abandoned."

"Oh, sweetie. I'm sorry you had to go through that." Paula was quiet a moment. "But if you think you love him, how can you not take a chance? The alternative sucks. If you can't have him and you don't want anyone else, then what are you? Alone."

"There's a difference between being alone and being lonely." She'd been alone for years. Oh, she'd gone out with different men, but never anyone serious or for very long. Like John, but in her own way, she'd avoided settling down. But seeing herself through Paula's eyes the future stretched out bleak and unchanging. That wasn't alone. That was lonely.

When she'd had cancer everyone told her to take the safe option, follow the conservative road. She'd taken a chance and come through. There was no gain without risk.

"Maybe I will go away with him," she said slowly. "Give him a chance. Give myself another chance at love."

This time she wouldn't avoid discussing their problems, no matter how upsetting or scary. If they were to have a meaningful relationship they needed to hash things out, once and for all. If they decided in the end that they weren't right for each other, at least they'd given it one last good shot. And having tried and failed, they would both be able to move on.

Paula picked up another piece of pizza and waved it at her. "If nothing else, you'll have made progress on your book."

"There is that. Okay, I'll do it." She laughed, giddy with the relief of deciding to do what her heart wanted.

Paula slid the phone across the table. "Go on, give him a call right now, before you chicken out."

Quickly Katie punched in John's speed dial number. At the sound of his rumbling voice saying hello her knees went weak. "Hi. I've decided to go with you and Tuti. It's time we talked things out."

"When the phone rang, I was hoping it was you, calling to say you would come," John said warmly. "And it was. I have a good feeling about this holiday."

"WE'RE GOING TO surf and swim," John said to Tuti in the rearview mirror. The car was packed with food, books, games and beach equipment. His surfboard was strapped to the roof and in the trunk was a brand-new boogie board for Tuti. "I'll take you to see the penguins and the koalas…."

"Will Katie be there?" Tuti asked for the fifth time.

"Yes, sweetie," John said patiently. "She has things to do first so she's bringing her own car. She'll arrive tonight."

"Yay!" Tuti bounced in her seat.

John laughed, his spirits as high as Tuti's. The sun was shining, the air was warm and it was nearly Easter. The beach was a great place to spend a week.

The two-hour drive passed quickly. Soon he was pulling into the gravel driveway of the three-bedroom weatherboard cottage that had been his family's since he was a kid. Across a quiet service road lay the beach. Leah usually came down over Christmas and Sonya and her family had been there toward the end of the summer holidays.

John unloaded the car, handing Tuti small things and carrying the heavy luggage himself. The cottage had all the basics but none of the frills. Painted floorboards and rag rugs, ancient overstuffed furniture, a wood-burning stove and a battered coffee table that had been the scene of many epic Monopoly games.

He opened all the windows while Tuti ran around exploring, claiming the girls' bedroom with the shells lining the windowsill. When they were settled in, he and Tuti went wading in the shallows to get her used to how cold the ocean was compared to the water surrounding Bali. Mutton birds wheeled above their rookery and waves crashed on the sand. They barbecued sausages for dinner and ate them between slices of white bread with fried onions and tomato sauce.

"When is Katie coming?" Tuti asked plaintively as he tucked her into bed that night.

"She'll be here when you wake up in the morning," he promised. At least he hoped so. He'd thought she would be here by now. He'd tried calling her a couple of times but her mobile just went to voice mail.

He hoped she hadn't changed her mind. He'd built up ideas about how they would bond over simple things like walks along the sand and quiet evenings by the wood-burning stove. He wanted to tell her about Tinman Island and get her reaction to the possibility of a future away from Summerside. Tuti was counting on her to come. He was, too. If for some reason, she didn't, these holidays would be awfully bleak.

IT WAS JUST SHY of eight o'clock and the sky was fully dark by the time Katie pulled into the cottage driveway. A light drizzle was falling as she crunched over the broken shell and gravel to the front door.

She *wanted* to do this, she reminded herself nervously. This was an opportunity. For years she'd been keeping John at bay, not realizing till recently that deep down she'd hoped they might get back together someday. And while she'd been helping Tuti learn to read, she'd learned to fall in love again.

Her heart beating fast, she knocked. While she waited, she went over everything she'd decided.

She would talk openly and honestly, listen to what he had to say even when it was painful to hear.

She wouldn't test him, not even on small things. She would give him the benefit of the doubt. Give the man a chance to show her he could change. Show him that she trusted him and that she could change.

But no matter what happened, she wouldn't fall into his bed right away. She would resist her desires long enough to talk things out. The chemistry between them was good and when she and John were sexual she tended to don rose-colored glasses when it came to their relationship. Sex wouldn't make the issues go away. In fact it could exacerbate them because they'd be ignoring the problems and pretending everything was fine when it wasn't.

If they could resolve the issues, then wonderful. If they couldn't, if the holiday was a disaster, so be it. The end. No more possibilities for her and John. God, she hoped that wouldn't be the outcome.

The slap of flip-flops on floorboards came closer. John flung the door open.

"Sorry I'm so late. Riley and Paula are looking after Lulu, my cat. I couldn't leave until they got home from work." Nerves had her words pouring out in a flood. "I tried to call you but you must be out of range—"

"Come inside." John reached for her hand, his fingers wrapping hers in a firm grip. His eyes filled with amusement plus warmth and affection. "You're here now. That's all that matters."

JOHN HELD TIGHTLY to Katie's hand, relieved she'd shown up and half afraid if he let go she would disappear back into the night. Her hair was tied back in a ponytail but wisps fell around her high cheekbones and her eyes were dark and smoky. "I just put Tuti to bed. Do you want something to eat? A cup of tea, a glass of wine?"

"Nothing right now, thanks." She gestured behind her, to the door. "My bag's still in the car." Her gaze searched his. "That's still okay, isn't it? You haven't changed your mind about me staying?"

How could she question whether he would welcome her? And yet he could recall other occasions when she'd been insecure around him, often masking it as anger. For example, the incident with Candice. He'd meant nothing by his banter but clearly Katie had seen it as "flirting with intent."

The truth hit him with a pang. This was the legacy of him "abandoning" her. He needed to reassure her, earn back her trust.

"Of course it's okay. It's more than okay. I've been thinking about you all day, waiting for you to get here." He kissed her lightly on the lips, brushing her hair behind her ear. Then leaned in for a deeper kiss. He felt Katie lift onto her toes to meet him.

"Bapa!" A high-pitched voice rang out. "Who's there? Is it Katie?"

John groaned. "Nice timing, Tuti."

Katie dropped to her heels, cheeks flushed. "Oh, good. She's still awake."

"She's dying to see you." Reluctantly, he released Katie, his gaze lingering on hers. "I'll bring in your suitcase while you say good-night to her."

"Okay. See you in a minute."

He heard Tuti greet Katie joyfully as he ran out to her car, raindrops dampening his T-shirt and wet grass brushing at his ankles. He grabbed her suitcase and her laptop bag, his mind leaping ahead to later tonight.

He didn't want to rush her. Or rush the evening. He would light the wood stove, bring out the good bottle of Shiraz he'd been saving and put on soft music. She deserved to be wooed. He wanted to woo her. If all went according to his hopes and plans, they would make love again here where they had sex for the first time. He badly wanted to show her how precious she still was to him.

Back inside, he started down the hall to his room then changed his mind and placed her bags in the hall. When it came to Katie he had to walk a fine line between showing her how much he wanted her and not scaring her off. Definitely it wouldn't do to make assumptions at this stage. If they weren't on the same page, well, she could always sleep in the third bedroom. But he hoped very much that they would be keeping each other warm tonight.

Tuti ran out of her room, her penguin pajama

bottoms rucked up around one knee, her excited face split in a wide grin. "We're going to play Snakes and Ladders!"

Katie came after, apologetic. "She wouldn't settle. I said she could stay up for one game."

"I don't know." John pretended to be disapproving. "Miss Henning tells me that children need routine, with a regular bedtime."

Tuti's face fell tragically. "Oh!"

Katie laughed at him over Tuti's head. "Don't be mean."

Tuti grabbed hold of his hand. *"Please, Bapa."*

"Okay, okay." John laughed. "One game."

"Popcorn, too," Tuti added happily, racing to the shelf below the window that held the board games.

Tuti and Katie sat side by side on the couch in front of the coffee table. John pulled up a stool. Logs crackled in the wood stove. One game stretched to two. Popcorn extended to hot chocolate. Wine for the adults. John found he couldn't object too strenuously, no matter how much he wanted to get Katie alone. He hadn't seen Tuti so happy since, well, since the last time she'd been with Katie.

Katie's dark eyes sparkled with warmth and humor and a deeper heat that made his blood thrum. She lifted her arm to push back her hair in an unconscious movement that drew his eye to the full curve of her breasts. Noticing the direction of his focus, she smiled slowly.

"It's your turn," Tuti urged him. "Roll the dice."

Dragging his gaze away, he barely noticed where his marker landed or Tuti's gleeful chortle when he slid down the longest snake and was back to square one.

Finally Tuti wore out and laid her head on Katie's knee, yawning and rubbing her eyes.

"Come on, Possum. It's time you were in bed." He scooped her into his arms and carried her down the hall as she waved good-night to Katie. He tucked her in bed and she was asleep almost instantly. With a kiss on her forehead he went out, leaving the door ajar.

Katie was putting the cups in the sink.

John came up behind her and slid his arms around her waist. "I'm so glad you came. I've waited for this chance for us a very long time." He kissed her lightly then nuzzled the soft skin behind her ear. Before she could reply he kissed her again, tasting, nibbling, teasing her lips open. "Come to bed with me."

He felt the sigh go through her as though he'd breathed it himself. Then she roused herself and eased back enough to look up at him. "We should talk first."

He knew she was right; he just had a feeling that what he was going to say wasn't what she expected to hear. "Go sit down. I'll put another log on the fire."

CHAPTER TWELVE

KATIE CURLED UP on the couch again while John stoked the wood-burning stove. So far the evening had been perfect. With luck and goodwill between them they could meet somewhere in the middle. John brought with him a sheaf of papers from a side table when he came to sit next to her.

"What's all this?" Katie asked.

He handed her a police newsletter open to an ad with a color photo of a tropical island. "Tinman Island in far north Queensland. I've applied for a job there, as commander. It sounds more important than it is. The point is, if I got the position, I'd be on active duty, not just pushing paper from my In tray to my Out tray."

She blinked at the ad, not comprehending. When she'd said she wanted to talk she meant about them and the issues dividing them. She was tired of sweeping things under the carpet and wanted to clean them up once and for all. Instead, he'd brought up a brand-new problem. "What's on Tinman Island?"

"It's a resort island but there's also an indigenous population and locals who work in the service industry," he explained. "Talking to you at Tuti's party helped me clarify my thinking. I badly need a new challenge and a change of scenery. When I saw this ad, I knew it was for me."

"So you meant what you said that day. You want to leave Summerside." *And her.* And she'd helped him come to that conclusion. A chill came over her. She rubbed her arms.

"Cold?" John pulled down a shawl from the back of the couch and wrapped it around her shoulders. "Is that better? I love the village. It will always be my home, but I've lived there all my life, aside from that year I spent surfing and traveling. A change would do me a world of good. *If* I get the job, that is."

Was this why he'd invited her to the cottage, to let her down gently? She tugged the shawl tighter around herself. How could she ask if they were breaking up? They weren't back together officially. "If you get the job, how soon would you need to go there?"

"Probably within a month. The incumbent commander has been hospitalized with serious health problems. They want to fill the position as soon as possible."

"I see. You said you weren't happy doing administrative work but will this be any better? What is this anyway, a promotion, a demotion, sideways shift…what?"

"Technically it's a promotion, but because of the small size of the station I would be more hands-on than currently."

The pit in Katie's stomach got bigger. It sounded exactly what he'd been looking for. "Tuti has finally settled into school. She's making friends and catching up to the grade with her English skills. Moving her again so soon would set her back."

"She's a smart kid. Resilient. She'll adapt again. And this time it will be easier since, as you say, her language skills are progressing."

"Your mother won't be happy to lose her newest granddaughter just as she's getting to know her. And do you really want to take her away from your sisters' kids?"

"I know my family is important to her, or will be. But frankly, Tuti doesn't get along with my mother all that well. And my sisters' kids are older so they don't play together."

"Give your mother time. She'll figure out how to reach Tuti. I think, after the birthday party, she's already starting to sort things out."

"Katie." He shook his head. "I thought you would understand. I thought you would be happy for me. For us. Why are you so determined to put up obstacles?"

"For us? Where is the 'us' in you getting a new job and moving to far north Queensland?" She swallowed. "It sounds to me as if you're gearing up to tell me goodbye."

"Goodbye?" Shock blanked his face. "Oh, Katie, no. You've misunderstood." He took her hand and held it between his. "It's my fault. I didn't explain properly. If I get the position, I'd like you to come with me and Tuti."

She laughed out of sheer relief.

"I'm not joking," he said, misinterpreting. "It would mean so much to both of us."

"You want me to come with you." She eyed him warily, not wanting to take anything for granted. "As a tutor for your daughter?"

"I'm really screwing this up, aren't I? Katie, I love you. I want you to come with me as my wife. Marry me. Please." He rubbed his thumb across the back of her hand. "I know this is sudden. I should have discussed the job with you before I applied. But I saw the ad and the closing date was that day. I shot off my résumé straight away."

"I don't know, John." *He loved her.* Part of her was tap dancing inside. Part of her was still wary. "We're barely friends again and you're asking me to marry you? And for me to leave

Summerside, my home and family. My students?"

"Tinman Island isn't the end of the earth. There are flights out every day. You could visit Summerside whenever you wanted. You could quit teaching and write full-time." His hand moved up to cup her jaw. "We don't have to marry yet if you're not ready. I don't even have the job yet. I just wanted to talk to you about this so it doesn't come out of the blue if I get it. Please, just think about coming with me. It'll be an adventure."

His excitement was infectious. Suddenly she began to see the possibilities of living in a tropical paradise with John and Tuti. Maybe this was fate. Maybe she and John were destined to get their happy ever after at long last. "I guess I could think about it."

"Fantastic." He curled his arm around her shoulders and positioned the newsletter between them so they could both look at it. "That's the police commander's residence," he said, pointing to a bungalow tucked into a palm grove close to the beach. "Rent is minimal and other expenses would be small. Mainly because there's not a lot to do besides laze in the sun, snorkel, fish, swim…"

"Write, read…" Katie gazed up at John,

searching his face. "It almost sounds too good to be true."

"It will be if you're there with me."

"You shouldn't count your chickens before getting the job," she cautioned.

"I'm not. But if this doesn't work out, something else will come along."

"When will you hear?"

"According to the ad, they want to make a decision soon. I should know by next week if I get an interview."

"Wow." Katie shook her head, dazed. "This morning I was wondering what this day would hold. But I thought I'd be discussing the past with you. I never dreamed we'd be contemplating the future."

She met John's gaze and his naked look of love and longing tugged powerfully at her heart. Her thoughts raced. She didn't want to get ahead of herself, but the more she thought about it the more excited she was. They didn't have to get married right away. They were still figuring out how their lives would fit together.

But this felt right. John felt right snug up against her side. And then he was kissing her, his lips seeking hers and his warm, strong hands stroking her arms, along her thigh…

But wait, was she managing to stick to her plan? *She would listen without prejudice to what he had to say*—check. *She would give him the benefit of the doubt*—check.

"I want more than just a week in a cottage with you," he said next to her ear, sending shivers down her neck and a warm glow through her heart. "I want love, marriage, family. The whole shebang. I want a second chance. We owe it to ourselves."

He took her mouth in another deep, drugging kiss. Her limbs felt heavy and her heartbeat sounded in her ears. *She wouldn't fall into his bed right away*—

Well, two out of three wasn't bad.

She eased away and whispered, "Let's go to bed."

He gathered her into his arms and lifted her to her feet. With his arm around her, he walked her down the hall to his bedroom, kissing her all the way.

Wind rattled the bedroom's windowpanes. Rain drummed on the tin roof. The table lamp's warm glow illuminated an old dresser and a quilt-covered white iron bedstead. Some places in Summerside held mixed memories but this room evoked nothing but love.

John stroked her hair. "Do you remember our first time?"

"How could I forget?" Nervous, eager, clumsy, awkward, tender, intense and emotional. That hot summer night, just the two of them at the beach cottage, had been the consummation of two years of affection, respect and growing passion. "We were so young, so innocent. We had no idea what lay ahead for us..."

"We still don't." He slipped the top button of her blouse free. "But we've learned a few things since then. We can make some better choices."

She stiffened. Was he referring to her illness?

Then he slid a warm palm inside her bra and cupped her breast, tenderly, protectively. "Like you on top, for instance."

She barely had time to smile before his searing kiss pushed thoughts of the past from her mind. His tongue plunged boldly inside her mouth, letting her know the time for teasing and dancing around each other was over. And she was more than ready. She tugged at his T-shirt, her fingers exploring hot skin, tracing bones and muscles, reacquainting herself with his body. The mole on his left rib cage, the scar below his right nipple where he'd cut himself on rocks in a wave surge. All so familiar, all so dear.

John broke away to tear his shirt off. In the glow of the table lamp she saw what her fingers had discovered—the new solidity of his frame, muscles hardened and developed over years into maturity. When she'd last made love to him he was barely more than a youth. Now he was a man.

With a man's needs and a man's desires. The intent heat in his gaze as he slowly undid her remaining buttons and removed her blouse made her shiver. With a flick of his fingers her bra came apart and fell to the floor. Her breasts bounced lightly with the release, making his pupils darken. She was proud of her breasts and she loved his reaction.

He leaned down and drew one nipple inside his mouth, sucking and teasing with his tongue. *She loved the way he loved them.* His other hand slid up under her skirt, stroking her inner thighs. She loved his slow hand. He hadn't forgotten what made her breath catch and what made her bite her bottom lip. His fingers molded her flesh, working their magic. Liquid heat spread between her legs, upward into her belly, making her knees weak and her limbs heavy.

Somehow she worked his zipper loose and pushed his jeans down. He got rid of her skirt, then her panties. He drew her against him, his erection throbbing against her belly. She took his mouth in another long, deep kiss and pushed him toward the bed. "Let's warm up those sheets."

He drew back the quilt and she slid between

the cool cotton while he found a condom in the drawer.

Katie plucked it out of his hands. Slowly she slid it over his thick hard member, loving how his eyes glazed over and his breath became more labored just from her touch.

"On top, you say?" Putting her hands on his chest, she pushed him down onto the pillow. Riding his hips, she kissed him, relishing the way he fondled and stroked her breasts and buttocks, building back the heat and urgency that had dissipated briefly while they'd been occupied with protection.

Their bodies moved together as if they'd never been apart. It almost felt surreal, being back with John. Yet here she was where she never thought she'd be again. Now she could admit to herself that all her fantasies over the years wore his face. All her longings were for his knowing touch. All her heart had ever wanted were *his* eyes gazing into hers.

In the tiny room where they'd first made love, the fire was reignited. He took her breasts in his hands and worshipped them with his mouth. She eased herself up and onto him, felt the push at her entrance, the slow filling and stretching while her gaze held his. Before she was fully sheathed she began to withdraw, her breath held, every muscle rigid.

"Katie." His voice was hoarse with need, his face taut with the effort of restraining himself. He took her hips with a bruising grip, his fingertips digging into her flesh.

Slick and hot, again she slid down partway. Again she withdrew, her breathing shallow. Tightness coiled in her like an overwound watch. Heat grew. Down, down, down. When he filled her completely, she let out a sigh that went all the way to her toes. She rocked once, twice, savoring the feel of him inside her, the delicious tension, balancing the urge to move with the fight for control.

"Enough." John flipped her onto her back with a wicked grin.

With that, the mood and the tempo changed. He thrust hard, stoking her fire, faster and faster until she was barely hanging on, biting his shoulder to stop from crying out, feeling herself spiral out of control, up and up—

Maddeningly, he slowed his pace again, taking evil delight when she hit him on the chest with an anguished thump.

"Got a problem, Katykins?" he teased, a light in his eyes. He looked younger than she'd seen him in ages.

A lump in her throat formed when he'd called her Katykins. He only used the pet term when they were alone, never in public. He'd coined the name the first morning they'd woken up together. Hearing him use the endearment now brought the past back, all the hope and happiness they'd once shared.

She pretended to pout. "You had me so close and then you eased off."

He braced his hands on either side of her head and started to grind in slow circles. "I'll get you there again."

The veins stood out on his arms, the tendons on his neck stretched. His technique had become more skillful in the years they'd been apart. Not so surprising considering how many women he'd been with since then. But she didn't want to think about *that*. What was surprising was that he recalled what drove *her* wild. Sucking on her earlobe while he played with her nipple, timing the rhythm of both with his thrusts so all three built and built, compounding the intensity of sensation. Within moments she was almost unbearably aroused.

He, too, was on the edge. She knew the telltale signs, the way his breath caught, how his heartbeat went erratic and his head fell back when he was moments away from release…

She lifted her hips, driving into his. She came explosively, rolling waves of orgasm after orgasm. She'd loved the things he could do to her, and the way they were together. Sex had never been like this with any other man. She'd never dared think she would find it again with him after all they'd been through.

And yet if anything, the lovemaking was better. Now they knew their own bodies better, knew better how to please a partner, had more control....

But who cared about the technicalities? She didn't want to think and analyze. She only wanted to enjoy the slow, languorous float back to earth.

After long dreamy moments when all she was aware of was the sound of his gradually slowing heartbeat, John turned his face to hers, a fraction of an inch away. "So...was it okay?"

She stroked a lock of blond hair off his forehead and smiled into his eyes. "Not bad. You?"

A corner of his mouth curved. "Fair to middling."

The spent look on his face told a different story. She grinned, knowing that, just like her, he'd been knocked flat. This was what they did. Had awesome, mind-blowing sex then made a contest out of downplaying it.

He leaned closer and kissed her. "We've still got it."

She gazed into the sky-blue eyes of the person who knew her better than anyone on the planet.

And yet somehow he'd missed understanding an essential part of her seven years ago.

Yes, they still had it. But even knowing each other as well as they did, their fundamental differences had torn them apart once. Would that happen again? Suddenly she wanted this second chance. She wanted it very much.

She lay in his arms, head on his chest, while he idly stroked her softly all over, her breasts, her belly, her thighs. In the quiet dark the only sound was their breathing and the distant crash of waves on the beach. Having stroked as far down as he could comfortably reach he returned to her neck and started over, trailing slowly down again to gently mold her breasts. The movement was tender and soothing, not sexual, and seeped into the crevices of Katie's soul.

His fingertips strayed near her lumpectomy scar. She held her breath, hoping he would move on before he touched the thin puckered line. After the physical and emotional closeness they'd shared she didn't want a reminder of the event that had torn them apart.

Closer and closer, his fingers stroked and molded. She tensed, trying but unable to regain that state of deep relaxation. He stroked the scar, moved on, paused, then her heart fell as he stroked back tracing the shape and length of the scar. Now she was aware he was holding his breath, too. The silence was electric. Would he speak and break the emotional connection between them by revisiting the past? Or would he ignore the scar and the issue, papering over the cracks already showing in their new relationship? She was torn, wanting first one thing, then the other.

He cupped her breast and with the utmost tenderness, kissed it over and over. A tear leaked out of Katie's eye and seeped into the pillowcase. She released her breath in a quiet shuddering sigh. Then John pulled up the covers and shifted position, settling in to sleep.

Not a word passed between them. Probably he hadn't wanted to ruin the moment either, not when their reunion was so new and fragile. So much for her vow to talk things out. Part of her was relieved a bullet had been dodged. Another part mourned a lost opportunity. Long after his regular breathing indicated he was asleep, she lay awake, dry-eyed, wondering what was going to become of them.

THE QUIET PIPE of a single bird on the fence outside the window woke John just before sunrise. Eyes closed, he swam up from the depths of unconsciousness, aware of feeling extraordinarily happy. A sigh came from the pillow next to his.

Katie. Last night hadn't been a dream.

He reached out to stroke her hair. His hand paused above her temple then retracted, letting her sleep. A wave of tenderness swept over him as he recalled last night when he'd touched her scar. He hated that she'd had to go through that. That he hadn't been with her the whole way.

Normally he wasn't one to shy away from confrontation. How else did a person air their thoughts and feelings and find out what the other felt? But having told her about a possible move to Tinman Island, he wasn't looking for any additional tension. He wanted to cement their emotional bond before they tested the strength of their feelings. During this time at the cottage, he hoped to build new memories that would erase some of the bad ones.

He got out of bed quietly and dressed. Peaking into Tuti's room, he found her looking at a picture book in bed. When she saw him she started to speak. John put a finger over his lips to shush her and came inside to sit on the bed.

"Katie's sleeping. Let's be quiet until she gets up, okay?"

Tuti nodded. "Is it raining?"

"Yes." He ruffled her already bed-mussed hair. "Don't worry. The weather is supposed to clear up later. We'll get you out on that boogie board this afternoon."

She gave him an odd look and sank deeper into the covers. "I'm going to read till it's warm."

"Good plan."

He left her, made a pit stop in the bathroom and carried on to the kitchen where he put on the kettle for coffee. Pushing aside the curtains, he gazed on to gray skies, a gray ocean and a fine but steady rain. This time of year the temperature was like that, up and down.

If they were living on Tinman Island, it would be hot all the time. Tuti would like that. It would make her feel at home. If they moved there she would have to learn to swim. All the local kids would be like little fishes. It was practically un-Australian not to swim. Not to mention dangerous on a small island known for water sports.

Pleasantly occupied with daydreaming their future, he got out the coffee and spooned grounds into the plunger. Then he pulled out his laptop and checked his email. There was an acknowledgment that his application had been received, promising to get back to him as soon as possible.

"*Bapa,* will you do my pigtails?" Tuti stood in the doorway, still in her pajamas.

"Sure. Go change and I'll meet you in the bathroom."

"Don't want to change," she pouted. "Want to stay in my jamas."

She'd behaved like a dream so far. He hoped she wasn't going to act up because Katie was here. Had they somehow ignored her in their focus on each other? He hoped not. The last thing he wanted was for her to become a wedge between him and Katie.

One thing he had learned in his stint so far as a father—don't sweat the small stuff. "Come on, then. I'll do your pigtails. You can get dressed later."

KATIE STRETCHED luxuriously in bed, feeling pleasantly achy and sated. In the bathroom John and Tuti's voices were muted but intelligible as they chatted over plans for the day ahead—puzzles, games, books, the beach if it stopped raining and a campfire in the evening.

It took her a moment to figure out what they were doing in the bathroom. Then she heard John ask Tuti to hand him the brush. Ah, the pigtails. He sounded so relaxed. Clearly he'd mastered the art. He'd come a long way in a very short time as a father. She wouldn't have believed it if she hadn't seen it for herself. He had become a different man altogether since Tuti had brought them back together. He'd grown and matured, shown sides of himself she'd hoped existed but hadn't known for sure.

The question was, was he a man she could see herself with long term?

On a practical side, their lives would mesh well, especially if he got the job on Tinman Island. Last night she'd overheard John tell Tuti they couldn't bother her during the day because she had to work. He got it, he really did.

She glanced at the bedside clock and groaned. It was after nine. This was the first day of their week here and already she'd slept in. Usually she was at the laptop or her sketch pad by seven.

John poked his head inside the bedroom. "Ah, you're awake. Ready for coffee?"

Tuti's head—with perfect pigtails—ducked under John's arm. "I won't bug you, I promise. Will you read me a story?"

Katie laughed. "Bring me the book. One story then we'll get up, okay?"

Despite the slow start Katie got a lot of work done that morning. John set up a card table beneath the window in the bedroom for her. He made her breakfast, brought her coffee then lunch. When the clouds cleared midmorning, through the window she watched Tuti and John cross the road to the beach for a walk along the sand. John's blond hair glinted in the sun. Tuti skipped to keep up with his long stride, her laughter lifted and tossed by the gusty breeze.

Could the three of them be a family? It all seemed too idyllic, too good to be true.

Why shouldn't good things be true? Why was she always waiting for the other shoe to drop and something really bad to happen to her? She'd fought cancer and survived. She'd made a life for herself. Why shouldn't she find happiness with the man she loved?

Just for a moment she allowed herself to entertain the idea of marrying John, of planning a future together. The thought was solid and warm and comforting. But she didn't want to rush into anything. They needed to get to know each other properly again. For now having John and Tuti in her life was enough. She certainly didn't want a repeat of their fight on Tuti's birthday. She needed to know that when they had differences they would talk things out and resolve them calmly and with mutual respect.

In the afternoon, John stopped by her makeshift desk and pressed a kiss on her cheek. "How is your writing day? Did you get much done?"

She slipped an arm around his waist. "Surprisingly yes."

"Why surprisingly?" He pushed her hair off her face before tracing a fingertip down her cheek and along her jaw.

"Because all I could think about was you."

She wound her arms around his neck and leaned up to kiss him.

"Oh, yeah?" John teased. "Every time I popped in you had your head down. Wouldn't even talk to me. Is that how it's going to be from now on? Because I'm not sure I like playing second fiddle to a computer."

From now on. Three little words that said *I love you* almost more than a marriage proposal. Despite her romantic daydreams the words caused a panicked flutter in her chest, reminding her that this interlude was temporary, that soon she might have to make firm decisions about the future. It was one thing to fantasize about an exotic island adventure, another to actually pull up stakes and move across the country. Last night she'd been caught up in the excitement. This morning, doubts were creeping in. Doubts she was afraid to express because John wanted the move so badly.

"A girl's got to do what a girl's got to do. What are you and Tuti doing this afternoon?"

"Going to the beach. Do you want to come?"

"Yes, that sounds great." She stood and stretched the kinks out of her shoulders and lower back. "If you want to go surfing I'll look after Tuti. She and I can explore the tidal pools at the point."

"Thanks, but I'm going to teach her to boogie

board. If we move to Tinman Island she'll need to improve her water skills."

Katie rummaged in her suitcase for her swimsuit. "But you wouldn't force her if she really didn't want to, would you?"

"Just because you never got into surfing doesn't mean she won't like it." He put his arms around Katie. "The only way to get past fear is to go through it. I'm a patient teacher. Don't you remember?"

"I remember almost drowning when you took me out too far the first time."

"You were never in danger of drowning. I was right there. Just as I will be at Tuti's side the entire time." He kissed her. "Trust me. I know what I'm doing."

She grinned against his mouth. "Famous last words."

CHAPTER THIRTEEN

JOHN SLAPPED KATIE on the ass just to hear her squeal, then laughed out loud because he hadn't felt so good in ages. When she pulled her shirt over her head to get changed he contemplated wrestling her onto the bed.

"Don't look at me like that," she said, laughing. "You said we're going to the beach. You get Tuti ready and I'll get some snacks together."

Ten minutes later he was leading the way across the road and down the sandy path through the dunes to the beach. The sand was cool underfoot and damp from the rain but the sun was hot on his head and shoulders, promising warmth for the rest of the day.

The path opened onto the beach. The bay stretched wide and blue beneath a clear sky. Pelicans flapped their huge wings low over the water. Small rollers hit the hard-packed sand with regularity. Perfect.

At the water's edge he dropped his towel and board and waded into the shallows where foam crept across the sand. "Tuti, come and see the crabs."

"What's a crab?" Tuti ran down to the water and crouched to peer at the tiny green crustaceans scuttling to their holes.

Katie picked her way daintily to the water's edge and waded out to him. He was about to reach for her when she bent over. Scooping a double handful of water, she splashed him, making him dance at the breathtaking chill on his groin.

"You'll pay for that." He picked her up and she shrieked, and kept on shrieking as he carried her out to waist-deep water and dumped her.

She went under and came up sputtering and laughing. First she feinted, then lunged. He let her take him under, their limbs a tangled slither of bare skin. When they came up Tuti was bouncing in the water knee-deep, waving her arms. "I want to splash, too."

John picked her up and carried her out. "Hold your breath." Her cheeks puffed out and she pinched her nose. He dropped her just above the water, making sure he pulled her up again immediately. She blew a jet of water, giggling. Her pigtails dripped and she wriggled out of his arms, falling back into the water. Katie brought her to the surface again, both of them giggling.

He caught Katie's eye. *See, she loves the water.*

Out of breath from exertion and laughing, the three of them found their way to shallower water.

John clapped his hands. "Okay, Tuti, time to put your wet suit on and try the boogie board."

Her little face, a second ago bright and glistening, wreathed in smiles, instantly shadowed. John looked up at the sky almost expecting to see that a cloud had covered the sun. No clouds, but the atmosphere had definitely chilled. Even Katie became subdued, retreating farther up the beach to grab a towel.

Tuti shook her head. "Don't want to wear a wet suit. Don't want to boogie board."

"The suit keeps you warm," John said patiently. "And it protects you from sand and board rashes."

Tuti shook her head again and glanced at Katie. Great. She knew Katie was a soft touch and was relying on her to intercede. Well, it wasn't going to work.

"Tuti, you're going to put on your wet suit." He stood behind her and physically picked up her legs and put them into the suit. It was like stuffing cooked spaghetti into a tube. "Boogie boarding is fun. Don't you want to have fun?"

Tuti shook her head. He zipped up her suit

and turned her around, chagrined to see her eyes wet with unshed tears she was battling to contain. He felt awful. But he couldn't back down now or she would never get over her fear.

Katie stood off to one side, her arms crossed over her stomach, an unhappy frown pulling her mouth. He wished she'd stayed at the cottage if she was going to be so negative.

He led Tuti into the shallows beyond the breaking waves and reviewed what he'd taught her in Bali about swimming. "Well done," he said when she'd floated on her back, and on her front and dog-paddled ten yards. "Now go get your board and bring it into the water."

Tuti ran through the foaming waves and up onto the sand. But instead of getting her board she veered off a little way down the beach and crouched to pick up a shell buried in the hard sand.

His jaw set, he waded through thigh-deep water after her.

Katie met him at the water's edge. "She doesn't want to."

"She just needs a little coaxing. How can she know she doesn't like it until she does it?"

"What are you going to do?"

"I'm going after her, of course."

Katie hurried after him. She grabbed his arm.

"And *make* her go boogie boarding? I can't believe you'd do that."

He stopped walking. "If you'd been more supportive she might not have run off."

"I think you're pushing her too hard. She doesn't like how the board wobbles and tips her off. I was watching. It scares her. Why not let her take lessons from a qualified teacher?"

"That's your answer to everything. Bring in the professionals. My dad taught me to boogie board. Tuti can learn from me. She's going to have to be adept at water sports if we move to Tinman Island."

Katie frowned. "Maybe Tinman Island isn't the best place for a girl who's afraid of ocean waves."

What was she really saying? Had she changed her mind about wanting to go with him? "A child can learn anything."

"She's not likely to get over her fear if you're pushing the boogie board on her."

"She's my kid. I know what's best for her."

"Oh, really? Is that the way it's going to be?"

"What are you talking about?"

The wind blew strands of her dark hair across her eyes. "Maybe we're not ready for Tinman Island."

"You mean, *you're* not ready. I get that it's all happening in a rush but sometimes you have to grab opportunities when they come up. I don't want to pressure you. But I would like an agreement in principle before I have to make the hard decisions."

"You might not want to pressure me but the fact is, you are—"

John cut her off with an upraised hand as he glanced around. "Where's Tuti?"

"Oh, no." Katie spun around, shielding her eyes from the sun with her hand. "I can't see her anywhere."

John swore. The empty beach stretched away in a curving bay to the rocky point and the tidal pools. How could she have gotten out of sight so quickly?

"Maybe she went behind the dunes," Katie said.

"Tuti!" John called. There was no one else on the beach. She would be perfectly safe as long as she didn't go in the water unaccompanied—which hardly seemed likely—but she was only six, after all. "Maybe she went back to the cottage."

"Wherever she is, I'm sure she's all right." Katie was trying to be calm but he could hear the tremor in her voice.

"Tuti!" he called again, louder. No answer. "You go back along the path through the dunes. I'll run along the beach. If she's not at the cottage—" He didn't want to think about that. "If you find her, yell out. Otherwise, I'll meet you at the end of the beach."

His feet pounded over the hard sand near the waterline, his gaze scanning water and beach. How could he have lost her? If Katie hadn't started arguing—no, it wasn't fair to blame her. Tuti was his daughter. He was responsible for her. He never should have allowed her to roam freely on the beach. But that's what kids did. It was all the more reason for her to learn water safety.

He wouldn't panic. They would find her. She would be all right. Even if she went in the water it was relatively calm with no rip. But there was no lifeguard, either.

Please don't let her have gone in the water alone.

She might simply be crouching out of sight, among the dunes. He slogged through the soft sand, warm now from the sun, to the top of a sandy ridge. Nothing but tufts of grass. No place for even a small girl to hide.

His gaze moved ahead, combing the rocky headland now only twenty yards away. Waves crashed over the black basalt slabs and foamed back into the sea. The area was riven with deep channels and dotted with tide pools. Every year along the coast drownings occurred when unwary fishermen were swept from the rocks.

Katie appeared at the top of a dune and waved to get his attention. “She’s not at the cottage or along the road.” From the height of her vantage point, she scanned the beach. Then she gave a cry. “There she is!” She started running toward the tide pools.

John began to run. A moment later he caught sight of two jaunty pigtails. Tuti was kneeling at the edge of a pool, peering in, oblivious to the waves crashing just meters behind her. Waves came in sets. Every so often a big one came in.... He sprinted. “Tuti!”

She looked up, then over her shoulder just in time to see a huge wave, so big it didn’t break but moved as a wall of green water, flowing across the rock. It picked her up and sucked her back out. Her small arms flailed, her eyes were wild. Katie screamed.

John sprinted across the sand then did a running dive into the water, battling the force of the surge. He popped to the surface. Tuti was barely a body length away, her arms reaching out to him in the roiling trough of the wave. He had to get to her before the next surge dashed her against the rocks. His feet found purchase on a rock and he pushed off, stretching out his hand...he tried to grab her but her wet suit was ripped from his grasp. His hand slid down her leg. He caught her ankle, held on tight and pulled.

She came up sputtering and coughing, her pigtails dripping. He circled her in his arms, shielding her as the wave pushed him onto the rocks. Pain sliced through his body. He couldn't protect himself or pull himself out. All he could do was stop Tuti from being bashed. Then Katie was standing above him at the edge of the basalt ledge, water swirling around her braced legs. He passed Tuti up to her and she hauled the girl out of his arms.

He was bleeding from half a dozen gashes, including his forehead. None of that mattered. Tuti was safe. He kicked hard, fighting to get away from the sharp-edged rocks. Then he let the next big surge carry him in and up. He grabbed on to a rock, clinging with his hands, even his toes as the water sucked out again. And before the next rush of water came he dragged himself out and collapsed on the rocks.

KATIE PACED THE the corridor of the Wonthaggi Hospital, waiting for John to come out from having his cuts and abrasions treated. This was a switch—her pacing a hospital waiting room for him.

Tuti, with barely a scratch on her, sported a

half-dozen cartoon bandages on her hands and feet. If she hadn't been in a wet suit the injuries would have been much worse. She sat in a plastic chair, swinging her legs as she played a handheld computer game. Every now and then she glanced up at Katie, and then at the door through which her father had gone fifteen minutes ago.

The Wonthaggi Hospital was smaller than the Frankston Hospital but the same odor of antiseptic and illness pervaded. Every now and then a wave of panic would roll over Katie as she flashed back to seeing first Tuti swept away then John pushed against the rocks like a rag doll.

He was lucky to be alive. Only his cool head, immense strength and his water skills had allowed him to judge the timing of the surge and use its force to haul himself out onto the rocks. Even then, he'd just lain there and she hadn't been sure if he was dead. She would never forget that moment. The world had stopped. Then he'd groaned and lifted his head. And the world began to turn again.

After the wave of panic came the anger. It was all his fault for forcing Tuti to do something she didn't want to do. Katie could have lost them both. Then what would she have done? She'd been fine on her own before. Yes, it was a little lonely at times but not *painful*. Finding and then losing them would be devastating.

But as the minutes ticked on the big wall clock over reception her natural honesty kicked in. If she and John had been watching Tuti instead of arguing they would have seen her run away. All that stuff about parenting issues had poured out, but really it was a power struggle not so different than they'd had years ago when she'd been sick. They both thought they were right and there was no room for compromise.

Unless they worked this out their old issues weren't going away anytime soon. Which meant they probably weren't ready for cohabitation, much less the bigger commitment of marriage. They could pack their bags and move across the country but their problems would tag along wherever they settled.

The doors opened. John walked out, bandages on his head, arm and knee. Tuti jumped up and ran to hug him.

Katie hung back. When he got closer she hesitantly leaned up to kiss him on the cheek. "Aren't we a pair? I'm finally off my crutches and now you're bashed up."

"I'm fine," he grunted. "It's only a few stitches."

"Spoken like a man." She stroked Tuti's head

then lightly tugged on a pigtail. "You deserve a medal for the way you rescued this little scamp."

"I'm not a scamp! I'm a girl." Tuti skipped ahead to "open" the automatic sliding doors to the outside. "And I'm not going in the ocean ever again!"

Katie glanced at John. "Reassure her. Tell her she doesn't have to."

The taut muscle in his jaw ticked. His response was low, in a voice not intended to carry to his daughter. "I'm not going to say that. She *will* have to swim in the ocean. Sooner or later."

Katie started to protest then decided to let the matter drop for now. Tuti was watching them, no doubt aware of the tension. She didn't want to argue with John in front of Tuti. Didn't want the strain between them to make the girl feel insecure with the two people she loved the most—in Australia, that is. At least she hoped Tuti loved her. God knows, Katie loved her.

If the day came when she and John weren't even friends anymore, she would lose contact with the girl. The possibility was so awful she couldn't bear thinking about it.

Nothing about today bore thinking about. No sooner had she and John got back together than cracks had appeared in their relationship. Not simple problems, either, but conflicts that threatened the very foundations of their still-fragile love. Tonight they had to talk.

Dinner was a mostly silent affair, a simple meal of hamburgers cooked on the barbecue. The warmth had gone out of the day and by the time the sun set, dark clouds again loomed on the horizon. Katie did the dishes while John put Tuti to bed early. For once the girl didn't protest. Her ordeal seemed to have drained her of mischief. She snuggled up in bed with her doll and a teddy bear.

Katie sat on the couch pretending to read a magazine but the words danced on the page. The hamburger lay like a lump of clay in her stomach.

John came out of Tuti's room. Instead of sitting next to her he took the chair opposite.

She set the magazine aside, bracing herself for the argument ahead. She would endure the anger and harsh words because she wanted so badly to connect with him. Hopefully, she could appeal to his rationality and keep the peace. Although her emotions were such a tangled mess she wasn't sure she had any rationality herself.

While she was mentally composing her opening remark John got straight to the point. "All that crap that came out on the beach when we were discussing Tuti was symptomatic of all our problems. I'm her father. I know her better than anyone. Yet you dismiss me as not having any valid viewpoint."

"I don't dismiss you—"

"You do. You did when you had cancer, too. Now you're doing it again with Tuti. You are the expert and I know nothing."

"When I—?" Her jaw dropped. "*I* was the one who was sick."

"Exactly. I was afraid for you. Terrified you were going to die. Do you know how that feels?"

"I have an idea," she murmured, thinking of what had happened in the water. Yes, now she had an inkling of what he'd gone through, but he went through it for months—not minutes. She should have been more empathetic.

He didn't seem to hear her agree. "Did you care how I felt? No, you were stubborn as hell. You went ahead and did it your way instead of getting the treatment you needed to ensure your survival. You wouldn't even get the genetic testing to see if you had the BRCA gene, the one your mother had."

"I already had cancer. What difference would testing have made? I had chemo, a lumpectomy and radiotherapy. Wasn't that enough?"

"You could have been tested. You could have had the mastectomy so the cancer wouldn't recur. You didn't do everything you could to save yourself. If you'd loved me, if you'd wanted a future with me, you would have done whatever it took to stay alive." His voice had risen with each sentence and now he was practically yelling. "All I wanted was for you to be alive!"

"That's easy for you to say now." Furious, Katie stood and began pacing between the tiny hall and the couch. She was trying to control herself but her voice was raised, too. "If I'd ended up with no breasts it might have been a different story."

"We'll never know, will we? Because you didn't give me the chance to prove my love."

"Oh, and I suppose abandoning me was your way of proving you loved me?" She flung a hand in the air. "Well, was it?"

"You pushed me away. Even before you were sick you wouldn't commit to marriage. Then when you got cancer, well, that was pretty convenient, wasn't it? Can't set a date when you don't know if you'll be alive for the wedding."

Katie gasped. "I can't believe you said that."

He didn't apologize, just went in for the kill. "You weren't willing to take a chance on our future. Why should I stick around for another serve of heartbreak? I didn't want to watch you die."

"I didn't. I survived."

"Through sheer good luck."

"Through good diet, exercise, natural remedies, meditation—"

They were toe-to-toe, in each other's face.

"Go ahead and believe that if you want."

"I do believe it. I'm living proof."

"You got lucky. That time."

"You're angry because I didn't do what *you* wanted me to."

"You're treating me like a bad person just because I disagree with you. You of all people should know how it feels to be lost and alone and frightened because the one you love best is leaving you. You must have felt that when your mother died. Just as I felt it when you were ill. *Who abandoned who?*"

Katie pressed fingers to her throbbing temples. "What are we doing? Where are we going with this? Let's not fight."

"Do you call this fighting? We're working things out."

"It's fighting and I hate it. Why can't you just love me no matter what? Why does it have to be conditional on me doing what you want? My mother and father were devoted to each other. I never heard them argue, not once."

"I adored your mother, don't get me wrong. She was the sweetest-natured person I ever knew. But she was so passive she wouldn't have said 'boo' to a goose. As for your father, I suspect he just agreed then did whatever the hell he wanted." John shook his head wearily. "Just because you didn't hear them argue doesn't mean their marriage was all sunshine and roses."

"They adored each other," Katie insisted. She sat and tucked her hands between her knees. "My father would do anything for my mother. Anything."

John met this statement with a cynical eye roll. "You do realize no red-blooded man would ever actually do that, don't you?"

"My father was a major in the army. Are you accusing him of not being red-blooded?"

"I'm saying, no one knows what goes on in a marriage except the two people involved. You're painting your mother as a saint and your father as a martyr."

"They loved each other."

"So do my parents. And they fight all the time."

"And that's what scares me." This whole conversation was scaring her. John wasn't listening to her at all. Just like his father didn't really listen to his mother. Nor had John ever seriously considered her side of the argument about her treatment, or about Tuti, for that matter. She didn't doubt he loved her. But did he respect her?

He couldn't, not if he refused to compromise.

He accused her of dismissing his concerns. Well, he wasn't discussing the issues so much as laying down the law. His law. He'd decided to move to Tinman Island and that was that. He was taking Tuti away from her new home, uprooting her again. Didn't he give credence to Katie's experience working with children? To her own desire to do what was best for Tuti?

If he didn't respect her, if he didn't think she was worthy enough to have a legitimate viewpoint on the important subjects of her health care and his daughter, then maybe that wasn't the kind of love she wanted. It wasn't the kind of love her parents had, where a couple worked through their differences and achieved a compromise.

John reached across the gap between the chair and the couch and took both her hands in his. "Katie, I'm going to lay it on the line. I need an answer from you before I hear about Tinman Island. I need to know..."

She swallowed. He looked so serious. "Yes?"

"I love you. I want to marry you. If I get the job, I want you to come with Tuti and me. You would make us both so happy."

Her throat was clogged with tears. He didn't get it. He just didn't get it. They were still talking around the real issue. Could she trust him not to leave her again if she got sick and didn't do things his way? "You're not listening to me."

"I heard every word you said. I woke up this morning with you in my bed and I was so happy. Come with me. Please."

Her hands lay limp in his. What was the point? He would never understand. So she talked around the issue, too. "Summerside is my home, where my people are. My history. Our history."

"Some of that history is hurting us. It's holding us back from taking the next step in our relationship."

"Which is?"

"Marriage. Children of our own. I believe a new home in a different location would be good for us. For all of us, Tuti included. We could be our own little family, starting fresh." The vulnerability in his eyes was devastating. "Katie, I need this. I'm dying in Summerside. I'm only thirty-five and my life is at a dead end."

She tugged her hands away and twisted in her seat. "You're pressuring me. Something this huge takes time to consider, to get used to."

"Last night you were all for it. What's changed? How much time do you need?"

She was silent. Maybe a lifetime. "How do I know we will last—that you won't leave me again? In the past seven years you've never been with any woman longer than six months."

"How do you know that?"

"Because I kept track!"

"I didn't stick with any of those women because on some level I was waiting for you. Face it, Katie. There will never be enough time for you to feel secure. Because you don't really want to be with me."

"Yes, I do!" The words flew out of her mouth.

Instantly he was by her side on the couch, his arms around her. "Then say yes. Say yes to us."

She wanted to so badly, yet still, she resisted. "I need time to think."

"Why?"

Why, indeed? Part of her was screaming to say yes. "I—I'm scared. I'm not as adventurous as you are."

"You are if you push yourself. You got hurt on your mountain bike but you said it was still worth it." Now he was nuzzling her neck, stroking her bare arms, kissing her behind the ear. "What happened to *que sera sera?*"

He touched her breast and squeezed gently. She recognized the signs that he wanted to make love. Instinctively she shrank away. How could he feel amorous when they'd just been fighting? They hadn't made up, not properly. The conflict between them simmered, unresolved.

She couldn't feel like having sex until that was fixed. And the conflict couldn't be fixed until they talked more. He seemed to be done talking.

"John, I don't…" Gently, she pushed him away.

The warmth in his gaze cooled. His hands slid off her. "Fine."

"I have a headache." She winced at the cliché but it was true. More than that, she was drained by their emotional exchange.

"Sure."

"And you're all battered and bruised."

"If you don't feel like it, you don't feel like it." The spark had gone out of him. He moved wearily. "Let's just go to bed."

"We can talk again in the morning."

"If there's anything more to say." Without waiting for a response from her, he got up and walked down the hall.

Katie followed him into the bedroom. She fussed with the curtains, waiting until he went into the bathroom to brush his teeth before changing into her nightie. A garment she hadn't worn since she got there.

He got into bed. "Did you take something for that headache?"

"Yes."

"Good night then." He rolled onto his side, facing away from her.

She lay staring at the ceiling, dry-eyed, her heart aching. What had just happened? How had things gone so wrong, so quickly? Most importantly, where could they go from here?

CHAPTER FOURTEEN

RAIN DRUMMING ON the tin roof of the cottage woke John the next morning. He moved his arm and winced at the pain. Memories of yesterday flooded back. Tuti swept into the ocean. Rescuing her, getting bashed against the rocks. Gingerly he touched his forehead. The bandage was slightly damp where blood had seeped through.

Then the argument with Katie. It had been pretty intense but he felt better for having vented. He glanced sideways. Her side of the bed was empty, her pillow still hollow from the impression of her head. He heard a noise out in the kitchen. It was her moving around, running water into the kettle.

What the hell had happened between them? He'd laid himself bare, told her he loved her, asked her to marry him, to share his life, to be a mother to Tuti…and she hadn't said no. But she hadn't said yes, either. Wasn't that just typical? What did she want from him that he wasn't offering her?

He thought he was giving her a gift—to be

able to write without worrying about making an income. She thought he was trying to… what—control her? That was her excuse when she didn't want to commit.

He rolled out of bed. A chilly draft was coming through the cracks in the window frame. Outside heavy gray clouds blanketed the sky over the bay. The last spate of autumn sun was over. The weather had socked in.

He put on long pants and socks for the first time in weeks. In the kitchen, Tuti was eating toast while Katie fiddled with the radio. She'd washed her hair and it was still damp, hanging in a loose braid over her shoulder. She found a clear station and they listened to the tail end of the news. The state government had approved a new freeway in the western suburbs and a rail link to the airport.

"Election coming up," John said. "They're splashing money around like nobody's business."

"Shh. Here's the weather." Katie held still to listen. The forecast was for continuing rain. Music came on. Katie turned the volume down.

John poured himself a coffee and leaned against the counter. "Not much point in sticking around here. The cottage isn't built for the cold."

"You're right." Katie added scrambled eggs

and a piece of bacon to Tuti's plate. Then she divided the rest between two plates and pushed one toward him. "If we pack up after breakfast we could be back in Summerside by lunchtime."

"I want to stay," Tuti said.

"Sorry, sweetheart. There'll be another time."

A ringing came from the other room. "Is that your phone?" Katie asked.

John grabbed his phone off the coffee table. "Hello?"

"Senior Sergeant John Forster?" an unfamiliar, official-sounding male voice said.

"Yes, speaking."

"This is Allan Barkin, District Police Commissioner of Queensland. I apologize for calling when you're on holiday..."

"That's no problem." This was it. It was starting to happen. John began to pace the room.

"I've looked over your résumé and I'd like to interview you now, over the phone. Would that suit you?"

"Yes, that's fine. Could you give me just a moment?" He went back to the kitchen. With his hand over the phone he spoke to Katie. "I'm on a phone interview. Could you keep Tuti quiet and occupied? I'll take this in the bedroom."

"Sure, no problem." She gave him a long, silent look, then turned to Tuti. "Eat up, sweetie, and we'll play Snakes and Ladders. Your daddy is on an important call."

Back in the bedroom, John sat at Katie's makeshift desk and found a piece of blank paper on which to take notes. "I'm back, sir. Please go ahead."

The interview went for forty minutes and covered a broad range of police procedures, regulations and duties, John's experience and his career aspirations, as well as the unique challenges of Tinman Island with its mix of aboriginal inhabitants, transient service industry workers and resort-goers.

"I'm looking for a fresh challenge," John reiterated when he sensed Allan Barkin was winding up. "I'd welcome the opportunity to combine leadership with hands-on policing. I've been reading up on local issues and I have some ideas about how to get the local communities involved and on board with police activities." He gave a deprecating cough. "And being keen on water sports, I have to admit the location appeals to me, as well."

"Plenty of water sports on the island," Barkin said in his gruff voice. "Do you fish?

"Fishing, scuba, sailing—I love them all. I don't have much time for that nowadays but I was a semiprofessional surfer in my youth."

"Well, John, I'm pleased to tell you I'm putting you on the short list for the position. Ordinarily I would consult with the rest of the panel before making that decision but we're on a short time frame. We need to make a selection by the end of the week. I believe I told you the outgoing commander is in the hospital after a major heart attack and won't be coming back. The officer acting in his position isn't interested in staying on. Can you get up here for an interview tomorrow morning?"

That soon? He could swing it. He and Katie had already decided to return to Summerside. Before he'd left town Sally, Tuti's after-school caregiver, had let him know she was available to look after Tuti as needed over the holidays. And he was still officially off work. "Yes, sir. I can get an early flight and be in Brisbane by midmorning."

"That will be fine. The selection panel is interviewing all day," D.C. Barkin said. "I'll slot you in for eleven o'clock."

"May I ask who my competition is, sir?" He wanted to know what his chances were.

"I suppose there's no harm in telling you since you're bound to run into at least one or two of them tomorrow." Barkin named a half-dozen names. Two of the men and one of the women being considered he'd never heard of but they all ranked higher than him. The other three contenders he knew by their stellar reputations. He was facing stiff competition.

"Thank you, sir. I'll see you tomorrow." John hung up and called Sally. When he had Tuti's care organized he went out to the cottage living room.

Katie was seated on the chair, Tuti on the couch. He threw Katie a glance and sat down beside Tuti. She looked up, brushing her bangs out of her eyes. He made a mental note to get her hair trimmed.

"I have to go to Brisbane tomorrow so Sally's going to look after you."

"Okay." She pushed the dice at Katie. "Your turn."

It was humbling how easily she accepted what he told her. She trusted him implicitly and here he was, possibly about to turn her life upside down.

Katie ignored the dice. She was watching him intently. "What happened?"

"I have an interview in person tomorrow."

She paled then reached for the dice but didn't throw them.

"What's an interview?" Tuti asked.

"It's to see if I get a new job. If I do we'll be moving up north to live."

"Will Katie go, too?"

"Maybe," John said.

"I don't know, sweetie," Katie said. "It's a long way from my home."

"We'll have to wait and see." Maybe he shouldn't have said anything to Tuti before he knew. But he had to prepare her. It wasn't that long ago he'd read her Katie's book on grieving and they'd had an emotional talk about Nena. Now he might have to prepare her for losing Katie. Hell, he might have to prepare himself.

Tuti's forehead wrinkled. "But Katie's my teacher."

"You would have a new teacher in a new school. No matter what happens Katie will still be your friend. Right, Katie?"

"Of course," she murmured.

"You can talk to her on Skype the way you do Wayan and Ketut," he added.

Tuti kept her gaze down, saying nothing. He hoped she wasn't going to stop talking again. "That's *if* I get the job. I might not. Then we'd stay here. And everything will be the same." Was that really true? If Katie drew a line in the sand and refused to even consider a move, would that make everything change again? Could they come back from her vote of non-confidence in their relationship?

"No matter what, I'll always be with you." He put his arm around her and hugged her. Still she said nothing. John massaged the back of her neck. "Okay, sweetheart?"

Tuti glanced up at him with sad eyes. She gave him a small smile and said, "Okay, *Bapa*."

"We need to go home now. Why don't you go pack your bag?" he said to Tuti. "Don't forget to brush your teeth first."

When she'd left the room, John glanced at Katie. "So, things are progressing. Have you thought any more about whether you would come with us?"

She started putting away the board game. "You don't even know if you've got the job."

"No, but a little support would help, going into the interview."

"I'm not sure I can give you what you're asking for." Katie's dark eyes clouded and the tiny lines at the corners became more pronounced. "Summerside is my home. It's where I belong, where I feel safe." Her voice cracked. "My mother is buried there."

John nodded, numb. She needed security. He got that. But he'd thought he was offering her security. The solid comfort of his love, a home and family. It wasn't enough for her. She wasn't willing to take a chance. "Tuti would miss you. I would miss you."

"I'm sorry, John—"

"Don't say no yet." He hated the desperation

in his voice but he plowed on. Their relationship had been brought to a head prematurely. It wasn't ideal but they would have to deal with it. "Nothing's set in stone."

"You got through the first hurdle." She smiled though her eyes welled with tears and reached out to smooth his shirt collar. "You are going to blow the socks off the selection panel."

"Whatever happens, don't let it mark the end of us."

Her smile faded and she searched his gaze unhappily. "You're obviously looking for something more out of life, something I, and Summerside, can't give you. I don't want to hold you back—"

"Shh, we won't talk about it anymore now." Their relationship wasn't over. It couldn't be. As long as she didn't say a definitive no there was still a chance they would get together. He'd waited seven years. He would wait seven more if he had to.

He pulled her into his arms and held her tightly. "We belong together. Tell me you'll think about it some more."

"Oh, John, I've been awake half the night, thinking." A tear escaped and she brushed it away. "I do love you. But I—I just can't do it. I can't go with you."

He buried his face in her fragrant hair, trying

to suck air into his tight chest. All he'd wanted was a lifeline. Instead he was drowning.

"LET ME GET THIS straight." Paula dished out Thai green curry from takeaway boxes onto three plates. "John asked you to marry him and go live on a tropical island. But you said no because you'd rather stay in Summerside."

Riley sipped his beer, shaking his head. "I always suspected you had a screw loose. Now it's confirmed."

"I do not have a screw loose." Katie was allowing herself to relax for the first time in weeks. She'd made her deadline by mere hours and the book and illustrations were on their way to New York. "I have obligations here. My students. Dad."

"Uh-huh," Riley said skeptically.

Katie dug into her curry. She was making excuses again. Her father and stepmother, Susan, were fit and healthy and planning an extended trip around the country in a camper van. And her students were going into grade two next year. She adored them but they weren't a lifetime commitment.

"On Tinman Island you wouldn't have to work for a living but could concentrate on your writing," Paula said.

"Which would be a godsend considering

you're under the pump with this contract," Riley added.

"Hey, ease up, you guys," she protested. "Do you think this was an easy decision for me? To say no and realize that John and Tuti might be going away and I'll only see them once, maybe twice, a year?"

Why did he want to marry her anyway? How could he love her when she put him through such hell? Had she become this unattainable woman, a conquest, and he wouldn't be happy until he got her?

More to the point, why was she being so stubborn? Why couldn't she commit? Riley had only been kidding about the screw loose but sometimes she wondered if she *was* going crazy. The thought of joining her future to John's scared her to death. It wasn't like being afraid of going downhill on a bike. This was a real, visceral terror of pouring her heart and soul into the one she loved. Only for that love to abandon her.

Katie stabbed her fork at a spring roll.

Like when her mother died.

Huh. Where had that thought come from? The spring roll dropped back to the plate. She'd been a young girl, on the brink of womanhood. Close to her mother, far closer than to her gruff military father. She'd believed to the very end that her mother would survive.

And then she hadn't.

Just as she'd counted on John being around forever, no matter how she treated him, or what condition she was in.

Until he wasn't.

She'd had similar thoughts before about John but without the added insight of her mother's death. Why would she? The two events didn't seem connected.

Maybe she had to accept some responsibility for John giving up on her. Oh, sure, he said he'd done it to try to save her. But had he really been trying to save himself?

She noticed suddenly that Paula and Riley had fallen silent and were watching her. Paula reached over and squeezed her hand. "We know you care about him. And that your decision must have been painful."

"How *is* John?" Katie asked, dreading the answer. She hadn't seen him all week. She'd been busy finishing her book, and hurting too much to be with him right now. If they still had a future it wasn't going to be the future either had hoped for. A long-distance romance on either end of a Skype connection wasn't her idea of a relationship. Temporarily, okay, but not for any duration. She missed him, and she missed Tuti. It was a taste of what was to come and she didn't like it.

"He's being all stoical," Riley said. "But he's hurting."

"How did his interview in Brisbane go?"

"He's on the short, short list. They've narrowed it down to him and another guy. Or I should say, a woman." Paula looked at her funny. "Didn't he tell you?"

"We had a fight at the cottage. I haven't spoken to him since." More than a fight, it had been a goodbye.

"You, fighting?" Riley said. "That must have been something."

"It wasn't nice." Katie grimaced. "Raised voices, practically yelling."

Paula exchanged a glance with Riley and bit her lip to suppress a grin. "Sounds desperate. What was it about?" she added more sympathetically.

"Tuti, to begin with. I know he's her dad and he has final say but if we married I would have a say, too. We are so at odds sometimes with how we approach parenting. If we can't agree on basics it would be hell to live together, both of us duking it out over who knows best. I've seen kids from unstable homes. They're not happy kids. I would hate to put Tuti or any child of our own through that."

"That's just fine-tuning. The main thing is, you both love her and want the best for her,"

Riley said. "Paula and I have been having discussions lately about Jamie. You don't have to always agree—"

"But if one parent lays down the law, the other one has to back him or her up," Paula finished.

"Exactly." Riley gave his wife a high five.

Katie smiled at their tag-team antics. She took a breath before admitting the rest. "Then...then we moved on to what happened when I was sick with cancer. It wasn't rational, just emotional. All sorts of horrible stuff dredged up from years ago."

"Maybe it was good that you got it out," Riley said.

"I don't know." She poked at her dinner with chopsticks, suddenly not hungry. "Mum and Dad never fought like that."

Riley shrugged. "Dad was a military man, used to being in command. And he has a temper. He's got it under control but I remember times he lashed out. Nothing abusive but he would stomp around as if he was giving his troops a dressing-down. Mum hated confrontation so she avoided saying anything that got him riled up. I recall a lot of tense silences."

Now that he mentioned it, her parents *had* spent a lot of time apart, her mother in the kitchen working on recipes for her next cookbook, her father in the shed doing some woodworking project. They'd done their own thing a lot—nothing wrong with that. She'd assumed they had different interests and gave each other space.

John was great that way. At the cottage he'd gone out of his way to give her time to write, making meals, bringing her cups of coffee and snacks. If he needed to find himself on Tinman Island, she wanted him to feel free to do that. She wished she could go with him, support him, but…

"Every couple fights at times," Paula said, breaking into her thoughts. "It's natural. When you don't air your grievances but keep everything bottled up inside, that's when your relationship is in trouble."

"Do you guys fight?" Katie looked from Paula to Riley, not prepared to believe it for a second.

"Yes, even we fight." Riley rolled his eyes. "You should see how pissy she gets when I leave my socks on the floor."

"That's not fighting." Katie waved away Riley's attempt at lightening the atmosphere. "The last time John and I had a big fight we didn't see each other for seven years. What if that happens again?"

"What did he do that was so horrible?" Paula asked.

Katie ticked off the crimes on her fingers. “He wouldn’t support my medical choices. He left me on my near-death bed. He went straight to another woman’s arms, had a child and went on to become a womanizer.”

Even as she spoke she realized it was all a long time ago. And in many ways, her actions had led to his actions.

He’d changed. She’d changed. How long was she going to hang on to the past?

“But you’ve fallen in love with each other again. That’s got to mean something,” Paula said. “Surely you can forgive and forget.”

“He’s moving away,” she said. “He’ll forget me.”

And with that, the fear came flooding back. She knew she was being irrational. She tried instead to think of the fun times—of which there were plenty—but she’d been in this mind-set for so long it was hard to break free.

Riley shook his head. “You are the most confident woman I know besides Paula—except when it comes to John. I just don’t get it. What’s holding you back? The guy is crazy about you. Always has been.”

“Yeah, well…” She didn’t get it, either. “He hasn’t called me since we got back from the cottage.”

“He knows you’ve been busy getting your

book finished." Paula pushed her plate away and wiped her fingers on a napkin. "You should call him."

"Don't screw the guy around," Riley said. "He loves you."

Katie reached for the spring roll again. Riley grabbed the box and held it aloft. "Not till you say you'll call John."

She withdrew her hand. "Changed my mind. I don't want any more spring rolls." When Riley lowered the box she grabbed a piece. "Ha-ha."

"Siblings. Honestly. How old are you two?" Paula rolled her eyes. "Makes me glad I'm an only child."

Riley slung an arm around her shoulders and hauled her close to plant a smacking kiss on her cheek. "You know you don't mean that. Katie's your sister now. You can give her crap whenever you want."

Paula pinched his cheek, the full wattage of love shining in her eyes. Looking on, Katie's heart ached with happiness for them and envy for herself. She wanted some of what they had. She threw a crumpled napkin at her brother. "Hey, get a room."

Riley and Paula drew apart sheepishly.

She'd experienced deep love with John. Her greatest longing was for it to be a lasting love. If only fear didn't get in her way. She rubbed her gritty eyes and stifled a yawn. Her book was done. Maybe all she needed was a good night's sleep and she would feel normal again.

"Do you guys mind if I call it a night?" She stifled another yawn. "I'm really tired."

As she was showing them out, Riley asked, "So, will you call John?"

"I don't know." She had a lot to think about. It seemed to her that her problems were bigger than what had happened between her and John. Was it possible she'd completely misinterpreted the nature of her parents' love and marriage?

Could *she* be the one searching for a love that was unattainable?

"JOHN, JOHN!" Patty rushed into his office on Monday morning, waving an envelope. She stopped short in the doorway, her red curls bouncing, and tried to look contrite. "I mean, Senior Sergeant Forster."

"It's okay." John glanced up from the stack of paperwork he was wading through, the flotsam and jetsam of a week away from the office. An envelope. If he'd been successful with the Tinman Island job he would have got a phone call from Queensland late Friday. No word had come through. Had Barkin sent a letter instead? Snail mail didn't bode well.

"What is it?" As calmly as he could he held out his hand.

"It's a letter from the Chief Commissioner." Patty gave him the letter then waited in front of his desk, her hands clasped, the toes of her high heels tilting together. "Are you going to open it? Is this the job you applied for? We're going to miss you, boss."

"Settle down, Patty. It's from the Victorian state government, not Queensland." John slit open the envelope. "It's probably the memo accompanying the quarterly budget, telling me to cut back on postage stamps."

"Oh." Patty's face fell. "I saw the government logo and thought… Would you like a coffee? I can run to the bakery for one of those pastries you like. Boss?"

John scanned the letter from the Department of Government Services. "I don't believe it."

"I can take the mail around to local addresses on my lunch break to save on postage if that would help," Patty said.

"Thank you, Patty, but that won't be necessary." John glanced up and grinned. "The building extension I applied for has been approved in the rush of government spending leading up to the election. To go with the new offices, we'll get five uniformed officers, two detectives and two admin staff."

Patty clapped her hands together. "And air-conditioning?"

"And air-conditioning," John said expansively. "Go spread the word. The dark days are over."

Patty hurried out. He could hear her excited squeals in the bull pen through his open office door.

Well. He'd applied for the upgrade to Summerside Police Department's facilities and staffing two years ago. Finally, it had come through. It wasn't the kind of challenge he'd been hoping for but if he stayed in town he would have his hands full in the next few years overseeing the building and the expansion of his force. Once everything was up and running a promotion would very likely be in order for him.

He could stay in Summerside. See where things went with Katie. Would she say yes to his marriage proposal if they were going to live here in the village?

He didn't know how long the phone had been ringing when the sound finally penetrated. Automatically he reached for the handset. "Hello?"

"John." It was the deep, bluff voice of Allan Barkin.

Here it came, the you-were-close-but-no-cigar speech. Well, he had a consolation prize—both the addition to the station and Katie.

So why did he feel let down?

He almost didn't hear what District Commissioner Barkin said. "I'm sorry. Could you repeat that?"

Barkin cleared his throat. "I said, the selection panel has unanimously decided to offer you the position of Commander of Tinman Island Police Department. If you're still interested in the job."

"I—" John leaned back, running a hand over his jaw. "Thank you, sir. It's an honor to be considered let alone be offered the job."

"I detect some hesitation, Senior Sergeant."

"It's all happened very suddenly. I have… family matters I need to consider. Could I have a day to think about it?"

"I understand. Well, you're aware of our time constraints. Let me know by this time tomorrow. Since it'll be Saturday I'll give you my private number."

"I'll do that." John rose to his feet, resisting the urge to salute his empty office. "And thank you again, sir."

He hung up and blinked dazedly. First the expansion approval. Now this. It never just rains, it pours.

He had overnight to decide. He picked up the phone to call Katie. Then hesitated. She'd already given him her answer. She wanted to stay in Summerside. The receiver clattered back into the cradle. No, this was something he had to figure out for himself.

He spent an uncomfortably wakeful night tossing and turning. Katie or Tinman Island? A professional and personal challenge or the love of his life? Even if he gave up Tinman Island for Katie there was no guarantee she would marry him.

Saturday morning he was rattling around his town house like the last bean in a jar, no closer to making a decision than yesterday. He would end up flipping a coin if he didn't get out of the house. There was nothing worse for a man of action than to be wavering over what to do. He couldn't think cooped up. He needed fresh air, open water.

He called his mother and told her his good news, getting the job at Tinman Island and the funds to expand Summerside police station.

"Congratulations," Alison said enthusiastically. "Which are you going to choose?"

"That's my big dilemma. I have to make a decision quickly and I need to think. Could you do me a favor and look after Tuti for the afternoon? I'd like—" Bowing his head, he pinched the bridge of his nose. "No, I *need* to go surfing."

"Bring her over anytime," Alison said. "I'll be here."

"I don't want to go to Grandma's house," Tuti complained all the way there in the car. "Can't I stay with Katie?"

"You haven't seen Grandma in over a week. She misses you. Katie needs time to herself. She's been working a lot lately."

"I wouldn't be any trouble," Tuti said earnestly.

"I know. But you're still going to Grandma's." He glanced in the rearview mirror at her. "She loves you, sweetie. Be nice."

Tuti sighed. "I try, *Bapa*."

At the house, John carried her backpack and held her hand up the walk, giving her words of encouragement. The door opened. He tensed, hoping his mother wouldn't expect Tuti to run into her arms.

But Alison kissed his cheek and merely smiled at Tuti before stepping back to let them in. "Have you got time for a coffee?"

"I'd rather get going if you don't mind," John said from the doorstep. "There's a three-meter break at Gunnamatta."

Alison turned back to Tuti. "I'm going to make scones. You can help me if you like. Or you can play on the trampoline. You decide."

Tuti hesitated, glanced at her father then back at her grandmother. "Scones?"

John smiled and bent to hug his daughter. "Good girl. I'll see you later this afternoon."

Tuti ran down the hall to the kitchen. Alison watched her fondly, and then turned back to John. Her expression changed as she peered into his face. "Is everything okay?"

"I'm fine. I just need a day to myself, clear my head."

"Things not going well with Katie?"

"You never liked her much, did you?"

"I adored her until she hurt you." Alison paused. "But even I have to admit, you've been happier this past month than I've seen you in years. Or maybe Tuti has caused the change."

"Tuti's part of it. But so is Katie. I feel as if I've grown up at the ripe old age of thirty-five, if that makes any sense. Katie doesn't know it but it's partly because of her that I applied for the job in Tinman Island. I wanted a fresh start." He gave a bitter chuckle. "Ironic considering the job might separate us."

Alison leaned on the doorjamb and gave him a commiserating look. "She won't go with you?"

"She's afraid we're not compatible. And she doesn't trust me after what happened seven years ago. We had a fight at the beach house and now she thinks that's the end because I didn't make up the way she thinks we should make up. I didn't talk things through and resolve the issues in minute detail."

His mother shook her head. "If your father and I split up every time we had a fight we wouldn't have lasted a week." She paused. "Although I must say, it bothers me that your dad won't talk things through. I know it looks as if I don't either but I would if I had any other choice. Your father thinks having sex is conflict resolution. Women need words, we need reassurance."

"Hmm." John winced a little, partly because her words hit home and partly because he didn't want to talk to his mother about her sex life. Or his. "She's scared I'll let her down again. I don't know what I can do to prove that I won't."

"There's nothing you can do. She either believes in you or she doesn't. She either knows you well enough by now...or she never will."

"Do you think I should stay in Summerside for her sake?"

"I think you need to do what *you* want."

"Isn't marriage about compromise?"

"Yes, but with Katie...will anything you do ever be enough?"

"You're good at answering questions with questions," he said, frustrated.

Alison gave him a hug. "I can't tell you what to do. What if I'm wrong? Take all the time you need for surfing. Tuti and I will be fine."

She hesitated. "One thing I do give Katie credit for—she taught me how to relate better to Tuti."

John got back in his vehicle, his surfboard strapped to the roof rack, and headed for the beach. It occurred to him halfway there that Katie had done the same for him.

CHAPTER FIFTEEN

AT GUNNAMATTA SURF beach John paddled out beyond the breaking waves to where three other surfers sat on their boards, waiting for a big one. A stiff breeze whipped the frothy tops off the waves. Gulls wheeled overhead. He'd barely gotten into position when a wall of blue water rose up behind him. Facedown on his board, he paddled and kicked, picking up speed. Then the wave lifted his board. He got to his knees and then into a crouch, arms outspread.

As he skimmed along the crest of the wave, he savored the wind in his hair, the fresh salt spray on his face. Water had always been healing for him. Something about the leveling nature of water and the vastness of the ocean put his problems in perspective.

He rode the wave all the way to shore, hopping off as the water turned to foam on the sand. Then he paddled back out and did it all over again.

Around midafternoon the waves petered out. He was ready to break for lunch then anyway.

He bought fish and chips from the kiosk and went back to his towel on the sand. With nothing between him and his thoughts, he stared out to sea.

What was he going to do about Katie? He'd tried so hard for so many years. Maybe she was right and their core beliefs were too different to mesh over the long term. But he'd held on to the hope of being with her all these years, even when he thought he just wanted to be her friend. Truth was, he'd never stopped loving her, and that hoping had become a habit.

She was the only thing in his life he'd ever lost that he truly cared about. Except for Katie's mother, Mary, but that wasn't the same. Maybe by trying to have a relationship with Katie, he'd held her back from moving on and building a life without him.

They certainly had different beliefs when it came to parenting. She was by the book. He was all about instinct. That applied to other areas of their lives. She was controlled, cautious, constantly hedging her bets with vitamins and health foods. Oh, he made sure he ate fairly well and got plenty of exercise but she was fanatical about it. He had to admit, though, she did take good care of herself even if it wasn't the way he would do it. With Tuti, Katie relied on what the experts said instead of her own excellent instincts. She just didn't trust herself to do the right thing naturally. No, that wasn't quite true. She thought there was one correct method and she had to do that or else disaster would strike. Not only that, everyone else had to abide by the correct "rules" whatever they were. Whereas he was more a play-it-by-ear kind of guy.

He drained the last of his cola and crumpled the can in one hand. So where did that leave him? He didn't want to make her unhappy.

But he did want a family. Since Tuti had come into his life he'd realized just how much he liked children. To be honest, at first he'd resented her presence in his life, turning his bachelor pad upside down. Now he couldn't imagine being without her. Her rapid and deep attachment to Katie wasn't surprising—she'd just lost her mother and Katie, while not a substitute, was a warm and caring woman who loved children, and Tuti in particular. Maybe he shouldn't have let Tuti get so close to Katie but in hindsight it was hard to see how he could have avoided that.

Katie didn't want to leave Summerside. He couldn't blame her for that. She wasn't the same as him, didn't have the same need for physical challenge and adventure. To her the pleasures of life came from more homey pursuits. If she couldn't come with him maybe she didn't love him enough.

But it wasn't about Tinman Island versus Summerside. If he truly thought they had a chance he would stay here and find his challenges in another form. No, their problems went deeper. She didn't trust him. He suspected that nothing he did, no amount of time, would fix that. He had to stop trying to reel her in like a fish on a line. As long as he was around she could blame him for whatever demons she was avoiding.

He'd vowed not to give up, to do whatever it took to bring her into his life. But if that wasn't what she wanted, he couldn't keep after her. Maybe he needed to let Katie go. Let her take her own path and hope that she found whatever she was seeking.

Having come to that conclusion, an ache started deep inside. She'd been part of his life since he was a child. Knowing it was over for good was like ripping out his heart.

Life went on. Look at Tuti. She'd shown resilience in the face of grief. Her mother had passed away but she'd soldiered on. He would, too. Somehow.

But when he thought about never holding Katie again, never seeing her eyes open to his in the morning, never hearing her laugh reverberate through his breastbone, never feel her move against him in the night. Never see her hold their newborn baby…

He knuckled away the moisture in his eyes and tried to suck air past the huge lump lodged in his chest. It would be all the worse seeing her on the streets of Summerside knowing his last chance had come and gone.

But he had to do it. He had to let Katie go. Ironically he needed to talk to her about it, needed her to know she didn't have to be torn anymore.

He pulled out his phone from his backpack and punched in her number. She answered and the sound of her voice lifted his spirits, as always, until he remembered why he was calling. "Would you have dinner with me tonight?" She started to demure and he quickly added, "Don't worry, I'm not going to pressure you about the move. I just want to talk."

She said yes. He put his phone away.

The wind had shifted. John scanned the horizon. Waves were rolling in with an east-west break. He had time for a few more sets before he had to leave to meet Katie. First he made another quick call to check in with his mother. She was delighted to have Tuti a little longer.

He hoped Katie would find love someday.

He hoped he could bear to watch and be

happy for her. It should be easier from the distance of the Tinman Island.

JOHN ARRIVED AT the exclusive waterfront restaurant first to make sure he got the table he'd reserved, next to the window with the best view of the bay. This goodbye celebration would be bittersweet. It was a new beginning for both of them. But it was also the end of a very long chapter in their lives.

Hearing footsteps behind him, he got to his feet.

Katie looked beautiful in a cherry-red dress that suited her dark coloring so well and highlighted her curves. He took both her hands and kissed her on the cheek, inhaling her special fragrance. "Thanks for coming."

She smiled up at him and turned her face to kiss him on the lips. Now he saw the shadows beneath her eyes and the tired lines at the corners of her mouth. She glanced around at the white linen, the bottle of champagne chilling in the ice bucket. "Are we celebrating something?"

He signaled to the waiter, who came over and popped the cork. John and Katie sat in silence while he poured. Somehow the gaiety associated with champagne now seemed wrong.

John raised his fizzing glass to Katie's. "To good times. And…good memories."

She set down her glass without drinking. "Did you hear something?"

"I got the job."

She froze.

"Plus the funding for the Summerside station expansion came through. Work can start next month."

"What are you going to do?"

He hadn't been one hundred percent certain until that very moment. Now he knew. For years he'd stayed in Summerside for her sake, not marrying, not moving on. He couldn't do it any longer. Nor could he accept a halfhearted love that always second-guessed his motives. If they were going to have a future together she had to make that leap of faith. For him to trust in *her* love it was time for her to compromise. And he couldn't ask her again. She had to offer.

"I'm going to Tinman Island." He searched her face. "It's really happening."

Katie opened her mouth. For one heart-stopping moment he thought she was going to say she'd changed her mind and wanted to come with him. Then she made a choking sound, burst into tears and ran from the dining room.

He found her on the beach below the restaurant. Her heeled sandals dangled from her hands as she waded through the shallows near the pier. Tear tracks streaked her cheeks.

"Katie." He folded her in his arms. "My love."

"I'm so sorry, John. I don't know what's wrong with me."

"Shh. There's nothing wrong with you." He stroked her hair. He was pretty sure the rending in his ears was the sound of his heart breaking. "I'm not pressuring you, or trying to force a love that wasn't meant to be. We gave it our best shot. This past month with you has been amazing. We'll part friends. Someday when we both have other partners and families we'll be able to look back on this time with affection and maybe relief at a narrow escape."

She turned in his arms. "Is that what saying goodbye to me is, a relief?"

He hadn't thought about it but now that he did.... "Not relief, exactly. But I'm at peace with our decision."

"*Our* decision," she murmured.

"Well, you decided first. I just caught up with you."

"Did I decide? I'm so tired. I can't think straight. I don't know what I feel."

"Don't feel. Don't think." He wiped the moisture from beneath her eyes with the pads of his thumbs. "Come back into the restaurant. Have something to eat. I'll bet you haven't been eating properly this week as well as not sleeping enough. Am I right? That rabbit food you subsist on wouldn't keep body and soul together."

"Rabbit food—" she began in outrage. Then seeing he was teasing she swatted his shoulder. "Oh, you. I *am* hungry."

"Come on then. Before the champagne goes flat."

Dinner was hardly a joyous occasion but John thought it went as well as could be expected. They spoke about keeping in touch. At least he did. Katie said very little and seemed fragile, her smile forced.

Afterward he walked her to her car. "You don't look too well. Would you like me to drive you home? I can pick you up tomorrow morning to retrieve your car."

"No, I'll be fine. Sorry I wasn't better company." She blinked and glanced away. When she looked back, her voice was steadier. "When do you leave?"

"The District Commissioner for Queensland is keen to get me up there as soon as possible. I'm going next week."

Her face dropped. "That soon."

"It makes sense to get Tuti started in her new school at the beginning of the term."

"How does she feel about it?"

John shrugged and scraped the toe of his shoe

on the pavement. “I told her she could get a puppy.”

“Typical parental response to cushion a child from a traumatic situation,” Katie said drily.

He bristled. “I suppose you think it’s a mistake?”

Katie smiled wanly. “I think she’ll love having a puppy.”

Well, he was glad she’d finally conceded he could do something right with regard to Tuti’s upbringing.

“I’d like to see her before you go,” she added.

“Of course. She would be devastated if she didn’t get to say goodbye.” A lump filled his throat. “I want to thank you for everything you’ve done for her—”

“Don’t.” Katie held up a hand. “I would have done it for any child in my class but especially for…” her voice broke “…a child of yours.”

He was struck mute after that, awash in pain. He kissed her forehead and helped her into her car. Then he waited in the parking spot until her Honda had climbed the hill and disappeared around the bend.

He walked slowly across the pavement to his car. At least he no longer had to wonder where he and Katie were going. The answer was, nowhere.

KATIE DROVE HOME on autopilot. She was numb from her hair right down to her toes.

This was for the best. Being free of John was what she'd wanted all along. She no longer had to worry about his feelings or whether he was teasing her or flirting.

She could get on with her life.

He could get on with his.

So why did she feel so awful?

She was losing Tuti. That thought brought forth a wail from deep inside. If she could have banged her head on the steering wheel without going off the road, she would have.

She thumped the wheel with her fist instead. She was going to miss that little cutie-pie. John was making a mistake taking Tuti away from her new home and everyone who'd come to love her. Of course Tuti would still have him. And she thought he was a good father, despite some of the things she'd said. Why hadn't she ever told him that?

She parked in her carport and went inside. The house felt empty and way too quiet. Funny, she'd never noticed that before. She was used to living alone and the quiet didn't usually bother her. In fact she liked silence. At least she used to—until John and Tuti had filled her life with laughter.

She changed out of her dress and into her

track pants, at a loose end now that her book was finished. The next book was hanging over her head but she didn't have to start on it today, not when the bottom had just dropped out of her world.

Maybe *she* should get a puppy. Something warm to come home to, to cuddle her and give her unconditional love. The kind of love she'd wanted from John.

She slumped onto the couch. The beautiful dinner John had treated her to sat heavily in her stomach.

He was at peace. Well, that was nice for him. She was all churned up inside.

You wanted him to leave you alone.

She jumped to her feet, clutching a cushion to her stomach. If that was true, why didn't it make her happy? She'd been happy, briefly, when she thought she had a second chance at the love of her life.

That second chance had just imploded in front of her eyes.

He'd asked her to marry him. She'd turned him down. Was she crazy?

No! Crazy would be giving up a great job, her own home, family and friends to go to a remote island with a man who let her down so badly she still hadn't recovered seven years later.

But she loved him, even more now than she

did back then. She had to get to the bottom of what was holding her back.

Her conversation with Riley and Paula had raised a few issues. Maybe she had more baggage than she'd thought. Maybe she was stuck, not just in regards to John, but further back. There was only one person who could give her the answers she needed. Katie grabbed her purse and headed back to her car.

Fifteen minutes later she peered inside the open double doors of the Men's Shed, a meeting place where men of all ages got together to build, repair, chin-wag and do other guy stuff. She scanned the long workbench along one wall, looking for her father.

The whine of a power saw vied with industrious hammering. No one would hear her knock so she walked in, passing a young fellow covered in tattoos nailing pieces of wood together and an elderly man painting a wooden rocking horse in dappled gray.

Her father was bent over the power saw, safety goggles and face mask protecting him from the wood shavings that flew off as the saw bit through the piece of timber. She waited until he'd finished making the cut before touching his shoulder.

"Hey, Dad. Susan told me where I could find you."

Her father pulled down the mask and pushed the goggles up onto his gray brush cut. "Katie. What brings you here?"

Katie understood why he might be surprised. She got along with her father, she just never sought him out. "I've finished my book and I'm at a loose end. What are you making?"

"I'm cutting out pieces for an Adirondack chair." He nodded to a stack of slats on the concrete floor next to the saw. "Making a set for Riley and Paula's wedding present."

"That's nice." She glanced at the far side of the shed. An urn was bubbling in the small kitchen and comfy chairs provided a setting for coffee breaks. "Want to grab a cuppa?"

Barry flipped the switch on the saw and covered the blade with the safety shield. Brushing sawdust from his faded navy overalls, he led the way to the coffee area. "Is everything all right?"

"Fine." She glanced over her shoulder. Some of the guys were looking in their direction. "Is it okay that I'm here? Will the men freak out at a woman in their shed?"

"Nah, no worries." Barry handed her a mug of steaming brew. "But we can go outside. Get some fresh air."

A couple of kitchen chairs were parked in a sunny spot between the gravel driveway and a tall hedge. Katie took a seat and stretched out her legs. "Still quite warm for this time of year."

Her father sat upright, his squared shoulders not touching the chair back. He gave her a shrewd glance over his mug's thick white rim. "You didn't come to talk about the weather."

"No." But now that she had his attention, she didn't know how to start. How did she ask personal questions about her dad's relationship with her mother? There simply wasn't a precedent for it in their reserved family.

"I hear you and John are back together," he said, when she didn't speak.

"Not anymore. He just got a job in Tinman Island." Trying to explain where she and John were at proved just as difficult as talking about her parents. "He asked me to marry him and go with him."

Her father's grizzled eyebrows drew together. "I take it you said no. Don't you love him?"

"I do, but..." Katie gazed past the road, beyond the fields and the bordering pine trees to the blue water of the bay. "Summerside is my home. I don't want to leave."

Her father snorted. "In the army I was stationed all over the country and beyond the borders. Your mother didn't like that much but as long as we were together, that was home. Of course that was before Riley and you were born.

Once you two started school I applied for a desk job so we could settle in one spot."

"I didn't know that." She was surprised, knowing how much he'd loved active soldiering.

"Your mother insisted." Barry gave a gruff harrumph. "She was right, as she usually was when it came to you kids."

"You were devoted to her, weren't you?" Katie leaned forward. "You would have done anything for her. I don't recall you and her ever fighting."

Her father gave her another shrewd glance. "Did you and John have a fight?"

She nodded, swirling the dregs of her coffee. "I know it's unrealistic to expect a couple will always agree, but he argues without talking it through to a resolution."

"Talk is cheap," Barry grunted.

"Maybe, but I can't imagine you and Mum ever letting an issue go unresolved."

"I wasn't much good at flowery words or the finer points of debating. Not much good at apologies either. When we had a fight, after I cooled down I changed the brake pads on her car or fixed the broken step." Her father twisted on his chair to face Katie directly. "Does he take care of you? Is he there when you need him?"

"That's rather the point—he wasn't, not when I had cancer," Katie said. "But when Mum decided not to have a third round of chemotherapy you supported her. You stayed by her side and held her hand through that whole terrible ordeal. You didn't argue and fight and then just take off."

"I stayed because I loved her but I also had no choice. There was you and Riley to look after. Believe me, that was no picnic. Your mum had done most of the parenting till then. I was too much of a hothead, too...regimented...she used to say. As for us not fighting, where did you get that idea? We used to have some doozies—over how to raise you kids, where to live, and yes, even her treatment. I wanted her to have more chemo. I ranted and raved, I yelled and cussed. She wouldn't listen." His voice broke. "She was a stubborn, stubborn woman."

Katie couldn't speak. She was in shock. "When did this happen? I never heard you guys fighting. Not once. Not a peep."

"Course you didn't!" Barry sat up even straighter. "Let the children hear the parents argue?" He harrumphed again. "Bad for discipline. Bad for morale. We 'discussed' things while you were at school."

"I had no idea," Katie said, shaking her head.

Barry cleared his throat and looked at the sky, his craggy face twisted by grief. "I tried everything I could to keep your mother safe.

And then…I couldn't anymore." He swallowed hard, his voice gruff. "Feeling helpless isn't easy for a man."

"It's not easy for anyone." Katie scooted her chair over and put a hand on his shoulder. She hesitated, then laid her head there, as she hadn't since she was a little girl. A tear rolled down her cheek. "I miss Mum."

He put an arm around her and squeezed. "I do, too. Susan's a wonderful woman. Don't get me wrong, I love her dearly—"

"I understand. You don't have to explain."

"I'm sorry I wasn't a better parent, both before and after your mother died," he went on. "That was one of our sticking points. She thought I was turning home into a kiddie's boot camp. I thought she was too soft."

Katie sat up and wiped her eyes. It all sounded so familiar. "How did you compromise?"

"We didn't. She took over raising you and your brother. I played a support role. After she was gone I struggled, not knowing you kids, not knowing how to handle you." He bowed his head. "Guess I was an absent parent a lot of the time."

Katie was silent. His emotional absence had been another wound in the aftermath of her mother's death. Something she hadn't thought about for years. Now she recalled wishing he would love her half as much as he'd loved her mother. With Mum gone, her father absent through grief and her brother going through puberty with no time for his little sister, she'd felt...abandoned. As if she wasn't worthy of love, as if she couldn't count on anyone to be there for her.

Only by constructing fantasies of a love so pure and perfect as what she believed her father felt for her mother had she gotten through her teen years. And who had her fantasies centered on?

John.

She buried her face in her hands. The poor man. She'd had visions of a relationship free of pain and conflict, the perfect marriage. Nobody could have lived up to her expectations.

But she'd tested him. Oh, yes, over and over. And found him wanting. So in a self-fulfilling prophecy she'd unconsciously pushed him away until even he abandoned her.

What he'd said was true. She'd condemned him before he had a chance to prove himself. She hadn't looked at it that way before. Even before she got sick. Not setting a wedding date, avoiding conversations about the future, brushing him off when he tried to make plans about where they would live. He'd wanted to travel and live in other cities back then, too. She'd refused to even entertain the idea. Her insistence on having her own way was just a ploy to make him continuously prove his love for her. Even now, he was being so generous, giving her everything he could possibly think of to help her and to make a family. And once again, she was pushing him away. He wanted one thing for himself, *one thing,* to have a crack at a different kind of job. And she'd refused to compromise. Oh, God. What had she done?

"I'm a horrible, horrible person."

"No, you're wonderful." Her father rubbed her back. "You're warm and generous and loving. And strong. You and Riley turned out bloody good considering how badly I messed up as a parent. We can thank your mother for that."

"You were the one who got us through our teen years. You are a very good father." Katie put her arms around him and hugged hard. "Don't ever doubt that. I love you, Dad."

"Love you, too," he said gruffly. Then he tipped up her chin and gave her a stern gaze. "You've got some of your mother's stubbornness in you. Be careful you don't push him too far. John loves you but there's only so much a man can take."

"I know." She jumped to her feet and hugged her dad again. "I've got to talk to him. Before it's too late."

As Katie hurried away from the Men's Shed she pulled her out her phone and punched in John's number. She wanted to hear his voice, tell him she loved him, tell him she would go with him to the ends of the earth. Oh, they had a few things to work out, make no mistake, but she loved him.

And where there was love, there was hope.

After four rings her call went to voice mail. She stared at the screen. He *always* kept his phone on, even through the night when he was sleeping. He was always available—for Tuti, for his family, for the police station. For her.

She rang the station. He wasn't there. Patty was on her day off and the temp didn't know where he was. Riley and Paula were out of the office.

He might be at his parents' house but she didn't have their phone number. She pulled out of the Men's Shed driveway and pointed her car in the direction of their house.

Alison would know. But would Alison tell?

CHAPTER SIXTEEN

JOHN HELD TUTI'S hand as they went through airport security, keeping her close among the throngs of passengers coming and going. They'd checked their bags and were on their way to the departure lounge.

He glanced at his watch. They had plenty of time. Getting to the airport early had seemed a better option than another hour moping around his town house over leaving Katie.

Tuti stopped dead, planting her pink jelly sandals on the shiny tiles. Her thin shoulders shifted beneath her backpack, heavy with books and toys. "I didn't say goodbye to Katie."

He'd already explained the whole thing to her twice. Patiently, he crouched in the middle of the concourse. "We're just going to look at our new house so we can decide what furniture to have shipped up. We'll be back in a couple of days."

"Can I bring Mummy's spirit house?" Tuti asked anxiously.

"Of course. Don't forget we're going to get you a puppy. Won't that be nice?"

"What about Katie?" Tuti's eyes grew shiny. "Is Katie coming with us?"

"I'm sorry, sweetheart. Katie is staying in Summerside. Her job is at the school. She can't leave her students, or her family."

"But I love her. I don't want to leave her."

John drew his daughter into a hug. All of a sudden he didn't want to leave, either. But he had to.

KATIE TUGGED DOWN her blouse and smoothed a hand through her hair. Then she rang the doorbell of Alison and Marty's house. She waited, long enough to admire the white and red geraniums in big pots and the flourishing garden beds and trim green lawn. Her finger was poised to ring the bell again when the door opened. Alison was dressed formidably in a blue silk dress that set off her coiffed blond hair. Expensive perfume drifted into the fresh outdoors. Damn, she was hoping she would get Marty.

"Hey, Alison," Katie began. "I—"

The older woman crossed her arms, her wrists and fingers heavy with gold. "He's not here."

Katie started to count to ten. She only made it to five. "Can you tell me where he is?"

"Why should I? So you can dig your knife a

little deeper? Maybe give it a good hard twist? I thought you were different this time. I was starting to like you again."

"I need to see him. Please."

"Why?"

God, this woman was hard. But she supposed she would be, too, if she were defending her child. She made an effort to soften her voice. "I want to accept his marriage proposal." To her horror, tears sprang to her eyes. She gave up all pretense. "Oh, Alison. I love him. I made a mistake and I need to tell him so."

"My dear." Alison dropped her hard veneer. "He's gone to the airport with Tuti. They're on their way to Tinman Island."

"They're not moving so soon!" Katie exclaimed.

"No, they're just going for the weekend, to look over the place and see their new house."

"Well, I need to be there, too, because I'm going to be living there with them." Katie dug her car keys out. "When is their flight?"

"Not till one-thirty this afternoon." Alison glanced at the regulator clock on the foyer wall. "If you hurry you might make it." Katie was halfway down the steps when Alison added, "Good luck!"

Katie ran back up the steps, ignoring the

twinge in her ankle, and hugged Alison. "I won't hurt him ever again, I promise."

The sixty-minute drive to the airport was a nightmare. Why couldn't she simply blink her eyes and find herself in the departure lounge, the way it happened in the movies? But no, there had to be an accident on the on-ramp to the freeway. And farther along, construction slowed traffic.

When she finally made it to the airport she parked askew across two spaces and raced inside the Domestic Terminal. She quickly bought a ticket and sped through check-in, easier since she had no luggage. Thank God, luck was with her and there were spare seats on the flight.

Reining in her impatience long enough to clear security, she grabbed her handbag off the conveyer belt and ran down the concourse. Naturally the departure lounge she wanted was at the very end. Puffing and panting, she came to a halt among the milling passengers lining up to go aboard.

"Katie! Katie!" Tuti jumped up and down on the spot. She tugged on John's arm. "*Bapa,* look!" Then she started to run.

Katie held open her arms. Tuti slammed into her, her backpack nearly throwing them both off balance. Katie scooped her up and hugged her tightly. “Oh, my goodness. I thought you’d left without me.”

“I missed you.” Tuti had a stranglehold on her neck. “I missed you so much. And we’re not even gone yet.”

“I’m coming with you.” Katie gave her another hug and let her slide to the floor. John was three feet away looking like he was seeing a ghost.

“Hey,” she said, suddenly nervous. “I know this is a horrible cliché, running to the airport at the last moment. But I had to tell you something.”

The other passengers filed slowly toward the Jetway.

“What did you want to tell me?” John asked.

She took a big breath. “I accept. I will marry you. I will come with you to Tinman Island.”

John just stood there, his jaw working.

“Please say something.”

He shook his head. For one horrible moment she thought he was refusing her. Then he took a giant stride forward and she was in his arms, her face pressed into his shirt. He rocked her back and forth. She couldn’t speak either for the tightness in her chest that closed up her throat.

He cupped her face and kissed her all over. “Katie, Katie. I thought I’d lost you forever.”

"No, no, the opposite. You've got me forever." She searched his face. "If you still want me?"

"Don't ever doubt it. I love you. I've never stopped loving you."

"*Bapa*. Katie," a little voice said. "People going."

"I love you." She rained kisses on his nose, his jaw of golden stubble, his beautiful mouth. "I need you."

"Last call for passengers of Flight QF68. Your flight is now boarding. Last call for..."

Katie broke apart and looked around. The departure lounge was empty. A pretty flight attendant, her auburn hair pulled into a bun, waited patiently at the entrance to the Jetway.

"Bapa!" Tuti tugged on his hand. "We have to go!"

"Have you got a boarding pass?" John asked as they hurried forward.

Katie fished it out of her purse. In a last-minute flurry they ran down the Jetway and went on board. The flight attendant closed the hatch behind them.

"Oh, no, we won't get to sit together," Katie said.

The attendant reached for their passes. "Let me see what I can do."

A businessman moved into Katie's seat and she was able to take his place. Tuti wanted the window so she could watch "the ground go away." Katie sat in the middle.

John still couldn't quite believe she was here beside him. When he'd looked across the departure lounge and seen her hurrying toward him he'd thought his imagination had conjured her out of his longing.

Could it really be true? Was Katie his at last?

The airplane began to back onto the runway. John twisted in his seat to kiss her. "Are you sure about us? I couldn't take it if you backed out now. Tuti couldn't take it."

"I won't," she said earnestly. "I've worked out some things…about my past, my mother's death."

"What made you change your mind?"

"I realized that all my life I've been waiting for the other shoe to drop. I thought that because my mother died of cancer, because I had it so young, that sooner or later I would get it again. And die, like she did." Katie's eyes filled. "But that's not necessarily true. And anyway, I can't live like that. I have to live bravely, with courage."

"You're braver than you give yourself credit for."

Now the airplane was trundling down the runway. The flight attendant came by and made sure their seat belts were fastened. Katie helped Tuti with hers then turned to John.

"How did you know my mother had the gene that predisposed her to breast cancer?"

"My mother told me a few years ago. Your mother must have told her. They used to have coffee together when Riley and I were little and we needed our mums to take us to play at each other's houses."

He wiped away the moisture clinging to her lower lid. "You could get the genetic testing. That might ease your mind."

"Or depress the hell out of me." She lifted her chin. "But you're right, it's better to know. I'll do it." Then she frowned. "And if it's positive..."

"We'll deal with that if and when we come to it."

She turned his hand over and traced the veins on his wrist. "I *will* promise that if I ever do get cancer again I'll do everything possible to get well." She met his gaze, her eyes shining. "I don't want to leave you and Tuti. I know how devastating that feels."

He folded her hand in his and brought it to his lips. "And I promise you that if you're ever sick again for whatever reason I won't leave you, not even if you push me away."

"I pushed you away because I was afraid of dying and leaving you behind—you and any children we might have. I won't ever do that again. We've missed too many good years being apart."

"We'll make up for that, don't you worry."

The airplane picked up speed as it moved down the runway.

Tuti glanced around, excited. "*Bapa,* Katie, we're going fast!" Then she pressed her nose to the window again.

Katie's deep brown eyes sparkled. "November sixteenth."

John was at a loss. That was months away. "What about it?"

"Our wedding day. You wanted me to pick a date. That's what I choose. We always wanted a spring wedding." Softly she added, "Remember?"

He remembered their plans, the dreams they'd shared. His throat closed thinking of how they could start making new plans, for themselves and Tuti. And children of their own.

He smiled. "I suppose you think you can rule the roost now that you've made me the happiest man alive."

"Well," she said coyly. "I do have some conditions."

"I knew it." He braced himself as g-forces pressed him against the seat back. The plane was nearing takeoff.

"I want Tuti to practice on the boogie board in a pool before she goes in the ocean again."

"Is that all? Whew, I'm getting off lightly."

"There's more."

He began to roll his eyes until he realized she'd turned serious. Outside the engines were screaming at high rev. "Go on."

"I know now that my parents didn't have a conflict-free marriage. But fighting upsets me. And to leave issues unresolved goes against my grain. I need to talk things through before I feel better. I need a period of talking without anger before I'm ready to…" she lowered her voice to a whisper "…make love."

The plane left the ground.

John let out his breath. "I'll remember." He brushed a lock of hair away from her eyes. "I hope you'll remember that just because I get mad sometimes and we fight doesn't mean I don't still love you."

"Can I get that in writing?"

"I'll have it tattooed on my forehead if it will make you believe in yourself and in my love."

"I believe."

"Are you sure you're okay with making the move to Tinman Island?"

"Que sera sera," she said airily. "I'm looking forward to taking time off from teaching, to give myself a shot at this writing gig. And I

want you to find the challenge you need in your life. I want to support you, be by your side every step of the way."

"In that case, Katykins, or should I call you Lizzy, we'll have to go on more adventures to give you something to write about."

Katie grinned. "Bring it on. I have a feeling being married to you will be my greatest adventure yet."

* * * * *